Have you found your true purpose in life? I enjoyed this story; it gave me hope for a better world for all of us, and Caipora embodies everything every teenage girl should aspire to be."
—Anne-Marie Reynolds for Readers' Favorite

"Thoughts have real energy ... Visualise yourself achieving your goal and you will achieve it. Believe in yourself and the power of your mind. Never doubt your abilities."

The author weaves gender roles, arranged marriages, culinary traditions, cultural beliefs, and spiritual rituals into an engaging tapestry of female empowerment and strength. The book provides a stark contrast between Caipora's low self-image and her indomitable spirit and resilience. The character development is both skilful and compelling. Burbeck leaves young adult readers with the clear but powerful message that they are capable of so much more than they could ever imagine.

—Joslyn Vann for the US Review of Books.

"Liene Burbeck's *The Power Within Her* is a colourful tale that takes readers deep into the heart of the Amazon rainforest. Burbeck's writing shines in near-cinematic descriptions of both the beauty and dangers of the wild. I love that Burbeck has made Caipora a fierce and resourceful heroine who has the fortitude and courage to overcome raging rivers and terrifying supernatural creatures, and put her trust in a cornucopia of strangers to save what she holds dear, and what so many depend on for their own survival. At its core, this is an environmental fantasy that doubles as a coming of age for middle-grade and above readers, and, as a girl dad, I absolutely appreciate Burbeck's fine work. The mix of myth and reality feels as organic as one would expect, and, although some of the action scenes are intense, they are never heavy-handed. Burbeck's ability to balance a message with real entertainment value shines brightly. Very Highly recommended. "

—Asher Syed for Readers' Favorite.

"*The Power Within Her* is a remarkable story that offers life-changing lessons about resilience, visualization, and self-belief. Although Caipora is a young girl thrust into a vast jungle with daunting challenges, her spirit is that of a warrior. Each time she confronts her fears, she learns to harness her inner strength and embrace her true potential. Her struggle with fate and its role in her destiny is relatable and will resonate with anyone who has ever questioned their purpose and ability to face adversity.

The story incorporates mythological elements from South American culture and folklore, featuring detailed descriptions of creatures and the jungle environment. The inclusion of maps and illustrations enhances the narrative, providing readers with a visual context of Caipora's journey. Liene Burbeck raises awareness about the importance of nature conservation and the interconnectedness of all living beings. I thoroughly enjoyed this book and highly recommend it to anyone who appreciates survival stories that promote personal growth, environmental stewardship, and resilience."
—Doreen Chombu for Readers' Favorite.

"*The Power Within Her* by Liene Burbeck is a wonderful read, a stunning tale of survival, freedom, and finding your true purpose in life. The action starts on page one, and the author's descriptive writing lands you right in the middle of the story, following Caipora on her journey as she fights to save her rain forest. Expect the unexpected in this tale as you follow Caipora on an exciting, terrifying journey, a tale of unconditional love and courage with an environmental theme running through it. This story will lead you to look deep within yourself and ask: are you all you were meant to be?

The Power Within Her

Liene Burbeck

Escarpment Publishing

*This book is for my grand daughters, Ruby, Ella and Indigo.
It was written through my love for them.*

Map of South America

Map of Caipora's Route

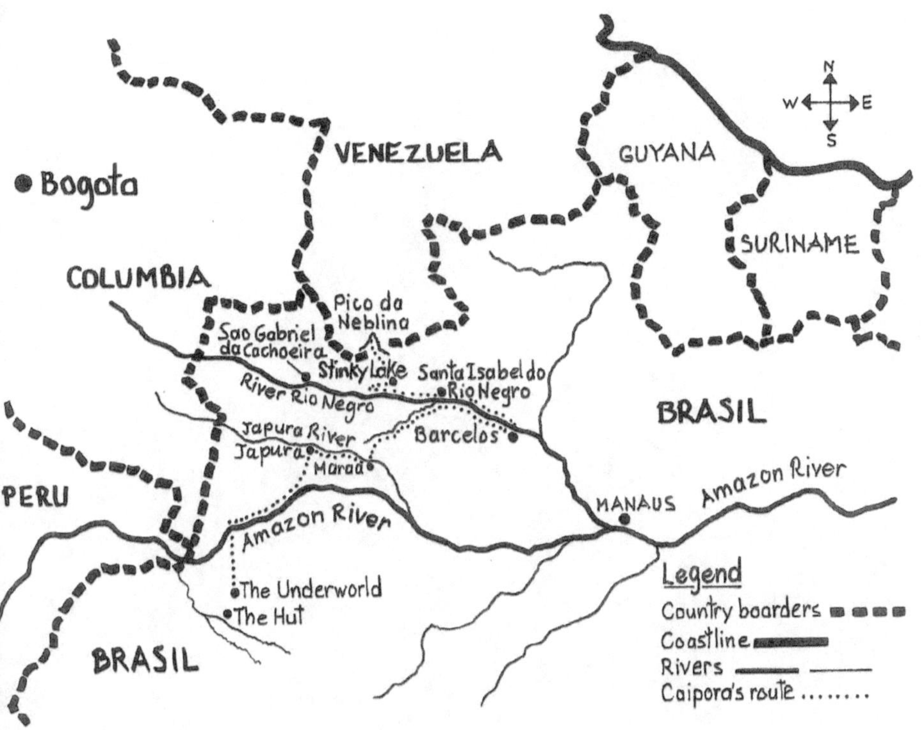

PART ONE

In The Beginning

CHAPTER 1
The Arrival

Keen eyes watched from the edge of the forest. They peered through tendrils of tangled vines, gigantic ferns and dripping umbrella trees at a figure making its way across a clearing by the river towards a hut on stilts, just a stone's throw from the eyes fixed on it. A canoe, tethered to a ladder reaching up to the landing of the hut, rested on the ground.

News had spread of a stranger moving through the land and the forest inhabitants had been on the lookout for days, curious, excited, somewhat fearful and on guard - as one normally is of the unknown. Now they watched the figure through the inky blackness, hearing its approach more than seeing it. Finally it stopped at the ladder, surveyed the hut and the flimsy landing with its crooked railings, the door slightly ajar as though someone were hiding behind it behind it, peering out unseen. Palm fronds covering the thatched roof, hung over the eaves and danced in the breeze above pane-less windows which stared like vacant eye sockets in the weathered timber walls.

The figure moved closer, pushed against two of the stilts, testing their stability. They stood firm. The small hands took hold of the ladder. It wobbled when shaken. Even so, the figure gingerly began its ascent, testing the strength of each rung before stepping onto it, and finally onto the landing. Boards creaked and the squeal of rusty hinges announced the figure's entry into the hut. Silence. Shuffling sounds. Something hard hitting the floor. Silence again.

Suddenly life sprang into the black eye sockets of the hut. Radiance punctured the night. It fell in yellow patches onto the clearing and fused with shafts of gold that speared through gaps in the walls and stretched like glowing fingers through the blackness.

"Ah!" from the edge of the forest, as if the trees had gasped.

The fat face of the moon peered over tall treetops and caught in its silver beams three small creatures scampering across the clearing towards the hut, skirting around the patches and fingers of yellow. Soundlessly they leapt up the ladder to the landing and crept to the windows, peered stealthily into the glowing interior. Countless moons had passed since a human had stepped into this place. Past experience had made the forest creatures wary of humans, yet they knew that not all humans were bad. Some had done good.

The orange light of a candle flickered over the brown satin skin of the figure. It danced through the long dark hair that fell to the shoulders and across the cloth covering the small breasts. Although her tribe had not used them, the girl had once seen a candle, seen it being lit and knew how to use the small sticks in the little box next to it. She dropped the woven grass sack from her shoulder, stepped over the collection of fruit that spilled from it, and lifted the lid of a large wooden chest by the wall. One by one she pulled out a small pot, a pan and a metal cup wrapped in cob webs. Nothing more. In a shadowed corner, a flattened mass of dry grass and ferns lay strewn across the grey floorboards; on top of it, a tattered blanket with more holes than thread to it.

The candlelight caught the rim of a dented metal bucket. The girl's eyes widened. She picked it up. A black rat sprang out, flew to the window ledge and was swallowed by the night. Rust had scarred the bucket. The girl peered inside, held it against the light, checked for holes. It was good. She turned and was at once at the door, pushing it open against its squeaky protests. The creatures at the windows screamed, scurried and collided with each other in their urgency to get away. Two landed on the roof while the third made its escape across the clearing and into the forest.

"You cheeky little monkeys! Have you been spying on me? You should have knocked! I would have let you in and you'd have had a much better view!"

The squirrel monkeys huddled together on the roof in terrified silence, tightly gripping each others fur, eyes like large black lumps of coal staring at the human. The girl made her way down the rickety ladder, bucket in hand. "I'll be back soon," she said. "No need to run away. I'm happy to have some company," but when she returned with the bucket of water they were gone: hurrying to the forest to spread news of the arrival.

Cross-legged on the floor of the hut, the girl feasted on the fruit she'd collected during the day. She wiped rivulets of juice from her chin with the back of her hand and, her hunger sated, curled up on the dried grass, pulled the tattered blanket over herself and blew out the candle. The night was still young when black clouds rumbled across the sky, smothering the stars and swallowing the silver moon. Lightning slashed through them as they clashed in thunderous wars and dropped their load onto the earth. The girl slept undisturbed.

First light fell on a hut surrounded by water, the tethered canoe turning this way and that at the whim of the current, like a captive animal struggling to break free from its restraint. The wet season had been under way for weeks, rivers rising with every downpour. This river now lapped at the second rung of the ladder.

The girl basked in the warming rays of the morning sun, her back against the splintered boards of the hut. On the run for months, she'd stopped only to gather food and to sleep. Every night she'd made a bed of grasses in the fork of a tree, out of sight of passers by, out of reach of prowling animals. Every night she closed her eyes only to see her parents dragged into the forest, struggling, screaming; towering flames engulfing her village; everyone running, shrieking in terror. Through the flames, she'd glimpsed his face - the face that always made her heart beat faster. And then he was gone. The nightmare haunted even her waking hours. Day and night her mother's voice shrilled, "Run! Run!" And she ran.

As she ran, month after month, tortured by the pain of loss and grief, a sense of liberation began to awaken in her. Had her village not been destroyed, she would have been married by now - but not to him. Not to Sema. Not to the one she'd grown up with, learnt to fish with, followed tracks through the jungle and lit fires with. Not to her soul mate. Out of the blue, against his will, he was married to someone else. She too, was to marry some one else as soon as she had her first period. For a year she'd managed to conceal the fact that she was menstruating. As soon as she was found out, arrangements for her marriage were made: arrangements for a life she didn't want; a life in which her sole purpose would be to have children, to produce warriors to protect the tribe from invaders. The fate of all the girls in her tribe: raising their families, foraging for food and preparing meals for her family. She loved her family and her tribe, but that life would have been for her a tight box, trapping her, stifling her, preventing her from growing. Her heart called out for her to run free; to find the seed within that was her essence; to nurture it and grow to become the person she was meant to be. She and Sema had planned to leave the tribe, to explore the world - but that was before he he'd been forced to marry someone else.

Leaning against this hut, she drew a deep breath and expelled it with a sense of relief. She mourned her family and her tribe, and her heart ached endlessly for Sema - but she had escaped the box. She was free. Obligated to no one. Responsible for nothing. This place offered her a refuge. She'd travelled far enough now, she thought, to be safe. Here she could try to forget the tormented screams that tortured her mind by day and made every dream a nightmare. Finally, she felt at peace. Her eyes closed and she surrendered to the warmth of the sun on her skin.

But peace was brief. A shrill squawking exploded above, shattering the serenity like glass, rendering the pristine blue sky broken and splattered with a flock of scarlet macaws and a multitude of sharply flapping wings. The girl squinted against the sun. Food had to be gathered and storm clouds already stained the sky above the tree tops on the far bank of the flooded river. She brought the canoe to the ladder, stepped in, and deftly plunged the paddle into the water, steering her way towards the flooded forest. The river had swallowed the undergrowth. Only tall trees stretched above the water. Some held aloft green canopies. Others stood with only bare branches, like the bony fingers of dead hands clawing their way out of their watery graveyard, calling for help. The girl skilfully manoeuvred the canoe around the tree trunks, leaning left, then right, ducking under overhanging branches that refused to give way to her push. Here and there a colourful bird offered company to a dead white limb. Other branches provided safe harbour to lizards, and to spiders waiting for their prey in the great webs they'd hung between the trees. The hut was long since lost to view behind the dense forest but still no land offered a foothold. Deeper and deeper she paddled into the watery forest. The canopy closed in overhead, smothering the light. An eerie mist crept through the air, silencing every song bird and buzzing insect. The girl floated soundlessly through the damp, sunless gloom.

A twig snapped, the sound tightening her fingers around the shaft of the paddle. She scoured the jungle surrounding her. Had they tracked her down? Had they not yet given up after all these months? The mist thickened. Something ahead moved, pushed through the undergrowth - not the sound of any animal she knew. If it were them, she reasoned, they would be charging her, not stealthily following her; if they had seen her, she would be dead by now. And whoever it was, *had* seen her. With that in mind, she paddled cautiously in the direction of the sound, peering through the mist, stopping to listen every few metres. An uncanny silence hung in the gauze-like haze. Then the sound of something moving again. No more than six metres ahead, an obscure shadow dissolved into the foliage. The girl paddled faster to follow it but jarred to an unexpected halt against a sudden rise in the ground.

She climbed deftly from the canoe, tied it to a tree and squelched a few metres through ankle deep mud in the direction of the shadow, then stopped. The sound was just ahead of her, as if the creature wanted her to follow it, moving ahead, then waiting, allowing her a fleeting glimpse of its dark form before disappearing again. On and on she followed it until she was out of the bog, on firm footing. She forged her way through tangled undergrowth, deeper and deeper into the jungle until the sight of lofty aguaje palms reminded her that she'd come in search of food, not to follow elusive shadows. Her mouth watered at the sight of the palms. They offered not only tasty, nutritious fruit, but also her favourite and most nourishing food: delicious Suri grubs living under their bark. The girl abandoned the shadow she'd been following and turned instead to sate her hunger.

Closer to the palm grove the ground turned muddy again, riddled with pools of water. She slopped her way to a lagoon from which there rose a myriad of aguaje palms. But with this welcome sight there also came the need for extreme caution. This was anaconda country. She'd witnessed more than once the disappearance of one of her tribe into murky waters, heard the crunch of breaking bones in the steely grip of the gigantic reptile. She wouldn't go in too deep. Too dangerous there. Although the air was now clear, encroaching storm clouds were eating up the light and the shadowy water revealed nothing of its contents.

Clusters of racemes hung from the crown of the closest palm, each more than a metre long and thick with fruit. The girl made a loop from strips of bark, stepped into it and held it taught around her ankles. She threw another length of twine around the trunk of the palm and tied it in a loop around her. Leaning back into it, she jumped onto the trunk, the loop around her ankles holding her feet in place. In one swift movement she leaned into the palm, threw the loosened loop around the trunk up higher, and leaned back to take another jump. Like a caterpillar, she made her way to the crown of the palm, cut down several racemes with her knife, and swift as an agile monkey, was on the ground again, tying the racemes together.

Suddenly the world around her exploded with a violent, turbulent thrashing of water. She swung round, knife at the ready to battle an anaconda - but there was nothing. Her heart a frantically beating drum, she scoured the murky water, then scampered up the palm again, surveying the lagoon from a height. Still nothing! But she knew well that just because you couldn't see something, didn't mean it wasn't there.

With one thunderous crack the black sky dropped its load, smashing it into the lagoon with a deafening noise that drowned all other sounds. Despite the deluge the girl was determined to secure her collection of Suri grubs. She moved the raceme of fruit to higher ground, quickly wove a grass basket, filled it with shredded bark and set it on top of the racemes. Then she pried back the bark of the trunk with her blade and uncovered a long, fat, cream-coloured grub, the length of her middle finger. Grasping its rear end, she pulled both gently and firmly, but the six legs under the black head clung defiantly to the grub's sanctuary. Longer and longer it stretched until finally the black legs with their little claws surrendered their grip and the shiny black head sprang like a shot from its hollow. Holding the head between her forefinger and thumb, the girl put the writhing creamy body into her mouth and bit hard just below the head and clawing legs, pulling the head off at the same time.

"Mmmm......." she chewed and licked her lips, then dug out another grub, and another, but these she put into the basket, buried them in the shredded bark and continued digging until she had excavated at least two dozen. She covered the lot with a large leaf and bark to keep the writhing collection from escaping. The delicious creatures lived off wood and it wouldn't do to have them loose in her canoe - they would quickly eat holes in it even before she got back to her hut! They would live for several days under the shredded bark. She loved them raw but liked them even better roasted on a stick over a fire. That was her dinner plan.

The red scaly skin of the aguaje fruit glistened temptingly in the rain. Just one, she thought, to refresh her mouth before carrying her harvest back to the canoe. The forest now reverberated with the deafening downpour; the lagoon, a turbulence of agitated, frenzied water. The girl deftly ran the blade of her knife under the skin of the fruit, water streaming over her face and body as she stood knee-deep in the lagoon. As she bit into the bright yellow fruit the water suddenly thrashed furiously around her! Something grabbed her leg. She plunged her knife into the anaconda again and again - but to no avail! The creature wrapped itself around both her legs and threw her off balance. Half submerged, the girl stabbed and stabbed, vainly trying to save herself. By now the gigantic serpent had coiled around her waist, caught her arms and strapped them to her sides. The end was near, yet she didn't scream, not in pain, not in fright, but tried instead to bite the reptile squeezing the life out of her.

Eyes watching through the foliage had never before witnessed such a valiant warrior. There was no surrendering. No giving up. But the end was near. The girl's struggles were futile. Her gasps for air, feeble. Suddenly a blast of shrieking, screaming howler monkeys burst onto the scene. Like lighting darts they zipped through the trees, each one seemingly going straight for the girl. Then, over the screams of the monkeys, a ferocious squawking exploded through the forest. Savagely beating wings thrashed around the girl, who, in her barely conscious mind, saw the jungle throwing every vicious thing it had at her. Arms pinned to her sides, all she could do to protect herself was to push her chin into her chest and squeeze her eyes tight. Then blackness engulfed her.

The snarling monkeys and squawking macaws launched themselves at the serpent, their teeth, claws and beaks biting, clawing and tearing at its flesh until the anaconda loosened its grip on its victim and finally lay inert. The girl too, lay half submerged, unmoving, in the murky water. The monkeys pulled her free of the dead serpent and dragged her onto higher ground, then, lifting their faces in unison to the sky, they let forth loud and woeful howls, over and over again. An uncanny silence followed as both the monkeys and macaws waited.

Soon, sounds of hurrying broke through the undergrowth and crackled through the forest. And the earth drummed with the thumping of rapidly approaching feet until there sprang into view a group of elven-like beings - naked except for clustered feathers hanging from a belt around their hips and more feathers sprouting from a band of anaconda skin around their heads. Dark ropes of hair interwoven with grasses fell to their shoulders. They were completely black, apart from long pointy ears which glowed a deep pink and protruded from the ropes of hair like beacons lighting the way in the dark.

A bedlam of squawking, chattering and babbling erupted at their arrival with much pointing and gesticulation at both the girl and the anaconda. Many of the elven-like beings prodded the gargantuan serpent with their stone-tipped bamboo spears. Some pulled blades from their sheaths and began to expertly strip the reptile of its skin. One grasped the handle of the girl's knife, pulled the blade from the flesh of the serpent and went to the girl lying motionless on the ground. In a show of respect for the valiant warrior, he knelt down beside her, slid the knife back into its sheath, and bent over her as if to whisper into her ear, words of praise she would never hear, his ear close to her nose and parted lips.

"She has breath!" he exclaimed. Gasps of excitement and relief sprang into a feisty commotion among the diverse gathering. The girl groaned, opened her eyes and sucked in a feeble gasp at the sight around her. Silence cut through the mayhem like the slash of a sword. No one moved. The girl lay wide-eyed, staring at the creatures surrounding her. Staring back were the near black eyes of the howler monkeys, big and shining in their serious old men's faces wrapped in thick fur and long beards. The macaws too, peered intently at her with their beady little eyes above large curved, sharp beaks. Those animals she knew, but the eyes the likes of which she had never seen before were narrow, black and slanting, with no white eyeball at all. They stared at her from thin, elongated faces below extraordinarily high foreheads and long narrow hooked noses, the tips of which stretched down to wide, thin lips. From long and pointy chins, there dangled the wiry threads of long sparse beards, ends tied in a knot. Everything about them was thin except for the shiny rounded bellies, protruding like black cooking pots above the belts on their hips. They stood on wide feet with webbed toes - feet for traversing wetlands and for swimming.

The girl tried to move but cried out in pain. She tried again but bit her lip against a muffled groan. One elven-like being knelt down, gently lifted her head and held a small vial to her mouth. She shook her head and turned her face away, but he waved the vial under her nose. It smelt good and even just a sniff, lessened her suffering. She looked into his black eyes and saw kindness. His already wide mouth widened further into a smile that stretched from pink ear to pink ear, revealing a row of dazzling white teeth. He held the vial to her lips again and nodded. She took a sip and her pain eased further. Two more sips and all the excruciating pain drained from her body! Never before had she felt so well or so strong! She glanced at the gigantic anaconda lying lifeless in the water. But for the monkeys and macaws she would be lying there with it. No, not with it - inside it. Swallowed whole.

The girl rose to her feet, profusely thanked all the creatures for saving her life and turned to collect her harvest but the elven beings, spears in hand, instantly blocked her way. They were small, a good two hands below her shoulders, but there were twelve of them and they suddenly looked fierce. A bolt of fear shot through her.

"You cannot go. Do not be afraid. We will not hurt you. We are wood elves of the Nevae tribe and we need your help."

Astonished and reassured by their words, the girl dropped her guard. Wood elves were protectors of the forest. "You need my help?" They nodded in unison. She would be dead but for them. "I owe you my life. Tell me what you need and if I can help, I will." It stunned her that she understood their language, and they hers.

"We will not tell you, but ask that you come with us to the one who will explain everything." Carrying her basket of grubs but leaving the heavy racime on the ground, she followed the elven beings through the dense jungle. Deeper into the forest, they passed stands of trees covered with foul smelling green slime, undergrowth brown and dry instead of lush and green, and were enveloped by pungent clouds of thick yellow mist. The forest was eerie, devoid of its usual sounds. "What's happened to these trees?" shocked and distressed, she asked the wood elves. "I've never seen anything like this!"

"The forest is dying," they replied.

"Why? How has this happened?"

"All will be revealed shortly." At last they found themselves on a narrow path which soon fell into a steep descent and led to a dead end marked by several huge boulders. Between two of these, at ground level, was a small dark triangular gap. The monkeys, the macaws and the wood elves had, in the blink of an eye, shrunk in size and disappeared into it until only one wood elf remained.

"You must go in," he said to the girl.

"How can I go in? I can't possibly fit through there!" she exclaimed in alarm.

"You will fit." He spoke confidently and pulled a small shiny rod from under the feathers of his belt. "It is the Underworld. We will be safe there." He reached up, touched the top of her head with the wand and pulled it down the length of her body to her feet. To her alarm and incredulity she shrank to less than half his size!

"What have you done?" she cried, craning her neck to look up at him. "I don't want to be tiny! You promised not to hurt me! How can I defend myself against enemies at this size? Put me back to how I was! Put me back right now!"

"I will put you back. I promise. But first you must go through this gap. Now you will fit." He spoke kindly and reassuringly, so that looking into his face, she believed and trusted him. She squeezed through the gap and stepped into total blackness. "Just keep walking," his voice echoed through the dark. She moved tentatively along a steeply descending path unable to see even her hand in front of her face. Suddenly her eyes snapped shut against a brilliant dazzle. When they opened she stood in the lustre of millions of sparkling fireflies: thick green moss on the walls of the spacious cave glittered with their brilliance; millions more flew about, shimmering sparkles in the air. Nooks and crannies held glass vials containing scorpions, centipedes and beetles in coloured liquids; fat bottles with large stoppers harboured small grotesque creatures in dark yellow solutions; small square jars contained exotically coloured powders. On shelves against the walls sat woven baskets piled high with miniature skulls and bones; beside them, tall jars stuffed with tiny dried hearts, bowls of green and purple berries and a vast array of pestles and mortars. Lizards crawled across the roughly hewn stone walls: bridled forest geckos, radiant in their orange and gold colouring; brown turnip tailed geckos and countless more, all hunting luscious insect delights. A toucan, its enormous beak forging the way ahead of him, threaded its way through the myriad of legs crowding the floor - the legs of unimaginable, mutated creatures, combinations of two or three different animals in one.

The cave reverberated with the rowdy clamour of excited voices, its occupants only moments earlier receiving word of the stranger who would help them. Suddenly they saw her. Silence fell like a hammer. Hundreds of eyes fixed on her and held time captive in their stares. Then it exploded! The uproar! The cheering! The furore! They swarmed around her, pushing their strange mutated faces into hers. They peered into her eyes and up her nostrils; pinched her cheeks; poked her with their strange digits and rummaged through her basket, disturbing the Suri grubs. They had never before been at such close proximity to a human. Their fingers explored the simple headband around her forehead and slid through the gleaming black hair covering her shoulders. They tugged at the woven grass belt and loin cloth around her hips, but when they went to the knife in its sheath, her hand closed firmly over it.

The roar and pandemonium reached an unbearable level. The wood elf who had shrunk her outside the cave pushed his way through the crowd and stood in front of her, arms in the air. The other wood elves surrounded her, protecting her against the barrage of invasive attention.

"Silence! Give us space!" he commanded and the crowd backed away. "Where is the Queen? Where is Caelia?" An instant hush blanketed the cave as all eyes turned to a wide tunnel in a far wall from which a wood elf shrouded in a glowing mist of fireflies, slowly emerged. "I am here, Ravan," she spoke in a gentle, yet authoritative voice. The crowd parted as the Nevae Queen approached the group of wood elves surrounding the girl. Her skin was as dark as that of her subjects but her belly was flat and she stood as tall as the girl. A leafy green cloak fell from her shoulders and a crown of leaves and ferns on her head trembled as she walked, satin black hair framing soft facial features cascading over shoulders.

"Greetings, Ravan."

"And to you, Your Majesty," Ravan bowed respectfully as the glowing monarch approached.

"You have brought a foreigner into our midst."

"Yes, Your Majesty. She is not of the Nevae, nor of any wood elf race. She is of the humans and has promised to help us."

"How do you know she can be trusted?"

"I know because I have looked into her eyes," replied Ravan.

Caelia stepped towards the girl and looked closely into

her eyes. The girl met the probing scrutiny unblinking. "I believe you are right, Ravan," the Queen spoke after some time. "What are you called by your fellow humans?" she asked the girl, continuing her intense examination of the foreigner.

"I am called Caipora," the girl replied timidly, overwhelmed by all that surrounded her, but still steadily meeting the Queen's eyes.

"Caipora?" the Queen's voice denoted considerable surprise. "And who gave you this name?"

"My parents, of course," replied the girl, taken aback by the question.

"That is very surprising. Do you know the meaning of this name?"

"No. No I don't."

"It means 'Goddess of the Wilderness'," said Caelia. "Goddess of the Wilderness......" she repeated thoughtfully, as if to herself. "How have you come to be in our land?"

"I was running away, escaping from a savage tribe that attacked my people and killed my parents."

"Was anyone with you?"

"No. No one. I escaped by myself. I don't believe there was anyone left alive in my tribe. Our village was burning to the ground as I ran. Everyone was screaming."

"You are all alone? You have survived alone in the jungle for how long?"

"Three moons have passed since I escaped," said the girl.

"Three moons is a long time to survive in the jungle on your own," Caelia nodded thoughtfully to herself.

"My parents and grandparents taught me many things," said Caipora.

"Yes....yes. Clearly they did, or you would not be here. Is it true, Caipora, that you have promised to help us?"

"It is true. I did promise. These wood elves, the monkeys and macaws saved me from the anaconda. I owe them my life and am indebted to do what I can to help, but I don't know if I can be of any use. I don't know what kind of help you need," Caipora replied.

CHAPTER 2
The Feast

The deep reverberations of a gong resonated three times throughout the cave, sending the fireflies into a frenzied panic. Everyone moved in an orderly manner into an adjoining, even larger cave and seated themselves on benches at two very long tables where the dancing fireflies threw a quivering light onto the freakish creatures.

Caipora stood, stunned at the sight. A being with the head of a peccary - much like that of a wild boar with small ears - and the body of a monkey, turned to look at her. Instead of straight spear-like canine teeth protruding downward from its wide mouth, they curled out sideways, rendering them useless for digging up the ground and finding food. Seated beside it was an animal whose top half was that of a hairy sloth and the bottom half, a lizard; there were animals half capybara, half crocodile; others bore the heads and enormous beaks of toucans with armadillo bodies. Amazed as she was at the variety of the grotesque and fierce-looking company at the table, Caipora was equally amazed that she could understand every word they said.

Caelia sat at the head of the longest table with Ravan to her right. "You will sit here, on my left," the Queen directed Caipora. The other Nevae sat among the rest of the Underworld beings, every one of whom burnt with a zealous desire to hear how the human had been discovered. A multitude of voices shouted questions and gasped with horror as word spread of the anaconda attack and how the girl had fought for her life. The air buzzed with increasing excitement, a feeling of great expectation. Of hope.

Again the gong sounded three times and again the fireflies flew into a frenzy. An instant hush swept over the cave. Caelia rose to her feet "We welcome into our midst tonight a special being: a being of human origin who has promised to help us in our terrible plight. Her name is Caipora, Goddess of the Wilderness. Let us show her our appreciation!" The Queen's voice resonated through the Underworld. The mass of extraordinary creatures raised their heads and arms or forelimbs to the roof of the cave and shouted: "A-ee-yo! A-ee-yo! A-ee-yo!"

"Let us eat and rejoice!" pronounced Caelia, At these words enormous trays laden with gourds of steaming tacaca soup appeared at the tables, the enticing aroma of dried shrimp wafting past quivering nostrils. Those who could hold the carved wooden spoons, used them. Others clutched the gourds in their paws and drank while still others simply lapped up the contents with their tongues. When the soup had been eaten, one way or another, the Nevae carried out more dishes. Every table groaned under their weight. Vibrant yellow peppers gleamed and dripped with anaconda oil. The paracress leaves, a strong favourite, brought streams of saliva flooding chins both hairy and scaly withing moments of eating amid sounds of profuse slurping and burping. Some wiped it on their arms, others in their fur and still others in wads of soft dry grasses supplied for that purpose.

Char-grilled Suri grubs piled high on bark plates glistened in the shimmering light, their mouth-watering aroma permeating the cave well before their arrival at the table. The delectable sight of roasted root vegetables, chayote, cassava, potato and gleaming hot peppers baked in coconut oil brought forth sounds of joyous appreciation while the spiky legs of grilled grasshoppers prickling over the rims of deep bowls stirred up great excitement. Piranhas stewed in coconut milk bared their needle sharp teeth in frightful grins as they stared with dead eyes at those around them. Great catfish lay on beds of leaves, their long whiskers trembling with every vibration of the table. There was arabu: a luscious dish of wild turtle eggs, raw or slightly cooked, accompanied by taro and yam and seasoned with salt. Platters of grilled tarantulas, their spiky legs sticking out every which way and dishes of frogs legs and snails in a sauce of fermented manioc were gleefully received at the tables.

When every morsel was devoured, the table was cleared and covered again almost magically with a vast array of succulent fruit. Greeted with oohs and aahs, it rapidly disappeared into eager mouths.

Her appetite sated, Caipora surveyed again the scene around her. Dismayed and concerned, she addressed the Queen. "Your Majesty, what has happened to all these creatures?"

The Queen turned to Caipora, eyes stained with pain, fear and anger, startling Caipora with her piercing look. "Three moons ago an horrific evil woke from a five hundred year spell and returned to the earth's surface as a gigantic toad. He is now cutting down the forest and selling the timber to build a castle and establish a kingdom with the money. He intends to take over the whole of Amazonia and use it for his own greedy, evil purposes. He is, as we speak, destroying our world.

We are sheltering these animals here because they can neither feed nor defend themselves in the wild. When the loggers the toad hired started cutting down the trees, the forest animals gathered defiantly in front of their machinery, blocking their way, and at night, while the loggers slept, they stuffed their engines with latex. So the enraged toad hired three supernatural evil spirits to help him in his dastardly work and they are now mutating every animal who stands in the way of the logging. As payment for their work, the toad has promised the evil beings a place in his castle.

Our only hope is Verita, the Goddess of Good. They have captured her, locked her in a glass cage and hidden her on the summit of Pico da Neblina. The key is in the pouch under the Toad's mouth. We need you to find the Toad, get the key, find Verita and free her."

Caipora stared at Caelia, thoughts tumbling, colliding, making no sense. Had she heard the words correctly? "W.....w....what?" she finally stammered in a half whisper. "Evil beings? Are you sure?"

"We have informants throughout the jungle. They hear and see everything. We know this for a fact. The evil entities are Boiuna, a gigantic shape-changing black serpent, the most powerful of all evil beings; Jurupari, the Amazonian Jungle Devil, god of darkness and evil; and Corpo Seco, a man so evil that even the devil himself refused to have him in hell - a dead man condemned to walk the earth until judgment day."

The elders of Caipora's tribe had often warned the children about these horrific beings. Their power was supreme, their evil unimaginable! And she was to be pitted against them? "But surely the evil beings will kill me at first sight through their stares alone!" Her words rapid and tight with terror.

"Humans are immune to the spells of the evil beings," Caelia explained. "They are also immune to the poison slime covering the Toad."

"Poison slime?" Caipora exclaimed, horror exploding through her voice.

"Yes. But you are immune to it. We, the Nevae, are not. Furthermore, the Toad is enormous: he would come up to your knees in height when you are your normal size."

"But I don't even know where Pico da Neblina is. I don't know where the Toad lives. How can I possibly help you? I don't now anything about..."

"We will train you," the Queen interjected firmly. "We will equip you and prepare you for the journey. You are strong. We have seen that you are a warrior. You know how to survive. Of course, you will be returned to your normal size." Caelia's eyes fixed on Caipora, determined, waiting for an answer, but the girl, brown skin almost white with terror, stared blindly into the space in front of her.

"Our lives and the future of our world depend on you! You cannot refuse us!" Caelia's voice, high and sharp, rang through the cave. It was an order. Not a request. Suddenly all the food in Caipora's stomach turned into an indigestible lump intent on returning to her plate. Ravan, on seeing her pale colour, leaned forward.

"You can do this Caipora," he said reassuringly. "The most important thing is to have courage - and to believe in yourself. We have witnessed your courage, Caipora. We have no doubt about that. If we did not know you could do this, we would not ask it of you. Do not be afraid. You will fare well."

Caipora stared disbelievingly into Ravan's narrow black eyes. She had only just arrived at the hut after running, running, running with no respite, no rest, from the savages who'd slaughtered her people and her soul mate. For three terrifying months she'd spent every night high in a tree, fearing every nocturnal sound to be a footstep coming after her. Her exhausted body was screaming for rest, for shelter; to feel safe and secure. She wrapped herself in the memory of her mother's comforting arms, heard her reassuring words in her ear.

"Caipora!" The Queen's sharp voice ripped the girl from her mother's arms and flung her into a place where, instead of running from evil, she was forced to to confront it, capture it and overthrow it. Couldn't they see she was only thirteen? What could they be thinking?

Time floated on a wave of silence that washed across every table in the cave. Even the fireflies seemed to hold their breath. Finally, as if in a trance, Caipora slowly nodded.

***

The following day the Nevae equipped Caipora with a bow and a quiver of arrows, a machete, a strong rope woven from bamboo fibres, and a wand. They gave her two vials of magic potions: the potion in the gold vial healed injuries; the potion in the silver vial would give her supernatural powers over her body and the bodies of others - she simply had to visualize what she wanted to achieve and it would happen. They made her a pudding which would provide nourishment and moisture and always grow back to its original size. And they gave her a hammock made from spider silk, fine and light but also warm and super strong.

Once trained in the use of the wand and magic potions, Caelia gave Caipora a map drawn on spider silk fabric, marking the route she was to follow. The only maps Caipora had known had consisted of a few lines drawn roughly in the ground. "We are here," said Caelia. "To read the map correctly, make sure the north arrow is pointing to actual north." With that information, Caipora was able read the map guided by the sun and the stars.

"From our cave, you will head north to the Amazon River, here," The Queen's forefinger slid across the spider silk to a long undulating line. "It is extremely wide and you are unlikely to see the northern bank when you come to it. Follow it until it turns directly east, then head north to the Japura River, here. It's not wide, but it is fast and treacherous. Continue north until you cross the Rio Negro. If you're on track, you'll come to the city of Sao Gabriel do Cachoeira on its northern shore, here." Caelia's finger stopped at a dot with writing above it. Finally, the Queen's finger was at the top of the map. "This mountain is Pico da Neblina, where Verita is hidden. Somewhere in this range of mountains south of Pico da Neblina is Stinky Lake, where the Toad lives. Stay away from this area here," her finger circled a part of the map south east of the mountains. It is Yanomami territory and those people are not known for their friendliness."

Finally the Queen looked up from the map and met Caipora's eyes. "Get as much information as you can from whomever you meet. But be careful: there will be creatures intent on stopping you but also those that want to help you as well. There is no sure way of telling which is which. Trust your instincts. And remember, the stench of Stinky Lake is so bad that it can kill you." With that, Caipora's training was over. She studied the map. She could not read the writing. In fact, she could not read at all. Her people did not have a written language. She memorised Caelia's instructions and the look of the words on the map.

All the cave dwellers gathered in the great hall to farewell Caipora with resounding cheers as she followed Ravan through the black tunnel and out into the forest where he pointed his wand at her feet, ran it up her body and returned her to her normal size.

"Take care, Caipora, Goddess of the Forest. May you be safe from harm, victorious in your mission and return to us with the Power of all Good."

PART TWO

Forests

CHAPTER 3
The Muiraquita Stone and the Ghoul's Demand

Day after day Caipora slashed her way through twisted vines and tangled undergrowth, clambered over fallen trees and squelched through bogs of rotting leaves and slippery mosses, ever on the lookout for scorpions, centipedes, snakes and deadly spiders. Every afternoon, black clouds above the canopy belched out ominous clashes of thunder and speared the earth with lighting bolts. Horrified as she was at the fate of the mutated animals and the destruction of the forest, Caipora's heart was not in her mission. Only three days ago she had arrived at the hut and felt she had finally escaped her enemy. Was free at last. But suddenly, out of nowhere, her newly gained liberty had been harnessed by the debt she owed the Nevae and she was obligated to repay it. But at what cost? Was she to give her life for it? She believed she was walking to her death. Days followed meaninglessly one after the other. Every evening she hung her spider silk hammock in the trees and searched for firewood in the purpled shadows of the creeping dusk. Every night she built a blazing fire and ate her pudding in the comforting glow of the flames that kept savage beasts at bay. And every night her thoughts went to Sema - the love of her life. Her soulmate. What hurt more? The injustice of his forced marriage to someone else or that he was no longer with the living? The pain of both was scorching.

One evening as Caipora lay in her hammock listening to the drip, drip, drip of drops through the leaves after the usual deluge, distant sounds of splashing touched her ears, then women's voices, bell-like, laughing and singing. Cautiously she made her way towards the sounds and, concealed behind a thicket of ferns, watched beautiful young women, star-sprinkled brown skin, diving and frolicking in a glittering moonlit lake. Soon the women joined hands, formed a circle and began an incantation, repeatedly calling for the 'Mother of the Muiraquita', and there emerged though the foliage on the far side of the lake, a woman whose long white tresses shrouded her shoulders and across whose face time had engraved the tracks of its journey.

Clad in an incandescent silver robe, the woman stood like a tall glowing column against the darkness from which she had emerged. Holding a woven basket in the curve of her arm, she made her way into the centre of the circle of young women. There, one by one, she took a small object from her basket and placed it into each outstretched hand. The women bowed their heads, uttered words of thanks and followed the Mother of the Muiraquita in single file to the shore of the lake. There, from the face of a large smooth rock, each woman took a leather thong and tied the precious object around her neck.

Suddenly, Caipora realised she was witnessing the legendary Icamiaba tribe of women, who, on certain nights of the year, celebrated their victories over the opposite sex. They paraded down the hill on which they lived to the sacred lake, Yaci Uarua, meaning Mirror of the Moon, and when the moon shone over the lake, the Icamiabas would dive into the water and, after purifying themselves, call upon the Mother of the Muiraquita, the 'mother of the stone', to bestow upon each of them a green stone carved in the shape of a frog or a fish or some other animal. The stones were soft when the women took them into their hands but hardened as soon as they stepped out of the water. Once hardened, they had powerful therapeutic and supernatural powers, protecting the women who wore them.

A long-legged hairy black spider dropped onto Caipora's shoulder forcing a squeal from her lips as she swiped it off. Instantly all eyes flew to the thicket from which the squeal had sprung, the women frozen in their actions, their voices stilled. Caipora stood motionless, panic-stricken. "Come forth and show yourself!" the voice of the Mother of the Muiraquita commanded fearlessly. "Do not hide like a coward behind leaves in the dark!"

Caipora hesitated, terrified, but with nowhere to go, stepped into the moonlight on the water's edge, eyes downcast, heart in her mouth. An eerie quiet fell over the lake. Even the forest held its breath. At last a voice, more reassuring than threatening, sounded through the silence. "Come closer girl," spoke the Mother of the Muiraquita. Slowly, head down, Caipora approached the group of women. "How do you come to be in this part of the forest? It is a long way from your people, of whom I know something. What brings you here?"

"You know my people?" Caipora cried out, wide

eyed, astonished.

"I know girl, that they no longer exist, so it surprises me all the more to see you here."

A lump rose to Caipora's throat: the horror of the attack on her people instantly vivid in her mind; the sight of her brothers and sisters, her parents, all slaughtered; the screams of her aunts and uncles as they were dragged into the forest; her skin burning in the heat of the flames engulfing her village. And Sema, disappearing behind the flames.

Feeling her, pain, the women gathered around Caipora, embracing her into their circle. "Come girl, sit with us. Tell us what brings you here," the ancient woman's voice soothed and comforted. And so, on the moonlit shores of lake Yaci Uarua, Caipora's story quietly unfolded. Her anguish, her heartbreak, her pain poured out of her. The women listened, compassionate, consoling. Then Caipora told them how she had been saved from the anaconda, and about the mission on which she now found herself. "I'm not the person they think I am. All I've ever done is grow vegetables and help my mother prepare meals. And I've caught a few fish. Nothing more. How can I be expected to fight evil monsters? I don't know anything about them! I can't even read the writing on the map! I'm going to die and Verita will be locked up forever and I'll be responsible for the destruction of our world!"

"The evil woke almost four months ago - at the same time your tribe was attacked and you escaped. There is a reason for that," said the Mother of the Muiraquita. "Your mission will not be in vain. And we can help you." The women told Caipora to take off her clothes, dive into the water and wash herself. Caipora did their bidding, even though her clothes consisted only of a loin cloth. She then stood with hands cupped in front of her while the ancient white-haired woman came towards her through the water. "Take this stone girl," said the Mother of the Muiraquita, placing it into Caipora's hands, "and wear it always against your skin where it will protect you from sickness and evil, as long as you do no evil yourself." As soon as Caipora stepped out of the water, the amulet hardened and the women hung it around her neck.

"This stone will help and protect you," the Mother of the Muiraquita reaffirmed, "but you can also help yourself. Use your thoughts," she said. "Thoughts have real energy. Believe in them and they will turn into actions. Visualise yourself achieving your goal and you will achieve it. Believe in yourself and the power of your mind. Never doubt your abilities."

"Can I bring back my soulmate through the power of my mind?" Caipora asked, choking back tears.

The Mother of the Muiraquita took Caipora by the shoulders and looked into her eyes. "No, you cannot bring him back from the other world, but you can talk to him." With those words the Icamiaba women embraced Caipora, turned and dissolved into the shadows of the night.

***

Caipora woke with her fingers around the Muiraquita Stone, the voice of the Mother of the Stone echoing in her mind: visualise yourself achieving your goals and you will achieve them; believe in yourself; you can control what happens to you through your thoughts. Caipora repeated the words over and over to herself until she began to truly understand what they meant: she had power - real power within her. The power of her mind. It had nothing to do with her physical strength.

A flock of macaws screeched through the canopy,

tearing into shreds the still of the morning. Time to move on. Equipped with her belongings, machete and knife at her hips, Caipora forged through the undergrowth with renewed energy. A belief in her purpose. No longer doomed to die. The distance she had to cover was immense and every day the evil in the forest spread further. Time was precious and everything depended on her. She visualised herself standing on the peak of Pico da Neblina, freeing Verita. The vision filled her with energy and touched the corners of her mouth with the whisper of a smile.

Days passed and Caipora's passage became more and more heavily impeded by enormous slippery rocks, gigantic fallen trees and ground so soggy that she sank into it up to her ankles. The strangely cool air reeked with the pungent stench of rotting flesh, the forest eerily empty of its usual sounds. She stopped, listened for danger. Nothing. She walked on, but climbing over a huge boulder, lost her footing on the other side and rolled down a slimy mound, stopping short of a thick wall of thorny vines - her way completely blocked.

A burning sensation on her chest brought her fingers to the Stone: it was hot - and glowing bright red! Strange, she thought, but her attention suddenly turned to the thorny vines which began to writhe about, their tight weave crackling and stretching open to reveal a massive, ghoulish abomination. Two stump-like things served as legs and two long appendages dangling by its sides served as arms to a shapeless blob with no discernible head. The thing consisted entirely of slime, thick, green and yellow, like a gigantic disgusting snot, dribbling and dripping all over itself, its surface rippling back and forth so that it was always moving - yet somehow held its shape.

A great terror of unearthly beings had haunted Caipora since she was old enough to understand the stories told about them. Now, facing the ghoul, she stood paralysed with fear, heart pounding. The ghastly being slowly squeezed itself through the thorny wall as if squeezing through a sieve, yet came together again as one slimy blob within arm's reach of her! She retched at its foul stench and threw up onto the slimy ground at her feet. Then, in spite of herself, she looked up at the features of the greenish-yellow thing towering above her. Two dark hollows formed what could only be the eyes, piercing her with their black, spine-chilling glare. A nose and ears were missing. Below the eyes and forming the base point of a triangle was another hollow which moved up and down, emitting a deep throaty rumble. With some difficulty, Caipora made out the words.

"What doeth ye want 'ere?" the monstrosity boomed at her, gravelly and threatening, making her want to clear her throat.

"I need to go through the forest," Caipora answered, looking straight into the nightmarish eye holes, amazed at finding a voice in her paralysed body.

"Ah! Ye wanth to go thwough *my* fowetht! Doeth ye, indeed?" The thing roared with such force that its entire jellylike mass shuddered with the vibrations. Then it slurped up the snot its roar had left dangling over the edge of its mouth hole. Despite its horrific appearance, foul stench and terrifying voice, Caipora was determined to hold her ground. Fingers wrapped firmly around the hot Muiraquita Stone, she was about to say, 'It's not *your* forest,' when it occurred to her that perhaps this was not the best time to argue that point.

"Yes. Yes I do," she replied instead with unwavering confidence, eyes fixed on its face.

"Well now, ye can't go thwough jutht like that! Nooah! Noah, noah noah noah noah! Therth thingth thath got to be

done firtht! Thingth thath got to be done! Thingth *oi needth*!"
The creature put a great deal of emphasis on the last two words
and continued rumbling incoherently to itself, as if trying to
work out some kind of problem. Certainly, Caipora could
not understand a word. Now and again it vigorously shook
its head so that bits of snotty slime went flying off sideways.
Finally, it turned its eye holes on her again.

"Oi needth four teeth fwom a bwack caiman cwocodile,"
it boomed at her. "Four good big teeth! Ye bwingth'em to me,
and ye can go thwough!"

Without waiting for a reply and still rumbling agitatedly
to itself, the abomination squeezed backwards through the
thorny wall and appeared to simply melt away, leaving the
vines dripping with its stinking residue. Caipora shuddered
and retched again. Surprisingly, her fear had vanished. All she
had to do, she reasoned, was get four teeth from a caiman,
bring them to the ghoul, and all would be well. It had not
threatened her in any way. As far as she could see, it simply
needed teeth. Quite reasonably, she thought.

***

From a rise in the land some distance back, Caipora had
seen a river to the east. If she moved fast she could reach it
before dark. Machete in hand, she cut and slashed her way
eastward through the jungle but was still some distance from
the riverbank when evening stole the light from the sky and
heavy clouds threatened an imminent storm. But she was close
enough. Sleeping right by the water's edge was dangerous:
jaguars liked to hunt there and crocodiles would be lurking
in the shadows, waiting for their evening meal.

A dense clump of low-growing palms forming a cave-like shelter beckoned to her with fronds already flapping in the growing breeze. She quickly cut gigantic leaves to shield herself against the coming downpour. The palms would hold back some of the rain, but not enough to keep her dry. She was in her hammock beside the blazing fire just as the storm hit, clutching her leafy blanket close while the wind howled and ripped around her, a menacing raging monster roaring and wailing through the forest like a tormented demon. Leaves and branches thrashed and slapped each other in a frenzied rage; palms lurched this way and that, fronds frenetically beating at one another. The entire forest screamed in pain.

Finally the storm exhausted its fury and left the battered forest sagging and sighing under its weight. A full moon peered through the branches of the canopy, admiring itself in the puddles on the ground. The calls of tawny-bellied screech owls punctured the night. A huge firefly hovered silently in the darkness for minutes at a time, as if considering its position in the world. A myriad of frog calls crowded the dripping darkness and now and again the potoo bird expressed its love for the moon, its eerie whistled notes decreasing in scale until they mournfully died. Separated from the one it loved, thought Caipora, saw Sema in her mind, and felt its pain.

She turned her face to the struggling fire. On the far side of the flames a tarantula crawled from its hole, long hairy legs making their way in Caipora's direction. She had eaten tarantulas in the past: crisp, crunchy and hot, straight off the fire. She and Sema used to hunt them. They'd poke a stick into the spider's hole and wriggle it until the spider lunged out at it, then they'd quickly press another stick down between its head and body, holding it firmly to the ground. In its effort to escape, the spider would rub its large round body with its back legs, flicking long stinging hairs into the air. They'd burn unbearably if they touched your skin and breathing them in caused excruciating pain. With a large leaf protecting their hands, and taking great care to keep their fingers away from the big fangs eager to give a painful and poisonous bite, the trick was to quickly gather up the front legs, hold them behind the head together with the back legs and wrap up the tarantula in the leaf, securing it with a piece of twine with which you then carried it. They'd skewer the spider on a stick and roast it above a hot fire, burning off all the hairs. It was ready when it started squealing - the noise of the air escaping from the cooked joints.

The tarantula crawled into the undergrowth in search of dinner. Caipora yawned and turned her attention to getting the caiman teeth. Slipping into sleep, images of animals living by riverbanks drifted through her mind: just as many capybaras as caiman's. She had a deep fondness for capybaras. She thought of them as gigantic guinea pigs - the size of an actual smallish pig. The gentle creatures happily spent their days with their families, grazing on the juicy grasses and succulent foliage by the water's edge. Her people used to eat capybaras, although her heart always sank when one was brought into the village after a days' hunting. But people weren't the only ones who ate them, thought Caipora: they were probably the caimans' favourite food!

The glow of dawn was only just seeping through the forest when Caipora climbed from her hammock with a plan in mind.

***

The river was so high that she barely walked fifty paces before arriving at the water's edge. Time to put her plan into action. Soon enough, she spotted a capybara contentedly feeding on a patch of succulent green grass. Not wanting to alarm him by suddenly appearing out of nowhere, she crouched down, slowly moving the grass from side to side and making soft chewing noises. The animal lifted his head, pricked up his ears, watched and listened warily from a distance.

Finally, slowly and very cautiously, the capybara approached the moving grass, pausing often to sniff the air and assure himself that all was well. With no scent of a known enemy, he finally came close enough to see Caipora, head down, face to the ground. He stopped chewing and stopped in his tracks. For a long time he watched her guardedly and waited. At last he grunted; waited; then grunted again, as if trying to elicit some kind of response from the strange animal huddling in the long grass. Caipora hesitated, then grunted back, imitating the capybara.

The animal's small eyes widened and his little ears pricked up. Then he barked - just one bark, like that of a dog, but neither deep nor menacing. More of a question. Caipora replied with a similar bark, and so it went on for some time. At long last the capybara gave his grey-brown coat a good shake and emitted a low purring noise from the back of his throat. It rose in pitch to a high trill and came down again, ending with a happy high-pitched squeal, much like that of a cheery bird.

Encouraged by this communication, but unable to imitate it, Caipora barked again, then said very softly, "Can you help me?" The rodent sprang back at the words and instantly dropped a wall of distrust between them. "Can you please help me?" Caipora pleaded again, head still down. The silence thickened with suspicion but the rodent did not retreat. Finally he spoke.

"What *are* you?" he asked, clearly puzzled and curious, allowing his guard to drop just a little at the request for help.

Caipora cautiously lifted her head and met the eyes of the gentle hairy creature some distance in front of her. "My name is Caipora. I'm a human."

"A human? A *human* you say? Humans kill us and eat us!" squealed the capybara springing back in acute alarm, eyes popping, fur on end like the needles of a porcupine. He had never before encountered a human but had heard of their horrifying eating habits through friends and relatives.

"I promise I will not eat you," Caipora pleaded earnestly. "We need your help - not just we humans, but all life in the jungle - and the jungle itself - it needs your help too. We will all die, even you will die, if I don't stop the evil Toad."

"Toad? What? What Toad? What evil? What's happening?" The capybara squealed in confusion and alarm, jumping about on all fours as though on hot coals, panicked eyes flying in every direction as if expecting the evil, whatever it was, to instantly spring from the bushes and slaughter him.

"Please don't be afraid. The Toad isn't here. He's very far away. If you will just listen, I'll tell you everything," Caipora spoke soothingly, trying to calm the greatly agitated animal.

Finally the capybara, his terror slightly abated by the fact that nothing had yet attacked him, agreed to listen. Caipora explained the situation: how Verita, the Goddess of Good had been captured and imprisoned by evil spirits that served the Toad and how he now reigned over and was slowly killing the forest and all that lived in it. The capybara was aghast at what he heard. "How can I help? What can I do?" he asked in shocked earnestness.

As Caipora explained her plan and the capybara's part in it, his horror grew with every word and finally exploded like a bomb from his whiskered mouth. "What? What? Are you mad? You promised not to kill me and here you are proposing to do precisely that! No! No, no, no, no! Absolutely not!"

"You just have to let the crocodile see you," Caipora calmly explained again, "then as you run towards the trap and jump over it, he'll fall into it and........."

"No! No! No! You don't even want an ordinary caiman! You want me to be chased by a great big black caiman, the fiercest crocodile of all!" The capybara raged hysterically. "He'll swallow me in one mouthful! *I have a family to take care of!*" he shrieked.

"Yes, I know you do. And so do all the animals in the forest. We will all die together with our families if we don't help each other. No harm will come to you, I promise."

"How can you promise that?" The capybara continued his frenzied protest. "Will you be able to get me out his jaws when he catches me? Will you be able to put my leg back on after he bites it off? And what about my head, if he bites that off? Will you be able to fix that?"

The capybara was, understandably, petrified at the thought of being caught and eaten by a crocodile. After all, he'd spent his entire life avoiding crocodiles at all cost - and had many narrow escapes! He'd seen his friends and relatives eaten and now this crazy human was asking him to throw himself in front of one! Caipora took the green Muiraquita Stone from her neck. "This Stone was given to me by the Mother of the Muiraquita. It protects everyone who wears it from harm. It will protect you from the crocodile. Let me put it around your neck."

"The Muiraquita Stone?" The capybara whispered in complete awe and astonishment. "You have the Muiraquita Stone?"

"Yes. I do." Even as Caipora approached him with the green Stone, the rodent became more subdued and as she hung it around his neck he purred and was calmed by its soothing energy. It wasn't long before he agreed to help.

The plan was that the capybara lure a black caiman out of the water. This would not be hard to do: he just had to let himself be seen. As the caiman chased him, the capybara was to run towards the noose of a tree spring trap which Caipora will have set and which would snare the crocodile and lift him off the ground. Once in the noose, Caipora would throw a magic potion into his mouth to paralyse him, then cut him free, pull out the four teeth and run for safety before the potion wore off.

Even though he had agreed to help, on seeing the trap Caipora had constructed, the capybara succumbed again to despair. "And you think this is going to catch and hold a black caiman crocodile?" he gasped, incredulous at the seemingly flimsy construction.

"I *know* it will," Caipora replied emphatically. "The important thing is that you jump *over* this loop. As the crocodile chases you, he'll step into it and dislodge the stick. Once the stick is gone, the vine will fly up with the crocodile in the loop. His weight will pull the loop tight and hold him off the ground - well maybe just his front half, depending on how big he is."

The rodent shuddered at these words. "Depending on how big he is," he repeated to himself, his bottom lip trembling at the image in his mind. Then an horrific thought occurred to him. "And what if he doesn't step into the loop?" Suddenly rigid, consumed by panic, his ears pricked up like small pointy turrets; little eyes popping out; the wiry hairs of his coat sticking up like millions of tiny darts.

"That's why you have the Muiraquita Stone," Caipora reassured him, putting her arm around the gentle, terrified creature. "You will be all right. Believe me." She felt the tremor running through his body. How brave he is, she thought. How very brave. After many more questions, many more reassurances, and many more promises of safety, Caipora and the capybara both agreed they were ready.

The capybara stood at the water's edge, eyes keenly scouring the surface for the slightest ripple denoting a crocodile. But crocodiles didn't always make ripples. And it couldn't be one of the smaller species of caiman: it had to be an enormous black one. The slimy ghoul had demanded big teeth! Soon the capybara spotted something in the water - but it wasn't black, so he scurried into the foliage to hide. Of course, it wasn't just caimans that hunted him. Leopards and pumas as well, were ready to pounce from anywhere at all.

Twice more the capybara ran to hide and and twice more he returned to the riverbank before spotting a black caiman lurking in the shadowy water. It had crept up silently as far as it could into the shallows. The rodent couldn't run and hide now. He stood in full view of his predator, feigning oblivion to the danger, his heart a wildly beating drum in his ears. Terrified, muscles quivering, nostrils flared, ears pricked, hair on end. Ready to run for his life.

He waited and waited, then finally looked back at the water. The caiman was gone! Not in the water and not on land! He knew it was creeping up on him through the undergrowth. It could come very close before he would know. It could get so close that there would be no chance of escape! The capybara felt something hot on his neck. He looked down: the Muiraquita Stone was bright red.

Exploding from the undergrowth, raging, hissing, jaws

wide open, dagger-like teeth bared, the caiman charged at the capybara! With one shriek the rodent flew across the ground towards the trap, the caiman snapping at his heels! The capybara turned to look back - and tripped! The caiman lunged, teeth bared, about to snap up the juicy animal when, with a thump on the caiman's back, there landed a huge green iguana! The long claws of its hind legs dug into the reptile's thick scaly skin and the claws of its front feet sank into the flesh around its eyes. At the same instant the capybara sprang to his feet and vanished into the foliage. Behind him, the caiman screamed in pain, unable to see a thing. The iguana, more than half the length of the crocodile, would not be dislodged, its powerful tail providing leverage and balance. The caiman thrashed violently to throw off the cause of his grief, but to no avail. He rolled over. In the water his attacker would have drowned - but on land, his roll proved useless and he threw himself back onto his feet. The iguana, horrifically fierce, a ridge of long sharp spines stretching down the length of his back, held on with a vice-like grip, his jaw a menacing grin packed with vicious teeth while a sheet of scaly skin hanging from his chin whipped from side to side in a frenzied flapping as his victim thrashed about.

It was clear that things had not gone according to plan. But, aghast as she was at the capybara's near death experience, and ignoring the caiman's ferocious snapping and thrashing, Caipora immediately came up with another plan: she cut a thin branch from a tree and tapped the caiman's snout with it. Unable to see a thing, the crocodile lunged forward, jaws wide open. Caipora swiftly threw a few drops of the magic potion from the silver vial into the enormous cavity.

Following Ravan's instruction that she clearly visualize what she wanted to achieve with the potion, Caipora focused all her mental energy on seeing the caiman quiet and still: paralysed. Instantly, he lay motionless. But the jaws holding his teeth were shut! The iguana reached across the caiman's long snout and pulled up his top jaw. "Get a sturdy stick in there vertically and be quick about it!" He instructed Caipora.

She whipped out her machete, cut a branch and propped open the jaws. Now for the teeth. Holding the sharp end of a stone against the base of an impressively big tooth, she hammered it with another stone until the tooth came loose, then twisted it out. Working rapidly, she removed the biggest tooth from either side of both the top and bottom jaw, still leaving plenty of teeth for tearing up food. The missing ones would grow back in a month or two. Caipora carefully wrapped the gleaming teeth in a large leaf and tied it securely with strong grasses. No sooner were they safely in her sack than the caiman hissed menacingly and flicked his tail.

"Run!" Shouted the iguana.

"Thank you so much!" she called to the enormous lizard as the branch in the caiman's mouth cracked behind her and the caiman's snarling and hissing ripped through the forest again. In the blink of an eye, the iguana was back in the tree where he'd been idly luxuriating in the warmth of the sun before the ruckus erupted. Having earlier overheard the girl explaining to the capybara her need for the caiman's teeth, he didn't hesitate when help was needed.

Relieved of the fiend on his back, the caiman hurried to the river to soothe the stinging burning skin around his eyes and console himself in his watery world. He could understand neither what had happened nor where his lunch had gone. Not only was his stomach still empty but there were now empty gaps in his mouth as well!

When the caiman had well and truly gone, Caipora cut the

vine for the trap so that a passing animal wouldn't be caught in it. The branch flew up to its rightful place, sending a flock of macaws screeching from the canopy. She watched them dissolve into the sky and turned to see the capybara slowly emerging from the undergrowth, his body visibly shaking.

"There you are!" she exclaimed, patting him on the back. "You were sensational! So brave! So courageous! Standing there. Unflinching. Waiting for that caiman! And you lured him out!

"I wasn't brave," his words trickled out in a trembling little voice, "I was terrified!"

"It's when we're terrified but still do what we have to, that we show our courage," said Caipora. "Our world will be eternally grateful to you! I certainly could not have got the teeth without you."

"And you very nearly didn't get them even *with* me! If it hadn't been for that iguana, I'd be in the slimy depths of that caiman's stomach now!" He looked up and gave a nod of thanks to the lizard basking in the sun above them. The iguana nodded in reply. "Well, I'd best be on my way," the capybara sighed, stifling a shudder and clearly exhausted. "I really do need to find my family and sooth my nerves. Good luck in your journey and I do hope for the sake of us all that you find and free the Goddess of Good." He turned to go but then remembered something. "Oh, I nearly forgot. You'd better have this back. Seems to me you might be needing it," and he handed Caipora the Muiraquita Stone.

"Oh! Thank you! How could I have forgotten that?" She watched a plump little tail waddle into the shadows of the foliage. "And just as many thanks to you too! You saved the day!" Caipora raised her eyes to the iguana. He nodded.

CHAPTER 4
The Tunnel

Guilt sat heavily in Caipora's heart as she made her way back to the slimy ghoul's domain. Her plan would have cost the Capybara his life had the iguana not saved him. He had believed in her and she let him down. His family would have waited and waited in vain for his return. How fortunate he was, she thought, to have a family to comfort him, to love him. Caipora's guilt over the Capybara mingled with the guilt she now felt for wanting to leave her family, to escape the shackles of the tribe with Sema. Yet she knew that neither he nor she would have been happy living the life the tribe demanded of them. Was it wrong to want to be happy? Was it selfish? The thought of Sema warmed her heart - fishing together, planning their lives. She saw him vividly in her mind, walking next to her. "I miss you," she said. It felt so good. So good to speak to him. "I miss you," she said again. "I miss you," she repeated with every step she took as the sun moved through the sky. Finally she heard "I miss you too." His voice was clear, close to her ear. Her skin prickled. She paused in her step. "I will always be by your side," Sema's voice promised.

The sun hung low when Caipora arrived at the foul-smelling forest. She shuddered at the thought of spending the night in the ghoul's domain and backtracked to a point where the air was more tolerable, hung her hammock and lit a fire. That night, Caipora's dreams wrapped Sema's arms around her. His kisses fluttered across her face and lips like an attentive butterfly. His loving words soothed her and his promises to meet again gave her strength.

In the grey light of morning, Caipora stood at the thorny wall, an eerie place empty of life. The heat of the Muiraquita Stone warmed her skin and out of nowhere a sudden strong breeze rattled the foliage. In its wake, deep throaty rumbles broke through the cold silence. Her fingers clutching the stone, Caipora watched the creature ooze his slimy being through the vines and thorns.

"Well'at woz quick, if oi doeth thay so me-thelf! Oi didn't ethpect ye back at all if the thwuf be told," he slobbered slime as the words splattered from his mouth. "Ave ye got the theeth then?" he leaned towards Caipora in eager anticipation, dumping his foul breath on her like a load of excrement.

"I have," she replied, holding her breath as she opened the parcel, put it on the ground in front of him and quickly stepped back.

"Hee, hee, hee! Haw, haw, haw!" the ghoul gleefully shook himself as his eyes fell upon what he'd hoped and dreamed of but never believed he would ever have. Caipora stepped back further to avoid the splattering goo.

With much grunting, he bent down and extended an arm towards the four big teeth glinting white against the green leaf. It wasn't an arm that would be recognised as such had it been on its own somewhere - more of an enormous, greenish-yellow thick snot with tentacles at the end. He touched a tooth with one of the tentacles and it stuck. He then lifted it to the hole that was his mouth and pushed the tooth into the soft slimy edge - and there it stayed! The ghoul repeated the procedure with the other teeth. Now Caipora faced an even more horrific sight: the creature's cavernous mouth gaping in a ghastly snarl, four large razor-like teeth gleaming against the black hole behind them.

"Hee, hee, hee! Haw, haw, haw!" Completely delighted the creature again shook himself and put the tentacles of one arm into the cavernous hole and bit down on them. As he opened his mouth and pulled his arm away the tentacles, now pierced by the teeth, simply stretched and stretched and would not come unstuck. The exasperated creature grunted and groaned, twisting his arm this way and that, stretching it as far from the teeth as he could, but to no avail. Finally he tried to pull them free with the tentacles of the other arm but they too, became stuck.

"Aaaaaaarrgh!" he snarled, bits of snotty goo dangling from his new teeth. "Theeth teeth ith yuthleth! Theeth teeth 'ere ith complethely uthleth! You gone done and thwicked me!" he lisped ridiculously and with both hands stuck to the teeth he turned on Caipora, growling, raging and splattering slime at her. She'd done her best, risking the life of an incredibly brave capybara and had secured four excellent teeth - teeth any caiman would be proud of - but which clearly were not suited to this slimy monster. It was not her fault but he was not going to listen to reason and there was no time to argue. He was coming at her. Turning and running was not an option: she had to get through the forest. The Stone burned on her chest again. This time it glowed bright green and a commanding voice spoke in her head.

"Jump over the wall. Run! Take a flying leap! Believe in yourself!" Caipora looked at the wall thick with thorns and a row of extra long spikes across the top. It towered above her. There was no way she could jump it. "Jump!" the voice commanded. What choice did she have? Fingers still grasping the Stone she ran at the wall and leapt off the ground just as the slimy monster lunged at her. Flying clear over the thorns she landed well away from them on the other side and charged on through the undergrowth without looking back, jumping fallen trees, crashing through bushes and spiky foliage, oblivious to the thorns stabbing and tearing her skin. Suddenly she came to an abrupt halt: huge webs of gooey slime hung between the trees, blocking her way in every direction.

Yellow vapours rose eerily from the ground, the pungent smell of decaying flesh thick in the air and the weight of death heavy in the silence. But there was no going back. No going anywhere but forward. Caipora fought back desperation. "I will get through this. I *will* get through this," she voiced her determination. "Thoughts have real energy. If I believe in them they will turn into actions," she repeated the words of the Mother of the Muiraquita, moving forward cautiously, seeking out gaps between the webs through which she could squeeze without touching them; avoiding puddles of slime. A constant dripping, splattering, low gurgling came to Caipora's ears and every so often a loud squelching punctured the air. Finally her eyes met the source of the sounds: iridescent yellow blobs oozing from trees, grew like balloons until they burst and threw their entrails onto a nearby trunk, sticking to it and forming a web between the two trees. The forest pulsated with slimy vibrating yellow webs.

Caipora's eyes fell upon a clump of large mushrooms a short distance ahead of her: purple and orange stripes radiated from their cetnres and tiny white specks crowded the edges of their caps. Strangely, amidst the foul stench saturating the forest, they gave off a wonderfully enticing fragrance. She bent down and breathed in the exotic scent.

"No! No! Don't do that!" screamed an alarmed little voice. Too late. "No! No!" the distressed voice screamed again. Caipora searched in astonishment for the source of the warning but saw nothing. What she did see however, was a forest green and lush with enormous red orchids on long stems bowing in the refreshing breeze; shimmering violet blossoms hanging from green and silver tendrils; exotic gold palms and huge multicoloured butterflies dipping into the nectar offered by the extraordinary flora. Everything exuded a sumptuous fragrance and to her great relief, just a little way ahead, a clear mossy path enticed her to follow it. Smiling, she hurried towards it.

"Don't go there! Do not go there!" shrieked the same voice again and it wasn't in her head.

Caipora stopped. "Who are you? Where are you? Why can't I go there?"

"It's not real! That path is not real! Nothing you see is real!"

"But I can see it and I can smell it. Everything is beautiful and wonderful."

"No! No! It's not!" the greatly dismayed voice shouted in Caipora's ear. Caipora tuned her head to a touch on her shoulder. "Aah!" Sitting on her brown skin was a glistening frog the size of her palm. Covered in bright green and yellow patches with dollops of striking pink, it looked at her with extraordinary gleaming black eyes bulging from the sides of its head.

"Don't move! Just don't move!" The frog insisted emphatically, a deep purple tongue flicking restlessly in it's open lip-less mouth. "If you follow that path you will walk into a thick web of slime. As soon as it touches you it will sting and burn like fire and slowly dissolve your skin, your flesh and even your bones, so that there is nothing left of you at all! And once it's touched you, you can't get away from it. It sticks to you and you'll be caught like a fly in a spider's web!"

"But I can't see any slime. The forest has changed and everything is beautiful now," Caipora argued, unable to understand what the frog was talking about.

"Nothing has changed and nothing is beautiful!" the frog shouted adamantly. "Everything is just as foul, horrific and dangerous as it was before! You sniffed a magic mushroom and it's made you hallucinate! What you're seeing is not real - it's a trick to get you to walk into the slime!"

"A trick? How do I know you're not a trick?" Caipora defiantly confronted the frog, confused and distrustful of the creature that had suddenly appeared out of nowhere, telling her she was seeing things that weren't there. "Why should I believe you? How can I know you're real?"

"Just think back to the stinky forest you were in a moment ago. What do you think made it stink?"

"Well, the slime of course!"

"Yes, the slime does stink, but it's more than that. Didn't you see all the rotting animal carcasses covered in slime. Skeletons covered in slime?"

Caipora thought for a moment. "I saw the slime and smelt the stench but I didn't see any rotting animals."

"Well, if you didn't see the rotting animals it's because they were so covered in slime that it was impossible to tell them apart from all the other mounds of slime."

"But I *didn't* see them, so why should I believe you?" Caipora persisted, her voice rising in frustration.

"You should believe me," said the frog, finally exasperated, "because I am Fyglia, your personal guardian. Some might call me your Fairy Godmother!"

"What? What's a Fairy Godmother? Oh, wait, I have heard of them. But aren't they supposed to have wands and wings and look very beautiful? You don't have a wand," said Caipora, asking and answering her own question, "and you certainly don't look....." but she stopped, not wishing to offend the frog.

"Don't make me laugh," the frog responded sarcastically. "Do you think that just because I don't have a wand I can't be as good as a Fairy Godmother? I can change my shape to be whatever I want whenever I want and I've been keeping an eye on you ever since you left the Underworld of the Nevae."

"If that's the case, why didn't you help me with the slime monster and the caiman?" Caipora demanded, taken aback by the frog's claim.

"Goodness girl! I can't do everything for you! You do have to fend for yourself as much as you can you know. How will you learn otherwise? If I believe you can get through a problem, I'll wait and only help at the very last minute, if I see that you need it."

"How can I know you're telling the truth? Why didn't Caelia tell me about you?" Caipora, stunned by the frog's claims, questioned the creature, remembering Caelia's words warning her of those who would want to help and those who would harm her.

"She didn't tell you about me because she didn't want you depending on my help. You just have to trust me."

"Trust you? How can I trust you or anything in a world where slime monsters squeeze through thorny gates and forests change from deadly to beautiful in the blink of an eye? If you really are my personal guardian and have been keeping an eye on me, tell me how I got this green Stone around my neck," Caipora challenged the bulging black eyes.

The frog described in great detail the lake and the Icamiaba women. She repeated word for word the conversation between Caipora and the tapir who'd come to shelter by the fire and outlined the scenario with the capybara who'd risked his life for the caiman teeth and the green iguana who'd jumped on the caiman's back to save the giant rodent. Caipora listened in amazement and watched as the frog's purple tongue flicked about rapidly disgorging the words from its mouth.

"All right. I believe you," Caipora finally capitulated, "and I'm grateful that you're here to help me. But how do I get out of this hallucination? How can I see things for what they really are?"

"Kiss me," said the frog.

"What?" Caipora, aghast and disgusted at the idea of kissing a frog, could not disguise her instant repulsion.

"Kiss me. I have a special secretion on my skin that will make your hallucination disappear. You will see the forest for what it really is and you won't walk into the slime webs."

Grimacing and with no choice, Caipora held out her hand. The frog hopped onto it and Caipora held it up to her face. It was actually quite a beautiful frog when you looked at it front on, she thought, but even so, the idea of touching its skin with her lips was completely abhorrent and it showed on her face.

"I'm really not that bad," the frog croaked resentfully, taking umbrage at being made to feel so repugnant. With a tinge of guilt at the offense she had caused, Caipora closed her eyes and kissed the top of the frog's head. Instantly she found herself back in the slimy forest, breathing in the foul stench and retching.

"There, that wasn't so bad was it?" asked the frog, back on Caipora's shoulder.

"No. Not nearly as bad as being back here in this stench!"

"Can you see the rotting carcasses now? That mound over there," Fyglia pointed with one of her long green digits, a bright pink suction pad on its end. "That's not a fallen tree, it's a slime-covered decomposing animal, although I can't tell you now what it used to be. And there's another, and another!" the frog's pink suction pad jumped this way and that.

"Oh! Those poor creatures!" Caipora, distressed and sickened at the sight of their carcasses almost sobbed. "And how on earth am I to get through this without becoming a rotting heap myself?" She looked around hopelessly, her way blocked in every direction by webs of deadly slime.

"There's a tunnel somewhere," Fyglia advised. "If you can find it, it will take you to the Rio Hamza, the underground river. It's very slow but you can follow that as it runs east, maybe even as far as the mountain where the Toad lives, although I'm not sure about that."

"A tunnel? How do you know there's a tunnel?" asked Caipora, both astonished and thrilled at this news.

"I just know things," said Fyglia, holding her head high and sounding a little smug.

"You know things, but you don't know where it is?" Caipora surprised herself with her challenging words.

"I didn't say I know everything, did I?" argued the frog, a trifle peeved and defensive.

"No, you're right. You didn't. I suppose the entrance might just look like a hole in the ground," said Caipora scouring her surroundings, regretting her adversarial words. A distant tree, partly obscured by a web of slime, caught her eye. Different from the rest, its bark was grey and dry, not green and slime-covered, and a narrow vertical fissure in it stood out like a dark wound against its pale trunk. "It's there! That must be it!" Caipora exclaimed. "That must be the opening to the tunnel!" She turned to the frog on her shoulder as if seeking confirmation - but she had gone. "Where are you?" Silence. "Well, so much for a Fairy Godmother! Can't depend on her!" She almost shouted hoping the frog, who she believed to be hiding somewhere behind a slime web might hear her and be offended, but there was no response and Caipora immediately regretted her ungrateful, petulant attitude towards the creature, after all, she was there when I needed her most, she thought to herself.

Caipora now stood facing the slime forest alone. "I have no hope of getting through this," she told herself, eyes fixed on her imminent death. "Why didn't they leave me to die in the coils of the anaconda? I was almost dead anyway and now I'll be slowly eaten alive by the slime! Why didn't the Nevae give me a potion with which to kill myself?" Her stomach twisted into an anxious knot and stress surged through her body, tightening every fibre of every muscle. Three deadly slime webs hung between herself and the grey tree. They were low but on careful assessment, not so low that she couldn't get under them. The ground beneath the first two was dry. There was a chance, she thought, that she could wriggle through on her stomach. The last web was high enough for her to get under it simply by crouching down - but it dripped slime and the ground beneath it was as slimy as the web itself.

Caipora gritted her teeth. There was nowhere else to go. She remembered the capybara, poor, innocent, meek animal and how it had stood unwavering, waiting for the caiman to attack him. He had believed in her. Now she had to believe in herself. Her memory spoke the words of the Mother of the Muiraquita. "Believe in yourself. Thoughts have real energy. Believe in them and they will turn into actions."

With those words in mind Caipora threw her equipment to a safe place beyond the first web, gripped the Stone in her teeth to keep it off the slimy ground and stepped towards the nearest web. Flattened onto her stomach, face to one side, she inched forward and under it like a worm. The space was tight. She almost touched a tentacle of the deadly stuff but held her breath, shrinking to almost nothing to crawl under it. On her feet again, she moved her equipment forward, flattened herself again and cautiously wriggled under the second web.

Finally she threw her equipment onto dry ground beyond the third web, dripping with deadly slime: the last obstacle before her refuge in the grey tree. She counted between the drops. They fell six to seven seconds apart but occasionally one would fall at five seconds. "The next drop. The next drop," she told herself and the moment it fell she was nimbly under the web, one leg stretched out to a slime-free spot on the right, and lunged forward with her arms to the dry area beyond the puddle of slime. She pushed forward with her back foot and was almost through when a drop of slime fell onto her leg! Instant unbearable pain seared through her like burning acid. She grabbed her equipment and ran to the dry tree. Leaning against it, she looked at her leg. A small blob of yellow goo just below the back of her knee was bubbling and quickly growing. Biting her lip against escaping screams of pain, she tried to think. How was she to save herself? Where was that frog when she needed it most? What to do? What to do? How to get this thing off her? It was impossible to think with the searing pain tearing through her.

"The vials! The vials! Get the vials!" The words rang urgently through her head. She fumbled under her belt. One was silver, one gold. But which one to use? She couldn't think for the burning pain. Which vial to use? They each held only a small amount. Using the wrong one would be a shocking waste. "Think! Think! What did Caelia say when she gave me the vials? What did she say?" Grimacing, Caipora squeezed her eyes tight, saw herself in front of the Nevae queen. "The gold one will heal your injuries. The silver will give you special powers. Use them wisely."

"The gold one! Yes! Yes! It's the gold one!" She pulled out the little stopper and let two drops fall onto the frothing slime. Instantly, the bubbles shriveled and completely vanished. Not only had the pain gone but not even a mark remained on her skin! "Thank you! Thank you! Thank you!" she called aloud to the Nevae and turned to the fissure in the grey tree trunk. The circumference of the tree was considerable but the fissure was narrow - long, but narrow. She peered inside. With her head blocking the light she could see nothing but was convinced this had to be the entrance to the tunnel. There was no hole in the ground anywhere. This was the only tree, dry or slimy, with any opening in it at all. Holding her bow and quiver in front of her, she squeezed into the blackness of the cavity. Once inside, a shaft of light fell through the fissure right onto the mouth of the tunnel at her feet!

A steep slope descended into an inky blackness. Caipora crouched down and pushed herself head first into it, arms stretched out in front of her. With little room to move, she inched forward on her stomach but could not bring her elbows under her chest to get good leverage. Nor was she able to bend her knees. When she lifted her head she knocked it against the roof of the tunnel. Her body took up almost all the available space and three metres in, claustrophobia overwhelmed her and panic began to set in. Would there be enough air further down or would she suffocate? She wouldn't be able to back out if there wasn't - but what was there to back out to? And what if she became stuck? Verging onto panic, Caipora fought to dismiss these thoughts and continued struggling forward on her bare stomach over roots and rocks protruding from the ground, across damp moldy-smelling soil. Her bow and quiver often caught on tree roots hanging from above and without room to use her arms to free herself, she had to jiggle back and forth and sideways until she came unstuck.

How far she had crept she couldn't judge, when cool fresh air slid across her face. At least breathing wouldn't be a problem! In a place devoid of sound and light, time cannot be measured against its usual markers. In a blackness so opaque that she couldn't see her hand in front of her face, Caipora felt as though she'd been struggling for hours. Exhaustion was creeping in with a growing sense of doom. Was she to be imprisoned in these moldy walls for days? Nights? So confined that she could neither eat nor drink? The air alone, vital as it was, would not sustain her.

Her head knocked against a low hanging root and she caught a mouthful of dirt. Choking and gasping, how she wished she had light! Just a faint glow would make all the difference. No sooner had she wished it than an explosion of white light flooded the tunnel with phosphorescent brilliance. She was both stunned and alarmed. Was an evil being coming to attack her? Nothing happened. The light remained steady and bright. Finally she saw the Muiraquita Stone: blazing white. "Thank you! Thank you! Thank you!" she cried out to the Mother of the Stone.

The light reached a good distance into the tunnel ahead of

Caipora and she saw that, not far ahead, it opened up in both height and width. She was soon making rapid progress on her hands and knees and after twenty metres more, rounded a bend into a spacious cave! The light of the Stone illuminated the walls and roof - but no way out! She had come to a dead end!

"No! No! It can't be!" Caipora cried in shock and despair. "If there's no way out of this cave, then there's no way out of the slimy forest! I will die and so will the forest and all life in it! It can't be! It just can't be!" fraught and distressed, she searched the cave walls, peering into every nook and cranny, craning her neck in hope of even the smallest hole in the roof - nothing! Suddenly the ground beneath her collapsed and she fell into a black hole.

Hours passed before Caipora woke to a burning sensation on her chest: the Muiraquita Stone glowed bright red. Something was crawling on her legs. Every part of her body cried out in pain as she struggled to sit up, holding her throbbing head in both hands. The red light of the Stone lit up dozens of small dark creatures covering her legs: Vampire bats, bodies no bigger than an adult's thumb, were lapping up the blood flowing freely from the cuts they'd made in her skin!

"Aaaargh!" She leapt to her feet, smacking at them with her hands. "Get off! Get off! Get off!" she screamed, her head spinning from the knock it had taken. The bats let go, some fluttering away, others falling to the floor and looking at her with startled black eyes, pointy ears sticking up, two large bloodied teeth protruding from under their strange squashed-up muzzles indented with u-shaped grooves which were their nostrils, making their faces something one would rather not look at.

"Aaargh!" Caipora screamed again, thrashing at the bats still stubbornly hanging on. Frightened by her screams, the entire cave now screeched in alarm, the blackness teeming with thousands of bats zipping this way and that, their noise piercing as thousands of sharp needles. They zoomed towards her, veering off at the last moment, saved only by their echolocation from smashing into the walls - and into her. She covered her face with one hand and took hold of the Muiraquita Stone with the other. She had to get out.

"Light. Light! Please, please give me light!" Again the stone radiated a bright white light, sending the bats into a frenzied panic, desperately seeking dark crevices to escape the blinding light burning their eyes. Those that had gorged themselves on her blood were too heavy to fly and had to pull themselves sluggishly up the rough surface of the walls with the little hooks under their wings. They made their way to the darkness of the roof to hang upside down for a good sleep after their satisfying feed, wings wrapped around their bodies, covering the light brown velvety fur on their bulging bellies. Some time passed before their hysteria subsided and they fell into a full-bellied sleep.

Caipora searched for an exit, every inch of her body aching, There was the hole in the roof through which she'd fallen but what good would it do to try to reach it? The only way out from that cave was back through the tunnel to the slimy forest. Clearly, the bats used an entrance to come and go but even if she were to find it and fit through, that too, would put her back in the slimy forest. The throbbing in her head grew with her anxiety as she scanned the walls for a way out. Nothing. Was she to be trapped forever in this blackness with the screaming bats? They would drain her of her blood every night while she slept and her 'forever' would be very short indeed. Finally a darker area under a ledge revealed itself: a narrow vertical gap, a metre and a half high and a metre deep opened into another space. Caipora squeezed through it, scraping her skin on the jagged surface in her excitement and found herself in a spacious flooded cave crowded with stalactites and stalagmites. In the light of the Stone, the walls glowed brilliant oranges, yellows, purples and greens. Their reflections shimmered on the rippling surface of the black water and danced to the tinkling rhythm of the drops that fell from the stalactites. She cautiously stepped into the visibly shallow lake. As she walked, a red circle spread out in the water around her. She looked down to see her legs covered in blood: it was still readily flowing, the draculin in the bats' saliva stopping it from clotting. She needed to sit down and rest, lower her heartbeat; give her blood a chance to slow down and clot. A small ledge came into view. She sat resting her head against the wall, legs in the cold water. Every part of her cried out in pain. Her fingers found a large and painful lump on her head. She'd fallen several metres onto the stone floor and was lucky not to have broken any bones. She washed the blood and draculin from her legs, leaned back and closed her eyes, the rhythmical dripping soothing her mind, and breathed in deeply, drinking in the peace around her.

Suddenly her eyes sprang open: the Muiraquita Stone was burning her skin! She was cold - very cold. She'd lost a lot of heat while she slept, she guessed for hours. She pushed herself to her feet, ignoring the pain, and fumbled through her bag for the pudding. Ravenous and freezing, she would eat as she walked: she had to warm up before hypothermia set in. She wound her way around the columns of stalactites and stalagmites, following the darkness that would always evade the glow of the Muiraquita Stone, vaguely wondering why the light was now red.

Gradually the floor of the cave rose out the water, making

her progress easier - and warmer. The stalactites and stalagmites grew more and more sparse and finally disappeared. Now as she walked, grotesque black shadows cast by the light onto the undulating wall, lurked in nooks and crannies like dark ominous entities waiting to pounce.

"Hiiissssssssssssssssssssss!" sliced through the silence. Caipora froze. Two narrow slits of yellow leapt into the black space in front of of her.

"Who comesssss 'ere? Who comesssss 'ere? What are ye? What do ye want?" Unattached to a body the high-pitched demanding words slithered across the walls of the cave, the yellow slits swaying from side to side just beyond the reach of the red light.

"Sssspeak, I say! Sssspeak and reveal your identity!" the voice shrieked with impatience.

"My name is Caipora......."

"I don't give a twit about y'name! Why are ye 'ere?" it demanded, hissing, menacing, the yellow jerking left and right.

"I'm here because I had to get out of the slimy forest, and I could find no other way."

"And why were ye in the slimy forest in the first place? What bussssinesssss did ye 'ave there?"

"I'm on my way to capture the evil Toad and free the Goddess of Good," Caipora stated clearly and factually, swallowing the tremor in her voice, hoping the darkness would hide the terror on her face. Her hand went to the Stone. Help me, Mother of the Muiraquita. Help me! She pleaded silently.

"Hisssee! Hissssee! Hisssee!" laughed the voice. "What! A! Joke! Hisssee! Hisssee! I haven't laughed like thisss sssince..... sssince.....no.....wait! I've never laughed like thisss before! Hisssee! Hisssee! Hisssee! Do ye seriously think that a short little wimp like yeeself can catch the evil Toad? Do ye 'ave any idea how many eeeevil ssspirits ee 'asss lookin for ye? Do ye know how poisonoussss ee 'imself isss? Hisssee! Hisssee! Hisssee!" The thing simply couldn't stop itself. It went on and on, the yellow slits lurching this way and that in the dense blackness as it hissed and laughed and laughed and hissed.

Caipora crept forward just a little, slowly, carefully, hoping to see the body that belonged to the eyes. The thing leapt back before the light fell on it.

"Hisssssssssssssssssssss! Move back if ye want to live, little girl!" the thing hissed, threatening and evil.

Caipora stepped back. "I just want to find a way out of this cave and this tunnel and get above ground. I don't want to argue with you or anyone else," she explained cautiously, hoping reason would do the trick.

"Do ye just? Don't ye just? How nice! How nice that ye don't want to argue, becaussse, ye know, ye really isssn't in a posssition to argue, isss ye?" Without waiting for an answer, the thing continued. "Well, lucky for ye that I don't want to argue either - well, not very much, that issss." Then the thing fell silent. Caipora watched the gleaming eyes sway from side to side and waited.

"Now, I wouldn't mind letting ye through," it finally spoke high-pitched and rasping. "But yesssee, there'sss not much life that passsses by 'ere, and it doesss get a trifle boring, 'ere in the dark, all on me own, night after night, week after week, month after month, year after year. There'sss not much to do ye know, guardin thisss cave. Personally, I sssee no need for a guard, really, but then, it'sss not my decisssion."

"Is the Toad making you do this?" Caipora ventured to ask, surprised to hear that the thing was not happy doing what it was doing.

"Ssssilence! Ye'll sssspeak when I tell ye to sssspeak!" the eyes leapt several feet higher as the thing shrieked at Caipora. She froze at the vicious piercing words.

"As I was ssssayin, not much 'appenssss in this cave, and I am in need of sssssome entertainment. Sssssoo, if ye can anssswer me riddle, I'll let ye through. If not, ye'll sssstay 'ere with me until I get tired of ye company and then.....hisssee, hisssee.....then we will sssseeee..... hisssee, hisssee." The thing laughed more quietly to itself this time, as if already having something in mind for Caipora should she fail to solve the riddle. Caipora held her silence as she'd been ordered, and waited. "Are ye ready?" the thing rasped.

"Yes, I'm ready."

"Then 'ere it issss: if ye 'ave me, ye want to share me. If ye share me, ye don't 'ave me. What am I?"

Caipora turrned the words over and over in her mind. The silence grew heavy and the weight of it stifled her thinking. The piercing stare of the yellow slits unnerved her. "She doesn't know it! She doesn't know it!" the thing's gleeful squeal shattered the silence. The yellow eyes jumped up and down in the dark. "Ye will keep me company 'ere for a hundred years! Hisssee! Hisssee! Hisssee!"

Caipora grew agitated. Her hand went to the Stone and her fingers closed over it, gently rubbing it. "Ye can't take forever! Ye doesn't know it! Ye doesn't know the answer! Hisssee! Hisssee!" the thing now screeched, it's evil eyes lurching from side to side.

Then a calm voice spoke in Caipora's head: "A secret," it whispered. "The answer is a secret."

"A secret," Caipora said, looking straight into the yellow slits hanging in the blackness. The thing stopped. It stopped squealing. It stopped swaying. It stopped hissing. Nothing moved. Not a single sound could be heard.

"Whaaaaaaaaaaaaaaaaaat? Noaaah! Noaaah! Noaaah!" its hysterical shriek pierced Caipora's ears. "Ye can't do that! Ye can't do that! Ye can't know the answer! Not fair! Not fair!" The thing threw itself into a frightful tantrum; the eyes disappeared then burst through the blackness again, jerking from side to side, jumping up and down and every which way, all the while shrieking it wasn't fair.

"Ye cheated! Ye cheated! Yeee'ssss not goin anywhere! Yeee'ssss sssstaying 'ere with me!" the thing raged in a blood-curdling fury.

"We had an agreement," Caipora said calmly, fingers around the Stone, determined to get through the cave. "If you make an agreement but don't keep it, the forces of natural justice will punish you. You cannot escape them."

"Punish me? Punish me!!" the scream cut through the blackness. The narrow slits widened as if to pop out of their sockets and bounced about in the dark like gigantic round fireflies gone mad. "I'm already being punished! O'w much more punishment can there be in this eternal blacknessss?" the thing both screeched and wailed, almost in tears. "All right! All right! Ye can have one more chance to get through the cave," it said, perhaps uneasy about the ghoulish penalty natural justice might bring upon it. Caipora was not going to argue that she'd already won the right to go through. Clearly, the thing was neither a fair nor a rational thing.

"The answer to my riddle was 'a secret'. Now ye have to guess what my secret is!" There was a surprising smugness in the voice. What secrets could this thing possibly have, Caipora wondered. Any number of unimaginable secrets could be lurking between those evil yellow eyes. But would there be anything worth knowing? That was it! That was it!

"Your secret is that you have no secret," she said,

calmly, confidently.

"Noooah! Noooah!" it shrieked. "Ye can't know that! Ye can't know that! Ye'sss cheated again! Cheated again!" It was beside itself, thrashing about hysterically. Caipora could hear the thudding as it smashed itself against the walls in uncontrollable rage. "Yeee'ssss not goin through! Not goin through! I won't let ye go through! Nooah! Nooah! 'Eere with me is where ye'll stay! 'Eere with me for a hundred yeeearsssss!"

Caipora took a step forward. The thing hissed and lurched at her. Long orange flames shot from beneath its eyes, almost searing her face. "Ssssstay where you are!" Its voice was low, slow, and menacing. The hysteria had gone. "Yeee'ssss not going anywhere!" it threatened through the dark.

"That's not fair. We had an agreement," said Caipora, calmly but firmly challenging the thing's command.

"Agreement! Shmeement! I'ssss not feelin very agreeable today..... night.....whatever it is! Who knows? Who cares? No one cares in this blacknesss 'ere!"

Caipora stood tall and straight and stared unblinking into the yellow eyes. "I *will* go through this cave," she said defiantly. "I promised to do everything I could to save the forest and its animals and that's exactly what I intend to do!" She whipped her machete from its sheath without taking her eyes off the yellow slits and took a step forward.

The eyes disappeared.

"Let me pass or prepare to do battle!" Caipora commanded, weapon in readiness. Deathly silence followed. Only Caipora's heartbeat drummed in her head.

"Hissssssssssssssssssssss!" The thing lunged out of the blackness and spewed a long tongue of red flame at her. "Prepare to die!" it hissed, lunging at her again and again, throwing its fire at her face - but always staying just out of the circle of red light radiating from the Muitaquita Stone. Caipora ducked this way and that, then charged at it, brandishing her machete. But the thing was quick. It leapt back and closed its eyes, vanishing into the blackness. Then it threw itself at her from a different direction, hissing, snarling, firing its flame at her again and again, all the while keeping out of the light. Caipora still had no idea what the thing looked like - no idea what she was fighting. Then the thing vanished completely. The blackness was suddenly silent; empty. Caipora stepped forward, then to the right, to the left, but the thing had simply disappeared.

An icy wind started up out of nowhere and from the distant blackness, a faint green mist rolled towards her, carrying an eerie howl that bounced off the walls in echoes which sent shudders through Caipora's body. Then another howl, and another. The cave reverberated with more and more howling and wailing until it became one piercing scream. Suddenly it stopped and in its place the sound of hooves clattered through the underground. Closer and closer, louder and louder, the green billowing mist galloped towards her until, when almost upon her, a dark form leapt from it and came charging straight at her. She gasped. Stood paralysed.

The creature had the body of a horse and the torso of a man - the Besta Fera! Behind him ran a pack of savage dogs, five or six, howling and wailing as the beast turned to whip them from time to time, as he does all animals he encounters. This was the creature her tribe believed to be the devil - the devil who leaves hell during nights of the full moon and gallops through villages until he finds a tomb into which he disappears. According to legend, if you see his face you will go mad for days before recovering.

The Besta Fera charged towards her, his long black mane flying violently about his head and the bull-like horns protruding from it. This is the end, thought Caipora. This is what the end looks like. She could not possibly escape two evil creatures at the same time. She grabbed hold of the Stone. "Help me! Help me! Please help me!"

But the Besta Fera was already upon her! She dared not look up at his face, but kept her eyes on his four-legged body instead. The torso bent down, snatched the machete from her hand, grabbed her and threw her onto the horse's back. The creature then reared up on his hind legs and cracked his whip every which way, turning violently in circles while Caipora clung to the torso in terror, lest she be thrown off and trampled to death. The whip cracked and sliced through the blackness until, with a brief flash of yellow, a horrific shriek cut through the blackness followed by a frightful wailing that went on and on and on. As if having achieved his objective, the Besta Fera turned and galloped back into the darkness from which he had come, Caipora's arms around the torso of the beast, nails digging into his flesh, wild dogs barking and howling behind them. It was as though time had stopped, the world had ended and the future didn't exist. Everything was swallowed up by the horror of this half man, half beast. It was the end of her. She would fight, but it would be the end of her.

The galloping hooves resounded through the cave, their echoes flying back and forth like rampant imprisoned demons. On and on the Besta Fera tore through the blackness, hair flying wildly in the wind of his own making. Suddenly the animal reared to a halt and let out a resounding snort. An arm around Caipora's waist lowered her to the ground. She didn't run or move. What was the point? Instead she stood trembling, eyes fixed on the ground so as not to look into the terrifying face. The hand that had taken her machete now offered it back to her. Without raising her head she closed her fingers around the weapon. Was she now to fight this massive towering creature from the ground with what suddenly seemed a very small knife?

Terror-stricken, Caipora waited for the end. The Besta Fera reared again, hooves kicking too close to her face, snorted and galloped into the darkness taking the green mist and howling dogs with him. Caipora's legs crumpled and brought her to the ground. Face cupped in her hands, she thanked the universe for her life. Could it really be that the Besta Fera had come to save her? The least likely of all creatures? She sat unmoving, unable to comprehend what had happened as diminishing echoes of galloping hooves haunted the inky underground.

When silence finally came, the depth of it was frightening.

Deprived of light and sound in blackness so thick you had to push through it, Caipora's mind sought solace in memories of her life with her tribe: of days fishing with Sema in gurgling streams; of tending to her garden, cooking with her mother; of sitting round the fire, singing, dancing, listening to stories told under the stars. Memories of her everyday routine, of fulfilling her duties and responsibilities comforted her and she now understood the security she had enjoyed. She saw herself by the riverbank, the sun tangled in leafy thickets, gilded reflections quivering in the blue-green current. She had visualised herself free as a bird, running through the forest with Sema, beyond the borders of their tribe where they would make their own decisions, their own choices; where she would be able to answer the call of her heart. She and Sema together escaping the shackles of the tribe and fulfilling their destiny. Restless and stifled, she had sat by the riverbank visualising herself free, but above all, believing that one day she would be free.

With that thought the words of the Mother of the Muiraquita exploded in her mind. "Thoughts have real energy. Believe in them and they will turn into actions. If you visualise your wishes happening, they will happen. Always believe in the power of your mind."

Like a thunderbolt it hit her: her intense persistent belief in her freedom had killed her people! The massacre of her tribe had set her free and she herself had brought it about through the power of her mind! She stared into the black space before her eyes at the nightmare that had revealed itself. Horror-stricken, her mind imploded, fell into oblivion to protect her from the unbearable realisation that she was responsible for the death of everyone in her tribe - even Sema! Numb, paralysed by the thought, she sat lifeless in the cold blackness. But time moved on and again her core body temperature fell dangerously low. In her semi-conscious state, her hand went to the Stone warming her chest, warning her of hypothermia. Her eyelids opened and the newly-discovered horror flooded her conscious mind. Chilled to the bone, nauseous at what the power of her thoughts had done, she could barely rise to her feet with the leaden weight of her heart. She had killed her family, her tribe. She deserved to die. Why not simply sit here and die? It would be so easy. So simple. But an unanswered question gnawed at her mind and moved her feet forward: why did the Besta Fera save her? Why had he wanted her to live?

Caipora trod heavily in the direction the Best Fera had taken her, her will to live ebbing from her as light ebbing from an evening sky. Despairing, forlorn, she wondered if this underground would ever deliver her to the river the frog had promised. And where was the frog now? Caipora stopped, her heart tearing itself apart with grief. "Where are you now frog?" she screamed into the blackness. "Are you keeping an eye on me now? Waiting to see me die? Did you know I killed my parents? My tribe? Is that why you sent me here to die?" her echoing screams disintegrated into heart-rendering sobs that flew back and forth between the walls of the empty cave. Again Caipora's legs gave way and she crumpled to the ground, face in her hands, consumed by agonising heartbreak.

The touch of a hand stroking her hair brought pause to her sobs. Then Sema's voice: "I miss you my love. My heart aches for you. Wherever you are, know that we will meet again. Believe that we will be together again." His words gave her hope and strength. Eased her despair. She hung onto them like a lost soul onto a guiding star in the wilderness and struggled to her feet.

How far she had walked when a faint sound stopped her in her tracks, she couldn't say. She held her breath and listened. Water? Or was it wind? Definitely water! The sound grew with each step and as she hurried round a bend her eyes squinted against the glare of millions of tiny lights. They sparkled in the walls and in the stalactites hanging from the glittering roof. A waterfall cascaded into a blue-green lake where the lights danced on water rippling around enormous green lily pads crowned with white blooms. The light of the glow worms reached into the distance where the cave narrowed into another tunnel and the lake became a river. Could this really be Rio Hamza, the underground river the frog had told her about? Would it rescue her from this cold black hell and carry her a long way towards her destination? There was only one way to find out. Caipora was an excellent swimmer, but the unknown length of the river and where it might lead concerned her and with the bow and quiver on her back, knife and machete at her hips and a sack across her shoulder, swimming any distance was not an option. She needed a canoe. No chance of that. But she remembered floating on a lily pad as a young child. Big and extremely strong, it would easily carry her weight even now. The biggest was near the middle of the lake. Caipora cautiously tested her weight on a smaller one by the water's edge, keeping her other foot firmly on solid ground. It held her well and she stepped from one lily pad to the next and finally onto the chosen one. Sitting cross-legged, she cut the stem anchoring it in the lake and manoeuvred the leaf into the slow-moving current. From there the water calmly carried her to the point where the cave narrowed and the lake became a river - and where the current traveled at a speed that flung Caipora left and right into jagged walls. The glow worms disappeared, the tunnel narrowed and the river threw itself violently around increasingly frequent and sharp bends in complete blackness.

Almost thrown into the water several times, Caipora lay down on the lily pad and, tightly gripping its upturned edge with one hand, clutched the Muiraquita Stone with the other and asked for light. Instantly, the Stone threw its light onto raging black water charging down a narrow chute but even more terrifying, a short distance ahead, the river disappeared! Before fear could take hold, Caipora plunged down a waterfall into a black abyss, swallowed by a mass of churning bubbles. Down and down she sank like a rock, her lungs screaming for air as she kicked and desperately thrust her arms upwards - but the bubbles could not support her.

"Swim to the bottom and away from the waterfall," spoke a voice in her head. "Swim to the bottom and away." Caipora dived down until her fingers clawed through the gravel at the bottom of the fall. There the water was solid and she swam away from the waterfall and up, popping through the surface like a cork. Gasping for air. A shaft of light hit her eyes! Light falling through an opening in the roof of the cave - an exit! She laughed out loud! All she had to do was get to the roof of the cave - but already the icy black water was sucking the heat from her body. Not only was it freezing but the current was pulling her towards another exit - an exit she didn't want to take: the mouth of a tunnel so small that she would be caught in it like a plug! If this was the Rio Hamza, it wasn't going to take her any further than this!

Caught in the powerful current, Caipora was within moments at the mouth of the small tunnel, arms and legs planted firmly on either side. She ran her freezing fingers over the rough surface of the wall, desperately searching for a handhold as the water snatched the heat from her body. Finally, above her head, her fingers grasped a rock big enough for both hands to take hold of. She leaned back, pushed her feet into the wall and took a couple of steps out of the water, then reached up for another handhold. Nothing! She scoured the wall in all directions. Still nothing! No! No! It couldn't be that her journey ended here! There had to be something! There had to be a way!

The rope she carried in her sack was of no use without a loop in the end. Tying one would take two hands and she had none to spare. Images of her equipment flew through her mind - and stopped at her hammock: she could throw it against the wall where it would catch onto handholds she couldn't even see! She pulled the hammock from her sack and flung it upward against the wall. Instantly it caught on several jutting rocks. She climbed the net and found a foothold and handhold on the wall above it, then threw it again until it caught on another rock and another. As she climbed she smiled at her good fortune to fall into this flooded cave while daylight lit the world above. Had it been night with no moon, no shaft of light would have shown her the way out. But progress was slow, the roof still a long way above her and already the jagged rocks had lacerated her fingers. Each time she grasped a rock and hauled her weight upwards she winced in pain. Each time she stepped onto the net it would swing back and forth, banging her knees onto the craggy surface.

Finally she reached the height at which the wall began to lean inwards to form the almost horizontal roof: a problem she had not foreseen, although, she thought to herself, it should have been obvious from the start. Again and again she threw the net before it caught onto a jagged rock only to fall free a moment later. Time and again she leaned out from the wall, holding on with only one bleeding hand to throw the net upward in the hope that it would catch onto something. Finally it caught onto a rock and held but hung down vertically from the roof! Caipora couldn't see how it could hold her or where she could go after stepping onto it: she would simply be swinging from the roof of the cave.

It was hopeless. She shook the hammock free, stuffed it into her sack with one hand while holding on hard with the other and crying out in pain. She considered her situation. Raw fingers and knees, and gashed feet hampered her thinking. Without the hammock her only option was to crawl along the roof upside down, gripping hold of knobbly bits and pushing on others with bleeding feet to propel herself along. Ignoring the pain, she reached out to a promising rock and gripped it tightly with both hands - but just as it took all her weight it snapped off, plunging Caipora ten metres into the icy water with a shattering splash!

As the swift current again swept her towards the small tunnel something smooth brushed against her leg and a light tickle slithered across her neck. She turned to catch sight of a small silvery dolphin leaping out of the water, gleaming briefly in the ray of light and diving into the wet blackness again. A dolphin! Strange, she thought, but the current demanded her attention. Again she fought to swim free of it - and this time she succeeded. Clinging to a handhold on the wall, Caipora reconsidered her options. What she needed was a ladder hanging down from the opening in the roof. Normally she would whip one up in no time but right now she wasn't in a position to make anything. Her rope was of no use. Even with a loop at its end, what could it attach to at the top of the cave? Her knife and machete served no purpose. The pudding was equally useless. The magic potions and... the wand. The wand!

She'd forgotten all about it! It had limited powers and wouldn't grant her just anything she fancied. It had to be a situation where nothing else could help. This was certainly that.

Her bleeding fingers searched through the sack and wrapped around the wand. There were certain words to be said, in a certain order. She had watched and listened carefully as the Nevae gave their demonstration and brought the wand to glow and pulsate with a bright blue light, ready for their command. Caipora closed her eyes, searching her memory for the words.

"Burn bright, power of light. Shine on my life, save me from this....." No, that wasn't it. "Shine on me oh brightest light...." Definitely not.

"Glimmer and glow, light of mine....," No. Nothing was happening. Then at last the words fell into in her mind.

"May your power burn bright, beacon of light. May your power burn bright and save my life!" The wand lit up! Glowed and pulsated with a bright blue light! Caipora's heart leapt and a smile sprang to her face. She drew a circle in the air with the wand as the Nevae had done, and gave her command.

"Make me a ladder from the mouth of this cave down to the water, so that I might climb out." All at once masses of long grasses grew down from the opening in the roof and formed a thick curtain all the way down into the water. Then, rustling and squeaking, the grasses began to weave themselves together, twisting over and under each other, wrapping themselves around one another until they formed two thick vertical ropes with horizontal rungs between them. Caipora watched in amazement as her escape route grew down towards her! But there remained still one obstacle to her climb to safety: the powerful current separating her from the ladder.

The current at the base of the waterfall was as wide as the

waterfall itself and not nearly as strong as it was running past the ladder in the middle of the cave. Caipora swam along the wall through the still water of the eddy to the edge of the waterfall and threw herself into the centre of the current. In an instant she was in the middle of the cave, hands on the ladder, her foot catching a rung below the water. She pulled herself up, grabbed hold of the next rung and the next and climbed out of the freezing water towards the now dimly lit opening above.

CHAPTER 5
The Mapinguari's Demand

Caipora crawled from the cave into a balmy evening, a purpled sky chasing a tinge of orange in the west. Early stars twinkled their greeting, looking as happy to see her as she was to see them, but already impending storm clouds hurried from the east to extinguish them. She stretched out on the grass, relishing the gentle breeze that soothed her bruised, exhausted limbs and savoured the fresh warm air.

She had climbed out into a small clearing at the base of a rocky hillside. On either side of the clearing a dense forest stretched to the edge of a cliff which fell into a deep gorge where a raging river roared through the serenity of the evening. Distant rumblings in the sky warned of the need for shelter and, as if in an effort to help, a cracking flash of lightning lit up a rock ledge in the hillside, exposing a small cave beneath it. Caipora roused her exhausted body and hurried to gather firewood.

In the warmth of the cave, behind a curtain of water glittering orange and red in the light of the flames, Caipora spread a few drops of the potion from the gold vial over her wounds and watched in amazement as they healed and closed. The wind ripped and raged through the forest as she devoured her pudding - not at all sodden after its time in the water - and deep throated clashes of storm clouds rumbled through the gorge. Physically and emotionally exhausted, she wrapped herself in her spider silk hammock and lay down on the bed of ferns she had made, the warmth of the fire and the droning of the rain soothing her frazzled nerves.

No longer under imminent threat, Caipora allowed her mind to drift through blissful days spent with Sema. His voice soothed her; his words calmed her; his laughter warmed her heart. He'd taught her all he had learnt from the men: hunting and tracking, climbing aguaje palms, making canoes, bow and arrows, machete. His presence in her mind comforted her and sleep came quickly, but her dreams offered no peace: all through the night she watched her tribe being slaughtered, screams shrill in her ears - knew she was responsible.

*****

From the moment Caipora crawled from the cave, five pairs of dark eyes had keenly followed her every move. They had watched her scurrying back and forth gathering firewood, tending to her wounds, devouring her pudding. Sheltering from the downpour in the thick foliage of the trees, they had seen the small cavern come ablaze like a hot sun in the black night.

"Do you think she's the one?" the oldest monkey asked no one in particular.

"Of course she is. Who else could she be?" squeaked another in reply. "Who else could survive the horrors of the underground and live to get out of that cave?"

"Who else could get out of that cave, even without the horrors?" And so they chattered quietly among themselves, asking questions to which there was only one answer: she was the one.

"I wonder if she knows what awaits her," pondered another.

"Of course she doesn't. How could she?"

"She's going to need help," someone added.

"Isn't that why we're here?" asked the littlest one.

Certain at last that Caipora slept, the monkeys crept down from the trees. The rain had eased and they squeezed through gaps in the lacy drizzle falling across the entrance to the cave. The fire was low. Sleeping on the ground, big flames were needed to keep predators away. The monkeys quietly stoked the fire with the wood Caipora had stacked against the back of the cave, then huddled around it, staring at her. Normally they would not come down from the trees at night but they wanted to be near the girl so that she wouldn't be up and away in the morning without them. Finally, propping one another up in a hairy heap, they fell asleep.

As the day yawned and stretched itself across the pale sky, birds threw their shrill calls against the calm of first light, shattering it like glass into thin shards. Caipora too, yawned and stretched, but sleep would not relinquish her. The sun was high when she finally opened her eyes and sat up - and gasped: five pairs of large black eyes set into five white faces stared at her, silent and unblinking.

"No need to be frightened," one little voice finally spoke. "Your Fairy Godmother sent us."

"What?" Barely awake, Caipora stared incomprehensibly

at the creatures, not entirely sure she wasn't still dreaming. The monkey's words made no sense. Finally, "The frog? The frog sent you?" she asked, incredulous at the words she'd heard.

"Well, she wasn't a frog when we spoke to her," replied the biggest monkey.

"Wasn't she? Well.... well....what was she then?" Caipora rubbed her hands over her eyes and face as if to shake off a hallucination.

"She was a monkey. Like us." a pert little one happily explained.

"Really?" Caipora, still not sure she wasn't dreaming, peered intently at the primates in front of her. "Why?"

"Why what?" they all asked in unison.

"Why did she send you?"

"She thought you might need some help," the oldest one replied, her voice carrying a serious and wise tone.

Caipora stared at them blankly. What *had* Fyglia been thinking? They were small capuchin monkeys - between thirty and fifty centimetres tall! They barely came up to her knees in height! They didn't have big strong limbs and they didn't even look frightening! In fact with their black coats, white chests and shoulders, white faces and smart black caps, they looked far too elegant to be a threat to anyone! Enemies were more likely to bow to them than run away!

"How could little creatures like you possibly help me?" Caipora asked, astonishment tinged with amusement ringing clearly in her voice.

Her words shocked the monkeys. Offended. Was she laughing at them? Was she diminishing and dismissing their abilities as fierce warriors? Was she questioning their loyalty to the cause? "Do not be misled by our size," the oldest one spoke slowly, her voice grave and stately. "We are warriors as fierce as fierce can be."

Instantly the cave exploded with a squall of hooting and whooping and the boisterous clamour of monkeys reaffirming to each other their prowess and unquestionable courage in battles past, recounting tales of unbelievable ferocity and glorious victories over their opponents. "Yes, we are! We are! We're very fierce! We're fierce and savage and afraid of nothing!" they shrilled in unison.

"All right! All right!" Caipora shouted over them. "I believe you! I believe you! It's certainly a lot of noise for such an early hour in the morning!"

"Early? I think not indeed!" asserted the oldest monkey haughtily. "Half the day is gone! We thought you would never wake! I do hope you don't intend to sleep in like this every morning or we shall never get things done!" she continued with her admonishments.

Ignoring her tone, Caipora leaned forward to peer out of the shelter. "Oh my! The sun *is* high. I was so tired I....."

"Yes, yes," cut in the oldest capuchin again. "Well I trust you are well rested now. I think I can speak for all of us when I say that *we* certainly didn't have a good night here on this hard ground, all falling into a heap over one another. Not our usual style or degree of comfort at all, I have to say, and at risk from savage beasts once the fire died out! But, these are the burdens we have to bear. Now, shall we get on?" Clearly, it was the group leader who had spoken. The others sat in silence, appearing to await her command.

"Do you mean to say you slept here the whole night?" Caipora asked.

"Yes, we did," all the voices replied in unison.

"Why?" Caipora asked, astonished.

"Why? Why? Well....... because we have to keep an eye

on you, that's why."

"Is that what the frog said?"

"She was a monkey. Like us."

"So is that what the monkey said?"

"Yes. It is."

"You do know that doesn't mean you have to stare at me all the time, don't you?" Caipora's words, tinged with annoyance, were met with silence. "You could have slept in your usual comfort in the trees instead of sneaking in here and frightening the daylights out of me when I opened my eyes!"

"Well......we..... er.....we wanted to see how the other half lived....." said one, with just the touch of a smile in the corner of her mouth.

***

Caipora stood at the edge of the cliff. Far below, the swollen river raged by at a speed that blurred her vision. She had no idea where she was. Countless rivers flowed through Amazonia but her map showed only the main ones. The wide and enormously long Amazon was clearly marked. This was not it, of that she was certain. The Amazon had to lie still some distance to the north and Caipora had to cross the furious, turbulent water at the bottom of this gorge to reach it. Clearly, that was not possible at this point. There had to be a place where she could climb down, swim across and climb up again. Turning around, she almost tripped over the smallest of the monkeys, standing right behind her.

"Good grief! What *are* you doing sneaking up behind me like that? I could have stepped on you and killed you!" Caipora exclaimed, feeling crowded and annoyed by the unexpected company.

"Sorry. I'm very sorry," he said meekly with a slight bow, "but that's exactly what I wanted to talk to you about."

"Exactly what?" Caipora questioned impatiently.

"Well, my life, that's what. Your Fairy Godmother promised us you wouldn't eat us, and I just wanted to check and make sure....."

"Eat you! Why on earth would I want to eat you?" Caipora almost shouted, irritated by the unwanted intrusion into her mission.

"Lots of Indians do, don't you know? They find us very tasty, so I just wanted to check....." his timid little voice trailed off, barely audible.

"No. You can relax," Caipora's voice softened reassuringly at the heartfelt concern the little monkey had for his life. "I'm not going to eat you, I promise. I've got plenty of food and besides, my tribe never ate monkeys, so you can stop worrying." The little one scurried back to his troop with the good news, greatly relieved, worries put aside.

Pushing her way through the undergrowth, Caipora followed the gorge, searching for a way down.

The monkeys followed her through the trees, chattering loudly, picking juicy pieces of fruit as they swung from branch to branch. Now and again Caipora stood at the very edge of the cliff, hoping to find a way down. Nothing. The sun was winking through the treetops when at last there came into view a bridge hanging across the gorge. The monkeys screamed with joy and hurried ahead of their leader - but their exuberance soon gave way to grave concern. The bridge hung on frayed and rotting ropes, in places, no more than threads. Most of the planks forming the walkway were broken or rotten, and just as many missing. Caipora arrived at the bridge to find the monkeys muttering in low voices, shaking their heads, white faces agitated.

"This bridge won't hold you," the oldest spoke grimly to Caipora.

"No, no it won't. It won't hold you. No, no. It won't hold you at all!" the others concurred, shaking their heads in mutual disapproval.

"We'll have to find another way," continued the oldest one.

"Another way. Yes, yes. Another way. A better way. This bridge is no good!" the capuchins again echoed their leader's verdict in troubled voices.

Caipora wasn't at all happy with the monkeys Fyglia had sent her. It seemed, even at this early stage, that they intended to take charge of her mission and make her decisions for her. While she admitted that it was pleasant to have some friendly company, she was her own person and would not be told what to do and what not to do, regardless of how well intentioned her new-found helpers might be.

"Thank you for your opinion, but I will decide whether the bridge will hold me or not," she said curtly. Gasps of shock thickened the air. No one had ever spoken to their elder like that! The monkeys gaped at one another, wide-eyed and open-mouthed at this defiance coming from the girl they'd been sent to protect. How could they do their duty if she was going to be disobedient and obstinate?

"I really must insist!" the oldest monkey said unyieldingly, incredulous at these words from the young girl. "We have taken on the responsibility of your welfare. We promised to ensure that no harm comes to you, as best we can! You *must* act upon our advice!" Her voice, half whispered, was insistent and forceful, like an urgent rush of wind determined to get through the forest.

Caipora met the eyes in the startled face, the eyebrows

that had leapt up to meet the rim of the monkey's black cap. "Thank you for coming to help me," she said calmly. "However, it is I who have been charged with this mission. It is I who have been trained and equipped by the Nevae to cope with whatever may happen, and it is I who will make the decisions concerning myself, where I go and what I do. I do not believe Fyglia meant for you to take charge of my mission. I think you must have misunderstood her instructions."

"Mis-un-der-stood?" the elder squealed indignantly, drawing herself up on her hind limbs. "Misunderstood?" she puffed out her chest haughtily and stretched herself as tall as was possible for any monkey to do.

"Yes. Misunderstood," replied Caipora. "I'm happy to have your company and should I need help at any time, I shall be grateful for it - but I will make my own decisions. If you cannot agree to this, I'm afraid we will have to part."

More gasps, sharper than before, burst from the small group. Wide-eyed looks of shock and disbelief flew between them. They shuffled away a short distance, huddled together, muttering among themselves, throwing an occasional glance in Caipora's direction, then put their heads together again to continue the muttering. Finally the elder stepped out of the circle and turned to face Caipora.

"You give us no choice," her voice was flat and resigned. "I have consulted with the others and, against our better judgment, we have decided to continue with you on your terms, even though we fear that you will place not only yourself, but all of us, in great danger."

"Danger is everywhere. If I run from it, I will achieve nothing and our world will cease to exist. However, I do not ask that you follow me into it." Silence followed. Clearly, there was nothing more to be said. They stood before the bridge under a dusky purple sky. Caipora knew the capuchins were right: the bridge did not look safe. It could well collapse under her weight even though she weighed little and she'd drop like a stone into the raging river, instantly swept away by the ferocious current.

"We'll spend the night in the forest and consider the best way forward in the morning," she announced. "We need wood for a fire." With those words the monkeys diligently gathered a plentiful supply of wood and soon the group sat around a blazing fire, Caipora feasting on her pudding, the monkeys watching: they'd eaten their fill of fruits, nuts, spiders, insects and birds eggs traveling through the trees during the day. Only when Caipora's appetite was finally sated and she lay in her hammock, did the capuchins settle in the trees above. But Caipora slept restlessly, tossing, turning, frequently waking. The night exuded an uncanny energy - oppressive, unnerving. The moon, a huge white lantern, hovered above the canopy and the stars glittered as usual but things were not as they should be. The jungle was bereft of its normal nocturnal sounds and in their place, eerie noises drifted across the gorge - sounds she'd never heard from any animal: long deep sighs, low moans and groans and a barely audible, deep murmuring. When morning light washed the stars from the sky, Caipora's eyes opened reluctantly. She had barely slept. The monkeys too, were unusually quiet and stayed close to her on their way to the bridge. When it came into view they stopped in their tracks and gaped.

"What's happened? Is this the same bridge? It can't be! It looks perfectly new!" Caipora exclaimed, incredulous at the sight.

"It must be the same one. It's in exactly the same place. Look, these are our footprints from yesterday!" the oldest monkey pointed out.

"Yes, it is in the same place! But look at the boards! They're straight and smooth and not one missing anywhere. And it's hanging taught across the gorge, not down in a big loop like it was yesterday. And the ropes are like new!" Caipora couldn't believe her eyes.

"Oooh! Look at the river, how beautiful and calm it is. Yesterday it was so wild it was really scary. I wasn't looking forward to crossing it at all!" said the littlest monkey, carefully peering over the edge of the cliff. Caipora looked down at the water and the blue sky and splendid bridge quivering on its glossy surface. How could this be the same bridge? There was no explanation other than that their eyesight had misled them in the twilight of the previous evening. Even so, the monkeys huddled together, murmuring among themselves, still perplexed by the inexplicable excellence of the bridge, dubious and anxious about its safety.

"I'm going across," Caipora announced and took hold of the rope, put her weight on the first board and tested it for strength. "It's good! Good and strong!" She stepped confidently onto one board after another and had covered some distance before looking back. The capuchins remained standing at the edge of the gorge. "Are you coming?" Against their instincts, tightly gripping the rope, the monkeys reluctantly followed their leader. She was half way across when a brittle crack of thunder shot darkness across the sky, a fury of violent winds screamed out of nowhere, battering the bridge from every direction, shaking it sideways, flapping it up and down, and threw Caipora flat onto her face. She struggled to her feet but the bridge was disintegrating. The rope fraying, unraveling in her grip! The boards were crumbling, falling into a now raging river - a mass of standing waves and churning whirlpools!

The monkeys shrieked, hanging onto ropes and boards with hands, feet and tails as the bridge tried to hurl them into the gorge. Now flat on her stomach, Caipora pulled herself along by what was left of the ropes and was almost at the other side when the bridge snapped in two and each half slammed into the cliff face on either side of the gorge. Hanging onto the rope, Caipora smashed into the jagged rocky face of the cliff. The monkeys went down with the other half of the bridge but had leapt onto the cliff face before they could be slammed into it and were already safely at the top. The violent wind died as suddenly as it had begun; the river peaceful and serene again. Caipora climbed to the top of the gorge hanging onto the frazzled remnants of the rope. Suddenly the monkeys began to shriek and jump up and down in frenzied hysteria. At the same instant, drowning out their shrieking, an horrific roar thundered through the jungle, shaking Caipora to her very bones.

She turned to face a towering, enormous ape-like creature, entirely covered in long red hair. Craning her head, she looked into one gigantic eye - no eyelid - glowering at her from the centre of a hairy forehead. Round and purple, it protruded from a patch of weeping, wrinkled red skin - something that should be covered up, not seen in the light of day. A glistening black lump of a nose squat in the middle of a flat, wide face dripped snot and below it, a foaming lip-less mouth bearing two huge curved fangs top and bottom, snarled at her.

To Caipora's added horror, a second mouth gaped from the middle of the hairy abdomen, just above her eye level: big and round, encircled by a lumpy red lip behind which a ring of small needle-like teeth flashed yellow. The mouth slurped as it rhythmically opened and closed, ready to suck in whatever came near. There was no sign of a tongue.

As the thing snarled at her, a long hairy arm reached up and an enormous hand with five clawed digits plucked a lizard from a branch above its head and began to stuff it into the now salivating mouth in its abdomen. The red wrinkled lip slurped up the struggling reptile. The sight was so grotesque that Caipora cast her eyes at the ground to avoid it. There her view met two gigantic feet, each with five toes from which protruded claws large enough to tear apart palm trees. The stench of the creature was so foul that she retched and struggled not to vomit. She knew at once that she stood before the elusive Mapinguari. Carnivorous, but for reasons best known to himself, he did not eat humans. Tales of the Mapinguari were widely known. The most terrifying thing about him was his stench: one man in her tribe was sick for days after encountering him and breathing it in, and never spoke again.

"Here you are at last! I've been expecting you for some time! What took you so long?" Even the ground vibrated as he roared. Caipora retched again from the extra load of putrid breath that he dumped on her and instead of answering, covered her nose and mouth to hold back the toxic stench.

"Never mind! No need to answer! Not important!" his voice thundered as fetid foam spluttered from his mouth. "I've been told you want to pass through my forest," he boomed, one enormous ugly eye glaring down at her. Too dazed and nauseous to answer, Caipora stood silent.

"Is this true?" he boomed again, bending down to her face so that all she could see was the one red-rimmed eye. She threw up at the Mapinguari's clawed feet.

"Never mind! Never mind! No need to answer!" he continued roaring. "Whether you want to come through or not, now that you're here, you'll do my bidding!"

"Yes, I do need to go through this forest," Caipora finally blurted out and instantly covered her mouth and nose again.

"No! No! No! Not *this* forest. "*My* forest," the Mapinguari corrected her. "It's *my* forest!" He thundered.

"All right. Yes, I want to go through *your* forest," she said obligingly.

"Good. Good. Now that we've got that sorted, I need you to do something for me before I let you through. There's something I need - needed for a long time, even before I knew you were coming," the Mapinguari finally spoke in a more reasonable voice. A silence hung between them as Caipora waited to hear what he needed, but he didn't speak. Still she waited. Then out of the blue he roared again. This time the trees shook as well as she herself. "Well? Don't you want to know what it is?"

"Well yes, of course I do," Caipora replied a little timidly, stunned at his unexpected aggressiveness.

"Then why don't you ask? Is it not important enough for you to ask?" he continued roaring.

"I was waiting for you to tell me," she replied defensively.

"You should ask! It's polite to show some interest you know!"

"I *am* interested. I am. Very interested. I would *very* much like to know what it is you need. Please, do tell me," Caipora spoke as politely and obligingly as was possible, not wishing to aggravate the ill- tempered stinking creature further.

"Thank you," he said with an air of smug satisfaction. "Then I will tell you," he continued, lifting one long and hairy arm to scratch an armpit, peppering Caipora with a shower of muck that fell from it. Shuddering, she backed away from the fallout.

"I need a hair brush," the Mapinguari said calmly, resolutely.

Caipora scanned the creature from head to toe. His hair certainly was dreadfully matted and lumpy, riddled with knots and tangles and crying out for a good wash as well as a thorough brushing. "I don't have a hair brush," she said quietly after a moment or two. "If I did, I would certainly give it to you - but I simply don't have one."

"No, of course you don't. And even if you did, I'm sure I wouldn't want it. I want a very particular kind of hair brush, you see. I want the tongue of a pirarucu fish!" the one eye glared at her, waiting for a response, but she could think of nothing to say. The tongue of the pirarucu is studded with teeth with which the fish crush the prey in their mouths. Caipora's people used to eat the pirarucu, although it wasn't their favourite as it doesn't keep long after being caught. They used to dry the tongues and use them to grate large seeds.

"Well? Do you know what the tongue of a pirarucu looks like?" he boomed again.

"Yes, of course I do," Caipora answered, surprised that he should think it necessary to ask such a question.

"Right then. Off you go. And when you bring me back a pirarucu tongue hairbrush - nice and big, mind you - you can go through my forest," the Mapinguari commanded and waived her off with a long and hairy arm from which a flurry of red hairs floated to the ground. He turned to leave but stopped. "Oh, one more thing. Be warned! This part of the river plays tricks on those who pass here: this is Boiuna's territory. Be alert and be careful! And make sure you come back - I need that brush!" Then he turned and was absorbed by the shifting shadows of the jungle.

Caipora had stood as if paralyzed throughout this encounter but now she doubled over and vomited up the entire contents of her stomach while frantic monkey screams flew across the gorge. She sat in a crumpled heap against the trunk of a tree, head in her hands, every part of her body seared with pain. Dizzy and nauseous, vision blurred, she retched again. It was very possible she would die. Not yet recovered from the horrors of the cave or the collapsing of the bridge, facing a future that promised more life threatening experiences and haunted day and night by the guilt of killing her tribe, Caipora's will to live was slipping away. "I deserve to die. So much easier," she told herself.

"Take the potion," a voice in her head spoke. "Take the potion in the gold vial."

"The potion...yes, there was that..." and her trembling hand pulled the gold vial from her sack. For some time the small stopper eluded the grasp of her shaking fingers but at last she pulled it free and sprinkled a few drops onto her tongue. Instantly her pain vanished and a life-giving energy surged through her body.

CHAPTER 6
The Pirarucu

Healed and vitalised by the potion, Caipora turned her focus to catching a pirarucu. The river flowed smoothly again and she searched for a way to get down to it. Rounding the next bend, an eddy bordered by a sandy beach came into view and right in front of her, a narrow animal track led down to the water's edge. Hurrying across its rocky surface Caipora lost her footing and were it not for a branch jutting from the cliff, would have plummeted into the river from a great height.

"What are you doing? For heaven's sake, be careful! Where are you going? Are you coming across to get us? " The monkeys clamoured across the gorge.

"I'm going to catch a pirarucu," Caipora shouted. Her hairy companions exchanged wide-eyed glances. Was she hungry? She'd had breakfast not long ago. It seemed odd to be wasting time and energy now to catch a fish, but they could only shrug their shoulders and wait. Caipora was halfway down the track when again, a vicious howling wind ripped through the gorge and whipped the water into a frenzied turbulence. The earth shuddered and with a thunderous rumbling the path beneath her feet fell away, plummeting her into the wild water which sucked her into its dark depths, tossing her about like a leaf at the whim of the wind. She kicked furiously to reach the surface - but which way was up and which down? Her lungs screamed for air and when she finally broke through the surface massive walls of water smashed her face from every direction and a tremendous roar reverberated through the gorge as a colossal tower of water surged towards her, on its summit a monstrous black serpent: Boiuna! In the blink of an eye the serpent changed into a ferocious monster covered in black, green and yellow scales. Six sharp red horns studded its head and massive black fins jutted from its spine and sides. Roaring hideously and blowing shafts of white smoke from cavernous nostrils, the gargantuan monster belted out red flames and lunged at Caipora, mammoth fangs on either side of its jaws. Its yellow eyes glared menacingly at her and as she was about to be snapped up she was lifted out of the water and riding on the back of a gleaming pink dolphin!

"Hold on!" the dolphin shouted. Caipora grabbed its dorsal fin, wrapped her legs around its body. They flew through the water at high speed and seemed to be making good their escape but looking back Caipora saw the monster right behind them, snarling fangs and foaming mouth ready to snap her up!

Then a second dolphin appeared beside them. "Have you got a rope?" she shouted over the roar of the monster.

"Yes!" Caipora shouted back.

"Make a loop and throw it in front of us. We'll grab it in our teeth while you hold onto it for balance. Stand up and put one leg on each of us," she said. "Two of us can pull you faster than one!"

Caipora pulled the rope from her sack and threw a loop in front of the dolphins. It was instantly between their teeth and she held onto it like a pair of reins, one foot on each dolphin. Her glistening pink rescuers cut through the water at fantastic speed but even so, the monster stayed close behind them.

"Take a deep breath! We're going under!" shouted one of the dolphins. Caipora gulped a mouthful of air and they plunged beneath the surface, Caipora lying down on them, speeding through deeper calmer water like shining pink arrows, then flying through the air again in a long arc.

"Breathe!" the dolphins shouted again. Caipora breathed in and they plunged once more into the dark depths. Again they broke the surface, flew through the air and dived once more. The third time they surfaced the gorge was quiet and serene. "I think we're all right now," said the male dolphin. "Is there anything behind you?"

Caipora looked. "Nothing! There's nothing! No monster. No waves. Nothing!"

"Then we've escaped the immediate threat - but the danger isn't over. We still need to be very cautious. Things are rarely what they seem in this part of the river," warned the female.

"You saved my life." Caipora said, now sitting comfortably on one of the dolphins. "I really thought it was the end and suddenly you were there....I don't know to thank you...".

"Oh no! No, no, no! We know about your mission to stop the Toad. You risk your life every day to save both us and our world. It is we who must thank you," said the dolphins.

"Well, the way I see it, we're all in this together," Caipora said thoughtfully.

"How did you come to be in the river?" the female dolphin asked and Caipora recounted her meeting with the Mapinguari.

"A hair brush? He wants a hair brush?" they cried out in astonishment, unsure whether to laugh or feel sorry for him. "We shouldn't laugh," said the female finally. "After all, we all groom ourselves to stay clean and healthy, and it seems the Mapinguari is no different. He can't help his stench and deserves our respect for wanting to improve himself. But how did you cope with his stench? It's been known to kill people - to make them very sick at the least."

"Yes, I was ill. Very ill," Caipora recalled quietly. "I thought I was going to die, but I have some magic potion which saved me." And said to herself "But I wanted to die...."

"Well, we'd better find a place where you can catch a pirarucu so that there can be a well-groomed Mapinguari in this forest and you can be on your way." With that they picked up speed and with playful leaps and bounds, flew across the water's surface. The sun was well and truly in the west before they spotted a small beach with an eddy. There was no time to waste.

"So, how do you plan to catch the fish?" the dolphins asked.

"Well, I've got a great hammock made from spider silk. There's nothing stronger you know, and it's perfect for catching fish."

"Oh really? I didn't know that," said the female in surprise.

"Yes, it's true. And there's no fish that's going to break through this net - not even a great big fish, which is what I want."

"But you don't want the whole fish do you? Just the tongue, isn't that right?"

"Yes, the Mapinguari only wants the tongue. We can eat the rest of the fish. You love fish and, as tasty as my pudding is, the thought of succulent fish for dinner is already making my mouth water. My monkeys will like it too."

"Yes, I've heard that some monkeys eat fish, but how is it that they're *your* monkeys?"

And so Caipora related to the dolphins how Fyglia had sent a group of monkeys to protect and help her, but with the bridge falling down, they'd been left on the other side of the river. "But now that we're all on the same side," she said, "they'll find me eventually."

"You're quite sure they'll follow you?"

"Absolutely! I couldn't escape them if I tried!" Caipora laughed and realised she was looking forward to seeing them again.

The dolphins watched from the shallows as Caipora tied each end of her rope to either end of her hammock, waded into deeper water and threw it into the current, letting the rope run through her fingers. When the current had taken it far enough she held the rope firmly and waited. The dolphins now lay still, as close to the bank as possible: if the fish sensed their presence they wouldn't come near for fear of being eaten. Every now and again Caipora felt movement in the net but knew from experience that it was only a small fish. She was waiting for a gigantic pirarucu: three arms long - about as big as they could get.

Then WHOOMPF! She flew over the water and disappeared head first into it - a vice-like grip on the rope and a whopper of a fish in her net. The pirarucu tore along the bottom of the river at ferocious speed. Grasses and weeds slapped Caipora's face and too often her knees scraped against sharp rocks. She was running out of air, but would not let go: letting go would mean losing not only the fish but her hammock and rope as well. Letting go was not an option. Suddenly the dolphins shot past her, launching themselves at the pirarucu. The fish was longer than them but the dolphins were stronger and more agile - and there were two of them! A frightful thrashing and smashing and twisting and turning ensued until finally, all was still.

Caipora too, was still. She floated lifelessly as river grasses waved back and forth around her body. The dolphins carried her to the water's surface where one supported her while the other firmly nudged her side again and again and again until at last she gasped, coughing and spluttering, and opened her eyes.

"Thank you," she finally whispered.

"All in a day's work," they said, "besides, what else can we do when you're so intent on killing yourself?" they squeaked with a little chuckle, making light of the situation. "We'll take you back now. You rest while we bring in your catch before someone else claims it!"

Alone on the sandy beach, Caipora sheltered from the sun in the shade of one small tree and tended her lacerated knees with drops of potion. Shaken and dazed, she fell into despondent gloom. "I'm not fit for this mission. Not qualified. It would be best if I were to simply die. I'd be with my family again in the spirit world. And with Sema." But how would she face Sema in the next life if she were to give up and die? His words flooded her mind: "You are special Caipora. You have a gift. We are all part of the universe, but your mind and your soul are directly connected to its energy. The purple specks in your brown eyes sparkle when it's flowing through you and I can feel it when my arms are around you. You must always use the strength it gives you to do good in the world."

Splashing and whistling and the return of the dolphins with her enormous catch washed Sema's words from Caipora' mind. She tucked her rope and hammock into her sack and set about gathering firewood and long thin sticks which she soaked in the shallows. The fire blazed as she scraped the massive pirarucu scales from the fish, cut it open and threw the guts to her pink friends who, had they had lips, would certainly have licked them with pleasure. When all the innards had gone she threw chunks of the fish over the water where the squealing dolphins leapt up to catch them. The fish was enormous: three arms long, she reckoned, and considered herself lucky not to have caught a bigger one which would certainly have ripped the rope from her hands and left her without fish, rope or hammock!

Finally the dolphins had their fill. "Enough! I'm too full to leap up any more!" cried one and the other feared he would burst at any moment. Caipora laughed and over her laughter came the calling and chattering of monkeys descending the cliff face in leaps and bounds, overjoyed to find Caipora alive and well.

"Greetings, my little troop!" Caipora called out. "What took you so long?" she asked cheerily.

"What took us so long?" asked one, astonished at the thoughtless question. "Did you hear that?" they gasped in unison, greatly offended at being called slow and incompetent. "Well I never....!!" They exchanged stunned glances, mouths agape, their joy at finding Caipora instantly nullified by her insensitive remark "Do you have any idea what we've been through in trying to find you? Scouring water and land searching for you?" demanded the oldest in a deep and serious voice.

"I nearly fell all the way down into the river trying to catch sight of you!" cried the littlest one, fighting back tears.

"Oh dear! I'm sorry you've had such a difficult time," Caipora lightly feigned compassion. "I, on the other hand, merely had a near death experience brought about by the Mapingurari's foul stench," she said flippantly, stifling a little smile, "and then I was almost devoured by a gigantic monster but was saved by my beautiful pink friends here," she threw a casual nod at the dolphins wallowing in the shallows, resting their fat bellies. "Then I was nearly drowned by a huge pirarucu but again saved by the same pink friends. However, I do understand that you must be beyond exhaustion from running along the top of the cliff," she winked at the dolphins with a twinkle in her eye, "so why not come and rest your weary little legs and have some of this tasty fish? It won't be nearly as good in the morning so eat all you can, and then some more, just as the dolphins did. After all, it's not every day you get to feast on pirarucu!" The capuchins didn't need a second invitation. Their trials and tribulations, woes and complaints all fell aside as they hurried to the chunks of fish piled high on a bed of river grasses.

In the purple light of the evening, Caipora threaded pieces of the fish onto wet sticks, cooked them over the fire and relished her hot meal while the monkeys recounted at length the harrowing events of their day. Her hunger sated, she turned her attention to the head of the pirarucu. By the flickering light of the fire, knife in hand, she considered how best to deal with it. It was important to get the whole tongue out in one piece without damaging it, leaving no cause for complaint from the Mapinguari. She slit the mouth on either side, opened it wide and avoiding the sharp teeth, cut the tongue from the back of the throat: it was big - very big, and the cut clean. Job done!

It had to be dried over the fire right away or it would rot - not so low that it would cook and not too high or it wouldn't dry. As if reading her mind, a capuchin who'd been quietly watching her called out "I know! I have a great idea! Make a thin twine from some grasses, tie the tongue to one end and I'll take the other end up into the tree and tie it to a branch above the fire."

"An excellent idea!" Caipora enthused and soon the tongue hung at the perfect height above the flames. Satisfied with her day's work, Caipora stoked the fire and the monkeys, who had thoroughly gorged themselves on the fish, hauled their distended bellies into the small tree they all had to share. Wrapped in her hammock, Caipora settled on a bed of grasses by the fire but with the ruckus and arguing over the best spot in the tree above, some time passed before peace ensconced the camp.

Hours later Caipora woke to a silence so heavy it seemed the trees were holding their breath. The fire burned low and in the blackness on the far side of the river, a dozen white lights danced slowly with their reflections in the satin water. Fireflies, she told herself. Just fireflies - but they rapidly multiplied a thousandfold and formed a wondrous sparkling bridge across the river. As Caipora stared at the mystifying spectacle, whispering voices slid through the silence of the night. "Walk across the star bridge and step into paradise. Come hither! Come hither dear friend and eternal happiness will be yours!" the voices whispered again and again, tempting her, coaxing, pleading with her to cross the river on the sparkling bridge.

Confused, bewildered, Caipora sat motionless, mesmerised by the glittering bridge hanging from the sky by starry ropes; bewitched by the whispering voices caressing her ears with tempting words. A strongly glowing light, larger than the rest, came gliding over the water and rested on her hand. She picked it up and at once it pulled her to her feet and, arm outstretched, into the water. Waist- deep in the river, she was about to step into the strong deep current when a voice she knew better than any, softly called her name and broke the spell ensnaring her.

"Caipora.....Caipora....." A vaporous apparition materialised out of the blackness. Incredulous, Caipora watched the translucent figure of her mother gliding towards her, dark shining eyes fixed on Caipora's. Closer and closer she came, arms outstretched, until she wrapped Caipora in them, enveloping her child in her unearthly, ethereal body. Caipora melted into her mother and together they moved out of the water. Soundlessly, the star bridge disintegrated; the hovering lights dissolved into the blackness.

Ensconced in her mother's arms, overcome with joy, guilt and regret, Caipora cried out, copious tears washing her face, "Mamma! Mamma! I'm sorry. I'm so sorry! It was all my fault! I wanted to be free and my wish caused your death!"

"No my child, it is not your fault," her mother held her close, stroked her hair, caressed her cheek. "Your wish did not cause our destruction. What happened was the work of Fate and had nothing to do with your desire to be free."

"Mamma, I'm frightened. I'm frightened and I want to die because I killed all of you! I am not worthy of walking this earth!"

"Listen to my words my child: you did not kill anyone." Her mother's voice was calm, reassuring and firm. "It was simply our time to die. Fate decides when we live and when we die, not you or me. Fate decides what we will do with our lives and when. No wish on your part had anything to do with our deaths. You wanted to be free and there is a reason for that. I knew you were different the moment I looked into your eyes when you were born. I saw that you were meant for greater things but as you grew, I didn't want to impose that on you. I wanted you to discover that for yourself and make your own choices. Our deaths were not your fault. Shed this guilt. It does not belong to you. Fate has given you freedom and given your freedom purpose. You are now doing what you are meant to do. But you must be brave. If you run from fear, it will forever chase you. To achieve your goals, you must face your greatest fears head on, grab them with both hands and do what needs to be done. You have to take risks to become that which you know deep in your heart you are meant to be."

"I will try Mamma. I will try." Caipora buried herself deeper in her mother's arms. "But Mamma, can you tell me why the Besta Fera saved me?"

"He saved you because he wants the natural order of the world restored but the shackles that order has imposed on him prevent him from restoring it himself." With these words her mother began to tremble and fade, but still held Caipora close. "Take my love my child. It is yours forever. Let it be your strength and your courage and know that I believe in you."

"Don't go Mamma! Please don't leave me! I don't want to be alone! Mamma! Come back!" Caipora cried and desperately clung to her mother's dissolving body.

"You are not alone my child. As long as you are helping others, you will never be alone." With those words the ethereal figure dissolved in Caipora's arms: the consoling comfort of her gone; the security gone. Caipora stood forlorn, aching for her mother's touch.

***

When first light stretched across the sky and a myriad of bird calls crowded the air, Caipora opened her eyes to find the capuchins snuggled in a hairy pile around her. Only the embers of the fire remained, warming the sand around them. "Time to wake up," she said, gently scratching one monkey behind the ear. "Why are you here on the ground with me?"

"We heard you crying in your sleep," the little one said, "and we didn't want you to be alone when you were sad."

"Why were you sad?" asked another, caringly running strands of her long hair through his fingers.

"Was it a bad dream?"

Caipora closed her eyes and was in her mother's arms again, words of love and reassurance in her ears. The pain of parting burned her heart, but the love and comfort was overwhelming. "I was thinking of my family and how much I miss them," Caipora replied quietly, thoughtfully, and wiped her eyes. "But I'm all right now. I feel very close to them now," and her mouth yielded the touch of a smile. "Who would like fresh fish for breakfast? What do you think?"

"A fish? Yes! A fish would be a good thing," they enthused in unison. "A very good thing indeed!"

"I'd *very* much like a fish. I dreamt about fish all night! I'd like another pirarucu," said the littlest one in a squeaky, hopeful voice.

"Well I very much hope it *won't* be another pirarucu! Why don't you get some more firewood while I catch our breakfast?" Caipora waded into the water and the dolphins swam towards her. "You'd better lie low if I'm going to catch any breakfast," she said.

"Why not let us catch it for you? We know exactly where the fish are and it will save a lot of time. How many would you like?"

"A great idea!" Caipora enthused. "I suppose six or seven good-sized ones should suffice." Soon enough, Caipora and the capuchins each held a fish skewered on a stick over the fire and ate until their bellies were full.

The pirarucu tongue had dried well and Caipora wrapped it in a wad of grasses and tucked it into her sack. Now, capuchin monkeys can swim, but being quite small, are not likely to win a fight against a strong fast current, so, with the aid of the dolphins, Caipora's rope was slung across the river and secured to both banks. Hanging onto this with hands, feet and tails, the monkeys crossed the gorge and scampered up the cliff face to travel through the trees while the dolphins carried Caipora upstream. Wary and vigilant, all eyes were on the lookout for the slightest sign of danger but this time nothing disturbed their progress. Arriving at the remnants of the bridge, Caipora swallowed a few drops of the potion before scaling the cliff for protection against the murderous stench of the Mapinguari - and a good thing it was, as he already stood waiting at the top when she arrived. Her hands flew to her face as she backed away from him, thinking again that, far more than a brushing, he really needed a thorough wash.

Without a word, and looking straight up into his one enormous weeping purple eye, Caipora held out the dried tongue to the Mapinguari on the palm of her hand. His reaction was astounding. "Oh me! Oh my! You've got my tongue brush! You've got my toothy tongue brush!" he squealed with joy, hopping up and down on the spot and clapping his great hairy hands in glee like a small child excited at a lovely present, causing a great deal of dust and hair and loose unpleasant stuff to billow from him in thick and plentiful clouds. He danced about, clutching the tongue with both hands, waving it around so that it almost caught in the branches above him. "Oh me! Oh my! I'm so happy! I'm so glad!" he rejoiced on and on, emitting not only clouds of debris and hair but also greater volumes of the murderous stench which his prancing clearly intensified.

"I wonder if you might move back just a little? I'm afraid you smell very bad indeed. The last time we met your smell almost killed me," Caipora dared to say, as politely as it was possible to say such a thing, moving back herself at the same time. Even though the magic potion would protect her from its effects, it didn't take away the stench itself. She expected anger, if not rage, in response to her offensive remark. Instead, the Mapinguari moved back and hung his head as if in shame. His flat wide face, black blob of a nose still dripping snot, looked glumly at the ground. The lip-less mouth sagged downward as did its partner in his abdomen.

"I know I don't smell nice," the mouth on his face spoke dejectedly, "but it's not my fault. I can't get down to the river to wash because I'm too big and cumbersome. I've never had a brush with which to brush out all the dirt and insects and other rubbish that's accumulated in my hair over my endless lifetime and I've always been on my own. I've never had anyone to groom me. It's not my fault I stink - I wish I didn't, but I know I do." So glum and sad and sorry for himself was he that the one inky purple eye reddened and overflowed with tears. The nose too, now exuded copious quantities of snot which caught in the fangs protruding from his lip-less mouth.

Caipora felt sorry for the poor creature. "Well, it can all be different now," she said encouragingly. "Now that you have a brush, you can stand in the rain and scrub yourself clean time and time again!"

"Yes! Yes I can! And I will! Every time it rains, I'll brush myself and brush myself, until I smell as sweet as a flower!" This thought clearly cheered him up no end as the ghastly mouth on his belly broke into an enormous, gruesome, toothy smile.

"That's an excellent idea," Caipora said encouragingly,

thinking to herself that aiming to smell as sweet as a flower might be just a little too ambitious, but not wishing to dampen his optimism and hopes of a brighter future, she said nothing.

The capuchins had by now arrived and were perched high in the trees a good distance from the Mapinguari. "Well, I must be off," said Caipora, eager to get away from the worsening stench.

"Yes, yes. You must be on your way. But be warned, there are many evil things that will stand in your path. Always be on your guard and trust no one. There is no one to trust in this dark forest" he warned her glumly. Caipora thanked him for his advice and turned to go, but the Mapinguari continued. "Surely you must know you can't possibly capture the evil Toad. He has countless malevolent creatures doing his evil work - the forest is full of them. You don't stand a chance."

"I have no choice," Caipora replied resolutely. "I have to save the forest and its creatures. I have to. Perhaps you could tell me which way is the Amazon River?"

"Well if you insist on going, then go north, that way," and he raised a hairy arm to point her in the right direction. And so Caipora and her troop of capuchins moved off into the sunless forest, leaving the Mapinguari in his new state of pure bliss, brushing himself this way and that with his fabulous pirarucu tongue hairbrush. It was clear when he got to that very difficult-to-reach spot in the middle of his back because he let out such a groan of ecstasy and relief that the very roots of the ancient trees trembled.

CHAPTER 7
The Toad's Council Meeting

When the Toad heard that a young girl was on her way to find him and bring him to justice, he laughed and laughed, bouncing up and down on his rotting mound of reeds until he rolled off and into Stinky Lake. Then he climbed out and laughed some more.

But when he heard how the girl had got the caiman teeth and escaped from the slimy guard at the forest gate, he didn't laugh quite so much. And when he heard how she had evaded the evils of the slimy forest, the tunnel and its horrors and crawled out of the cave, he laughed even less. And when he was told that she'd got the pirarucu tongue for the Mapinguari, survived his stench and survived the river monster, he stopped laughing altogether and through a messenger, summoned the three evil spirits to a council meeting. Furthermore, he ordered that Boiuna make for him lots of large glass jars to be filled with a smorgasbord of his favourite foods - flying insects, beetles, slugs, spiders, worms and any other tasty morsels she could think of - and brought to the meeting.

"And a good quantity of anaconda oil from a market somewhere as well. And a small cauldron," the Toad instructed his messenger.

The evils spirits did the Toad's bidding and made their way to the meeting place - a dank cavern under Stinky Lake. The Toad arrived early and sat reclining his greenish-grey lumpy body on a mound of damp reeds, his fat blotchy belly heaving up and down. A narrow shaft of murky light fell through the doorway, catching the green vapours rising from cracks in the floor, illuminating the cavern with an eerie glow. Clusters of brown and yellow fungi grew in the moldy silence, disturbed only by the sound of water dripping through the roof and splattering on the floor. The Toad was not happy but made an effort at controlling his anger as getting into a rage was bad for his digestion.

At last three figures stood silhouetted at the entrance to the cavern, cutting the shaft of light into thin shards and throwing the cavern into a muddy duskiness. "Where are my glass jars? You'd better have brought them!" The Toad spewed out the words in his gravelly voice.

"I have them here master," Boiuna spoke meekly, setting down five jars in a row in front of him. She'd come as a woman, so as to have hands with which to carry the jars in the bag she'd made for that purpose. The Toad smiled a crooked slimy smile and picking up one jar after another, peered into them, saliva dribbling from the corners of his mouth. A dozen large moths fluttered about in one, agitated at being confined to such a small space. Another jar contained beetles of varying sizes and colours; a third was well filled with an assortment of spiders crawling over one another, struggling to find a way out. A good quantity of worms, slugs and delectable larvae writhed about in the remaining jars.

The Toad pulled out the tuft of grass that served as a cork for the jar of moths and waited for one to escape, following it with his protruding eyeballs until it flew past his head and then, faster than the eye could see, he shot out his long sticky tongue, snapping up the moth as it flew by. His sticky saliva made swallowing difficult and he had to close his eyes and pull his protruding eyeballs back into his head, making him look strangely ridiculous. The pressure of the eyeballs in his head made his saliva more liquid and swallowing much easier. Satisfied with the delectable morsel, he licked his lip-less mouth with great relish and feasted on several more flying insects, after which his taste buds called for a change.

"I feel the need for something hot now," he grunted, slurping up drips of saliva. "Get some wood and light a fire. I'll fry some of these slugs in hot anaconda oil." So wood was gathered and a fire lit. When the small cauldron of oil was smoking, the Toad poked a thin pointy stick into one of the glass jars, speared a slug and dipped it into the boiling oil where he let it sizzle for a moment. Taking it out, he blew on it once or twice, stuck out his long tongue and wrapped it around the crunchy creature. Again he pulled in his protruding eyeballs to allow him to swallow. And so he continued to snack on the slugs, spiders, larvae and other delights until he could swallow nothing more and sat, big and bloated, seemingly oblivious to the smelly drops of water that fell from the roof of the cave and splattered on his head with predictable regularity. Finally, he let out a colossal burp - so foul-smelling that even the evil creatures pulled away, grimacing at its stench. Then he lay back on the mound of reeds, his blotchy body so distended that it looked as if it would burst then and there, and fell asleep.

The light outside was dim when he woke and the fire around which the evil spirits were sprawled and snoring as if they never intended to wake, had died down to embers, but the cauldron of oil sitting on them, still smoking.

"Get up you lazy lot! I didn't ask you here for a sleep-over!" he bellowed. They jumped to attention as if hit by lightning. "I called you here to tell you that you'd better do something about that girl or there will be no place for you in my castle! I want her stopped! Do you hear me?" the Toad raged at the evil beings. "You all have powers - use them! It's no good just following her and watching her get through all the dangers you've put in her way! Make her stop!"

"Yes, we do have powers," agreed Jurupari defensively. "But she's immune to our spells and....."

"Then do something else!" the Toad bellowed, jumping up and down through the green vapours, foaming at the mouth and throwing a Toad tantrum.

"We've done lots of things, but something always saves her. That Fairy Godmother of hers is a real nuisance, always turning up just when things are going well and ruining everything!" Boiuna complained, sulkily pouting her wrinkly lips.

"Well if she's a nuisance, get rid of her! Surely you can manage that! She's just a tiny little thing!" screamed the Toad, thumping the wall of the cavern with his fist, smashing a cluster of juicy mushrooms which splattered into his eyes.

"She's a tiny little thing when she's herself, but she can change into anything she wants, just like Boiuna, and become fearsome and savage!" Corpo Seco whinged through his rotting lips.

"Oh you poor zombie! She can become fearsome and savage can she? Frightens you does she? What on earth did I hire you for? If you're just going to make excuses and be a wimp, you can leave my employ right now and forget about living in my castle!" the Toad raged on....and on. "Get some other evils involved if you can't cope with this little girl on your own. You've just been sitting on your backsides doing nothing but enjoying the easy life, thinking she won't get very far. Well I can tell you this: I don't want her getting any further! Is that clear?"

The evil spirits sat, heads bowed, feeling chastised and incompetent. To be threatened with exclusion from the Toad's castle was a shock. They'd already begun to plan their lives there: imagining what their respective rooms would look like; whether there would be a swimming pool, and how they would entertain themselves through their long lazy days.

Boiuna had also informed Corpo Seco that if there were to be a pool, he would on no account be allowed to swim in it. Bits of his foul rotting flesh would fall off and the water would be full of it - too disgusting for anyone else to use. Corpo sulked for days after hearing this but then had the excellent idea, he thought, of asking the Toad to build a pool just for him. He had intended to bring this up with the Toad that very day but the way the meeting had gone, with the Toad calling him a wimp and suggesting that perhaps he should leave his employment, Corpo decided that this was not the right time after all. Instead, he sat quietly by the fire, trying to make himself useful by counting the flames.

Jurupari, on the other hand, after some minutes of despondent silence, put on a good show of power, grit and gutsiness in response to the Toad's admonishments. He jumped around flapping his scaly wings so fiercely that they fanned the embers and reignited the fire and he completely lost control of his tail which flicked so wildly that it hit Corpo in the face, knocking off one of his rotting ears in the process, all the time gritting his fangs while alarming guttural noises issued from his throat.

"We'll get her! We'll get her for sure! I have a plan - I can feel it coming!" said Jurupari, leaping about ever more energetically.

"Oh, good! Do be sure to tell us when it gets here!" the Toad raged sarcastically, pink patches on his blotchy skin brightly iridescent.

"I think I can do something to trick her," Boiuna said quietly, almost to herself.

"Trick her? Trick her into what? Into believing she can't do the things she clearly can? I don't want her tricked! I want her stopped!" he screamed in exasperation until he finally croaked, "I'm exhausted from all this arguing! My nerves are frazzled and my throat hurts! I'm going to bed!"

He was on his way out when he turned and threw himself into another bellowing frenzy and accidentally knocked over the cauldron of boiling oil, much of which splattered onto his feet. Screaming and whelping and cursing, he hopped out of the cavern and launched himself into Stinky Lake, slowly making his way back towards his putrid mound. Half-way there he turned around, stuck his head out of the slimy water and yelled, "What are you waiting for? Get off your backsides and off my mountain and start doing something about that girl!"

CHAPTER 8
The Mohana's City

Caipora and the capuchins had been making their way through a dense and gloomy forest for almost two weeks with no sign yet of the Amazon River. As she walked, Caipora's memory wrapped her mother's arms around her and echoed her words: "Fate decides when we live and when we die." What more did Fate control, Caipora wondered. Had Fate chosen her to save the forest and its creatures? Had her wish to be free also been Fate's plan and had Fate already decided what future choices she would make? If so, her life was predetermined: she had no free will, no true freedom. And if everything is predetermined, why bother making plans, nurturing hopes and dreams?

A cluster of gigantic mushrooms blocking her way jolted Caipora from her thoughts. Despite the lack of light the forest brimmed not only with gigantic funghi but with enormous flowers and other huge plants which were normally minute.

Few of the mushrooms were edible but even the size of those was astronomical: they reached her shoulders in height. The others she believed to be poisonous: purple trumpet-like mushrooms, yellow funghi imitating flower petals, others indigo or white-stalked and mottled; long thin-stemmed funghi with bright red balls on top and still others wearing brown caps sitting on thick rough stalks resembling tree trunks. They had one thing in common: their gigantic size!

As Caipora stopped to look more closely at one particularly weird blossom, a sound in the undergrowth caught her ear. She bid the monkeys be quiet and watched in amazement as an enormous insect the size of a small capybara crawled out from between the ferns, a cluster of small red and black fungi on her back. The sight of the six-legged creature with its broad nose and brightly coloured body left them speechless. "I thought I heard footsteps," the insect squeezed her words out in a thin crackly voice. "But I certainly didn't expect a human! You want to be careful walking these parts," she continued. "Look at what's happened to me and the other animals here and all the plants: I'm so enormous these skinny legs can barely support me and I need far more food now than I used to at my normal size. And I'm not the only one. There are many of us this size and we're eating far too many plants just to stay alive - but in staying alive, we're slowly killing the forest. But what can we do? If we don't eat what we need we'll die and so will all the life that depends on us weevils. It really is very difficult indeed," the insect squeaked and moaned simultaneously at the end of her lengthy monologue, thin legs quivering under her weight.

"Oh, goodness! You're a weevil!" Caipora cried out. "But weevils are tiny little creatures and so well camouflaged they're difficult to see. Is it the evil Toad who's done this to you?"

"Of course! Who else would do such an abominable thing? He wants to destroy all life in the forest and the forest itself. This is going to be the end of us all - a very slow and painful end......" her squeaky voice trailed off into a barely audible little whine.

"Well, I'm going to fix that," said Caipora, pleased to announce that the weevil's dire proclamation was not inevitable. "I'm going to find that Toad and free the Goddess of Good so she can restore this part of the world to what it should be."

"Oh! I'd heard someone was coming this way for that very purpose. I just didn't expect it to be a mere little girl like yourself!" exclaimed the weevil, most surprised.

"I am a girl, but I'm not a *mere little* girl!" Caipora retorted, taking great umbrage at being called a mere anything, let alone a *mere little girl!* "I'm tough and strong and I'll get that Toad, just you wait and see!"

"Oh, I didn't mean any offence. It's just that you don't normally see children taking on a fight like like this. Children should be with their parents, cared for and protected, not out in a dangerous world fighting evil."

"Yes....well.....I did have parents.....but they were killed," Caipora spoke softly, more to herself than to the weevil.

"I'm so sorry to hear that," the weevil, genuinely sympathetic, looked up at Caipora. "Well, I must get on and find something more to eat. I do wish you all the best of course, as my life and all life in this forest depends on you and I am more grateful than you can imagine. I can offer you one piece of advice in your journey: don't eat anything around here, and don't talk to anyone - except maybe another weevil of course. Oh, and one more thing: get through here as quickly as you can." With that the weevil crept back into the cheerless shadows of the undergrowth.

The light was dimming and a steady drizzle of rain beaded the air but taking note of the weevil's advice to get through that area as quickly as possible, Caipora forged on, pushing into the encroaching darkness, slashing through thick undergrowth with her machete while the capuchins swung through the trees. It was some time before the growth thinned and with that, Caipora found herself squelching through a rancid swamp, every step sinking deep into filthy mud.

Hours passed before she climbed out of the bog onto dry ground. The gigantic plants now behind them, she considered herself in safer territory and searched for a place to camp. She had not gone far when there came into view a pale blue mist glittering in the moonlight, illuminating a small clearing. Ethereal, enticing, it beckoned Caipora, drawing her near with strains of exotic and sublimely beautiful music - a string instrument, softly playing an exquisite tune. Rounding a thick copse of trees, Caipora froze: a barefooted man in white man's clothing and wearing a hat sat on the stump of a tree in the misty clearing, playing a cavaquinho. His skin was brown but not as dark as hers and he hummed along to the tune he played. He looked up, smiled, and continued playing without interruption, seemingly unsurprised by her presence.

His music saturated the forest, the air, the ground and took possession of Caipora's very soul. She stood motionless, transfixed by the melody. When he had finished his tune, the man placed the cavaquinho on his knees and turned to her. "Come closer, come closer. No need to be afraid. I have no weapons other than my instrument," he laughed. "My goodness, you do look a mess," he said on seeing Caipora's mud-encrusted legs. "I take it you didn't see the bog in the dark?" he asked. He was the first person Caipora had encountered since escaping from the murderous tribe that killed her people. Terror stole her words and paralyzed her limbs. "A shy girl are you?" the man asked lightly, beginning again to casually strum the strings of his cavaquinho.

Finally, as if reassured by the music, Caipora's mouth released a few words. "No, I'm not shy at all. You've merely taken me by surprise, that's all," she replied, although somewhat timidly. Never before had she heard such breathtakingly enchanting music. Without a pause in his strumming the man plucked an exotic flower from a bush beside him and extended it to her. "Have you ever smelt anything as exquisite as this?" he asked.

Caipora breathed in the intoxicating fragrance and was immediately imbued with complete happiness, a sensation of pure relief and joy, without a care in the world. Still strumming his cavaquinho, the man asked if she would like to wash the smelly mud from her legs. "Oh yes. That would be lovely," she replied.

"Follow me. There's a river nearby. The water there is cool and fresh." Without one questioning word or a glance back at her monkeys in the trees, Caipora followed the man with the hat through the glittering blue mist and disappeared.

***

When Caipora opened her eyes, she was clean from head to foot, resting against an earthen wall on a bed of grasses by the edge of a wide, slow-moving river which ran through an enormous, endless cavern. Her immediate thought was "The River Hamza! Found at last!" The cavern sparkled with the lights of billions of glow worms and countless small caves punctured its walls on either side of the river, each glowing with the flickering orange light of a fire. Rope bridges, from which hung numerous cages and baskets, were suspended across the river between most of the caves. Where a cave had no bridge at its door, it was accessed by a ladder. The cages hanging from the bridges contained guinea pigs, chickens and other birds and the baskets brimmed with fish, corn, potatoes and manioc. Fruit was also plentiful: acai berries, passion fruit, bananas, mango, papayas, guava, avocado, coconuts, cashews, Brazil nuts and vanilla nuts - and finally, countless baskets of enormous mushrooms and other fungi. The delicious aroma of toasted suri grubs permeated the air. Senses alert, Caipora sat up, mouth watering, just as a young girl appeared before her offering her a small basket of the delicious morsels. Caipora took the basket without a word, as though expecting it. One by one she put the delectable crispy grubs into her mouth and crunched through them while the air in the cavern increasingly thickened with mouthwatering aromas and the growing sounds of human voices.

Young women, naked except for a loin cloth and a headband and strongly resembling Caipora, descended ladders, filled urns at the river and carried them up to their caves. They crossed bridges back and forth bearing baskets on their backs and heavy urns in their arms. Others cast nets into the black water, pulling them out laden with thrashing fish to be divided and hoisted up to the caves by way of pulleys. Young men, weighty sacks slung over bare shoulders, small picks tucked into belts holding up loin cloths, appeared from around a distant bend in the river, all heading to one place where with loud rattling, they emptied the gleaming yellow contents of their sacks into wooden wheel barrows.

A pod of shimmering dolphins leaped through the air and splashed into the river again, streaming through the water with great alacrity, then swimming back more sedately a short time later, protectively surrounding a very small young dolphin. Caipora observed the increasing buzz of activity as everyone went about their communal duties. The harmony, contentment, their helpfulness towards one another, woke in her mind a time long ago when she was part of a coherent, tranquil community but her dream melted with the return of the girl who'd brought her food earlier, this time offering Caipora fruit and nuts and water.

She sat with Caipora while she ate. "If you are ready, I will take to you to your dwelling," the girl said when Caipora had finished eating. "The Master will come and see you after you have slept." Nothing surprised Caipora and it didn't occur to her to ask any questions about the Master or anything else. Sleep was beckoning and she willingly followed the girl up a ladder, across a bridge, up another ladder and into a small cave in which a warm fire flickered. A comfortable bed of grasses welcomed her and within arm's reach of the bed was an urn of water and a basket of mushrooms. Another basket held exquisitely fragrant

flowers, identical to those which the man with the hat had given her to smell - but Caipora didn't remember anything of the man with the hat. A large stack of firewood took up most of the end wall.

Caipora thanked the girl as she left and wished her a good night.

"And may you also have a good night. A bite or two of the mushrooms will help you sleep very well indeed," the girl advised. "Do not fear the Master. He will do you no harm," she added, as if trying to allay any concerns Caipora might have had. But Caipora had no concerns - none whatsoever. She had eaten well and looked forward to eating well again. As far as she could tell, she had all the comforts one could ask for: good food, a soft bed, and the company of her own kind around her. She lay down, made herself comfortable and closed her eyes.

It seemed she had not slept a wink when someone shook her by the shoulder. "Caipora! Wake up! You must wake up!" urged an alarmed whispering voice. Caipora opened her eyes to meet those of a girl so close that her long black hair brushed her cheek, but deep sleep pulled her eyelids shut again. "Wake up Caipora! Wake up!" the voice continued frantically, as did the shaking.

"Why? Why must I wake? I only just fell asleep. What's happening?" Caipora mumbled sleepily, eyelids still closed.

"You are in grave danger Caipora," the girl whispered urgently. "We need to get you out of here immediately - without being seen by anyone!"

"What danger? What do you mean? Everything is so nice here. You wished me good night a few moments ago and now you want me to get out of here. Why?"

"I am not the girl who wished you a good night! I'm Fyglia and I'm here to save you from....."

"Fyglia?" Caipora exclaimed, sitting up abruptly. "But you were a frog the last time I saw you!"

"Yes. Yes, I know that. I can be anything I like, only not for very long. Now you must get up at once. The Mohana is coming!" As Caipora rose to her feet, Fyglia held a vial of liquid to her nose. "Breath in deeply," she instructed.

Caipora breathed in, was momentarily dizzy before the words 'the Mohana is coming' rang vibrant and clear and she understood that this was not a place where she should be and that the danger was very grave indeed. "You were hypnotized by him and his music and made to feel happy and content. Have you eaten any of the mushrooms over there?" Fyglia asked, greatly concerned.

"No. The girl said I should, but I wasn't hungry."

"Well, it's a very good thing you didn't. They would have put you in such a deep trance that I'm not sure I could have got you out of it. That's why everyone here looks so peaceful and content: they don't know the reality of their situation because they eat the mushrooms every day. They don't know they have families and friends who still grieve for them. They are always drugged and remember nothing of the real world and their past lives outside the Mohana's City."

The rope ladder leading to the door of the cave gave out a painful squeak. "Take my hand, quickly!" whispered Fyglia. The moment they clasped hands both were instantly no bigger than an adult's finger and hid behind the basket of mushrooms. The firelight flickered over a figure in the doorway wearing western clothes and a hat: the Mohana had come to check on Caipora and instantly exploded with rage. "Where is she? Is this the right cave? Where is she? Who is responsible for this?" His bellowing resonated throughout the cavern. Alarmed and frenzied activity ensued. Panicked and distressed, women and girls hurried across the bridges, climbed ladders, rushed from cave to cave, calling and searching for the missing girl. Men ran about frantically scouring the surface of the dark water for a sign of something other than dolphins.

Relentlessly the Mohana hurled abuse at them threatening all manner of ghoulish punishments should they fail to find her. The poor girl who had led Caipora to her cave was taken personally to task. Head bowed and quivering at his accusations of carelessness and incompetency, tears glazed her cheeks as she responded to his ferocious interrogations with trembling, barely audible words.

"Search the river banks! I'll search the river myself together with the pod!" the Mohana shouted as he hurried down the ladder, across a bridge and to the water's edge where, with great alacrity, he stripped himself of his clothing and his hat, revealing a bald patch on the back of his head. Caipora peered through the entrance of the cave at the very moment he changed into a dolphin and dived with a great splash into the river. The cavern reverberated with his high pitched call, instantly answered with a myriad of similar calls and the water was at once alive with dolphins leaping and diving and swimming at great speed in every possible direction.

Caipora had, of course, heard of the Mohana. Every mother told her children about the Mohana and warned them not to talk to strange men in white man's clothing, especially those wearing a hat and playing a cavaquinho. "You will know for certain that he is the Mohana if you take off his hat: he will have a bald spot on the back of his head," Caipora's mother had warned her. "He is an evil naiad whose true form is that of a dolphin, but who disguises himself as a man to allow him to live on the earth's surface when it serves his purpose. He will hypnotize you and take you to his underground city to work for him and make him rich." How could she have forgotten these words?

"Now is our chance!" said Fyglia snatching Caipora from her thoughts. "There's a tunnel out of here but since you don't have wings it will be almost impossible for you to reach it while you are so tiny. I'll make us both normal human size and when we get to the tunnel, I'll shrink us again, as I'm sure they'll be searching that too," she whispered. "Take my hand," and they instantly returned to normal human size. "If we hurry and appear as agitated as the rest of the girls no one will notice us, but if they do, take my hand and we'll shrink to almost nothing again!" They hurried down the ladder, scurried across a bridge and down another ladder to the ground. Fyglia was right. Everyone was frantically rushing about and paid them no attention as they leapt over abandoned baskets and crates of food. Nets brimming with thrashing fish lay strewn along the riverbank and guinea pigs and chickens ran freely about with much wing-flapping, squawking and squealing as they desperately tried to avoid being trampled in the frenzied rush around them.

Caipora stayed as close as possible to Fyglia without stepping on her heels. Together they ran to a point where it seemed they were about to hit a wall but instead, ran into the blackness of a tunnel, so well camouflaged was it. Their ascent up the incline was rapid and they had covered some distance when sounds of hurried footsteps and rattling wheels came bearing down towards them. "Take my hand!" Fyglia instructed abruptly and they were instantly tiny again and pressed themselves firmly against the wall. Through the darkness an unattended cart rattled down the gravelly slope towards them, a girl waving a flaming torch chasing after it. The out-of-control cart veered at the wall and came crashing into it at the very point where Fyglia and Caipora stood flattened against it. Caipora screamed in fright. It's difficult to imagine how her scream could have been heard over the noise of the crashing cart, but it was and the girl holding the torch above her head was right behind it, searching for the source of the scream. Caipora and Fyglia stood motionless. Suddenly the light fell on Caipora. Fyglia had disappeared.

"Oh me! Oh my! Just look at *you* then!" the girl exclaimed in great astonishment and before Caipora could blink she was snatched up, brown fingers wrapped tightly around her.

"Where oh where have *you* come from? I've never seen anything like you - you're just like me, only tiny!" she continued in complete and delighted amazement.

"You need to let me go!" Caipora pleaded desperately.

"Do I? Why would I need to do that?" the girl amusingly feigned interest with a little high pitched laugh.

"Because I have to save the forest from the evil Toad who wants to kill everything and everyone in it!" Caipora's distressed words flew out fast and shrill.

"What on earth are you talking about? I've never heard

such nonsense! There's no evil Toad! Everything in the forest is fine. We are all very happy and have everything we want," the girl, eyes wide with incredulity, blinked at Caipora.

"No! No! Please let me go! I have to save the forest!" Caipora cried, helplessly struggling against the firm grip of the fingers.

"No. I will not let you go. You will stay with me in the Master's city and be my toy. No one else has a toy of any kind! I shall be the only one! Time does not always pass quickly and you will provide me with excellent entertainment. Can you dance? Or sing? Or perhaps you can do both? Now that would be a real treat! We shall see!" The girl held Caipora in one hand and the torch in the other, but quickly realised she was two hands short of managing the cart.

"Please let me go! I beg you, please let me go!" Caipora pleaded, but the girl was now focused on resolving her problem of how to transport Caipora, the cart and the torch to the city all at the same time. She stuck the torch back into its holder on the side of the cart, but was still left with her precious treasure in one hand. Suddenly, quite out of nowhere, the Mohana appeared before them! The girl holding Caipora froze, speechless, terrified. Caipora felt the fingers tighten around her, squeezing the breath out of her.

"Give her to me," demanded the Mohana, holding out his hand. The girl meekly placed the tiny Caipora onto the palm of his outstretched hand without a word and he curled his fingers around her. "Now get back to your duties," he instructed. The girl quietly obeyed, immediately grabbing the cart with hands which were now both free and hurried down the tunnel to the city.

Paralysed with fear, Caipora could neither move nor speak as she was held up to the gigantic face of the Mohana. Terrified of being hypnotised again, she covered her face with her hands.

"Caipora, it's all right. It's me!" a familiar voice sounded from the Mohana's mouth and in an instant Caipora found herself in Fyglia's hand.

"How do you do this?" Caipora cried out, astonished in realising that Fyglia had changed herself into the Mohana to fool the girl who'd captured her.

"It's my job," she replied.

"Well, it's a good thing it is. I'm sure I would never have seen the outside world again if it hadn't been for you."

"Let's not dwell on what might have been. We're not out of this yet. Give me your tiny hand," and Fyglia took it between her fingertips, instantly bringing Caipora back to her normal size.

"We need to get out of here as fast as we can, before another cart comes rattling down," Fyglia spoke quickly as they hurried through the dense blackness up the incline of the tunnel. "This isn't the only tunnel they use," said Fyglia. "I saw a number of entrances while I was making my way to your cave. I suppose each tunnel takes them out to a different place on the surface where they can get different kinds of food."

"It's a very difficult way to get food!" said Caipora, thinking of how easy it was to simply pick fruit from a nearby tree. "But if they can get out of the Mohana's city, why don't they escape and go back to their families?"

"I told you: they're kept hypnotized through eating the gigantic mushrooms and breathing in the scent of those fragrant flowers. They have no memory of their families or of their lives before being brought here - no idea that another world even exists. They're quite content. They have everything they need: warmth, comfort and good food and they happily raise their children within their peaceful community. The women provide food while the men dig gold out of the walls of the cave for the Mohana."

"Can't we help them somehow?" Caipora asked Fyglia. remembering the beautiful life she had led with her family and tribe - unable to understand now why she had wanted to be free of them.

"It's not possible to help those who don't want help. They are sedated, subdued and happy and won't believe you when you explain what's happened to them. Forcing help on them would only make a bad situation worse. Now you need to think about the task ahead, not dwell on what we've left behind," Fyglia stated decisively.

And so Caipora focused on putting one foot in front of the other through the seemingly endless darkness. Much time passed before tree roots tangled in their hair and at last a faint light glowed through the blackness ahead. From that point the tunnel narrowed until they had to crouch down and crawl over a rough wooden surface to get out into the forest. Looking back, the entrance to the tunnel revealed itself as a large hollow tree trunk covered in thick moss and colourful fungi. No one passing would ever guess where it would take them were they to crawl into it and beyond.

With a deep breath of relief, Caipora imbibed the fragrance and serenity of the evening into which they had arrived. Moonlight splashed through the canopy and lay in silver puddles on the forest floor. A silver beam also glinted on something lying in the palm of Fyglia's hand. "I wonder if you might find this useful," she said, a touch of irony tinging her voice.

"Where did you get *this*?" Caipora gasped.

"Where did you lose it?"

"I don't know! I can't imagine! I didn't know I *had* lost it!"

"I saw it around the Mohana's neck and took it from him. He didn't feel a thing," Fyglia smiled a wry little smile. Annoyed with herself for being so careless, Caipora clutched the stone tightly and searched her memory for the moment when she had been separated from it. She'd had no warning from the stone about the Mohana before he hypnotized her, so she didn't have it then and no warning about the Mapinguari, so she didn't have it then either. Nor was she warned about the river monster or the bridge falling down. Before that she'd spent her first night with the monkeys after climbing out of the cave. Yes! The last help she'd had from the stone was in the cave: it had given her desperately needed light. The image of a dolphin leaping from the water after she'd fallen from the roof flashed into her mind together with the feeling of something slithering around her neck.

"It was the dolphin in the cave! He was the Mohana! How could I not have known it was the stone slithering from my neck? Will you help me put it on?" but when Caipora looked up, Fyglia was nowhere to be seen.

"She's done it again! Just vanished into thin air! You really can be exasperating!" Caipora said to the missing Fyglia, irritated at her tendency to disappear without a word.

"We'll help you put it on!" cheery voices called out in unison and her capuchins dropped through the foliage onto the ground in front of her. "We've been so worried about you! We didn't know if you'd ever come back!" they all spoke at once.

"I didn't like that horrible man who took you away. I didn't like him at all!" squealed the littlest one.

"But why didn't you help me? Why didn't you stop him?" Caipora asked, stunned to see her troop again.

"We couldn't do anything! We knew he was the Mohana

and if we'd come closer he would have hypnotized us too!"

"Worse than that!" cried the littlest one again. "We would have been eaten for sure! Made into soup or stew or just roasted or........."

"For heaven's sake! Will you stop? I can't bear to listen to your frightful stories any more!" screamed one capuchin in alarm and desperation. "They make my stomach turn and I break into a cold sweat hearing your words of horror!" But her pleas were ignored as all the monkeys loudly voiced the unthinkable atrocities they might have suffered, clamouring over one another about what end they might have met had they been captured by the Mohana.

"Stop it! Stop it! Stop it!" screamed the hysterical one again. "I can't stand it anymore!"

Ignoring the blustering ruckus, the leader of the group approached Caipora. "Sit down and I will tie the stone around your neck. We couldn't help you but we did see where he threw your equipment and we gathered it up as soon as you disappeared into the tunnel." The Mohana had removed Caipora's bow and quiver from her shoulder together with her knife, machete and her sack with all its valuable contents. He'd simply flung them into the forest as she walked with him. She had noticed nothing.

PART THREE

To The Amazon &

Beyond

CHAPTER 9
Through the Deadly Forest

Eager to get away from the entrance to the tunnel before someone from the Mohana's city should come out and find them, the capuchins quickly retrieved Caipora's equipment and the group hurried away. Within a day of walking they found themselves in a bleak forest engorged with the smell of decay and almost bereft of foliage. Nothing moved or uttered a sound. For weeks Caipora trudged through grey mould and slime blanketing the forest floor, each night hanging her hammock in a tree and sleeping with the capuchins; each night pondering the question of Fate: was it Fyglia's decision to rescue her from the Mohana or did Fate bring it about? If Fate did have plans for her, could the power of her mind overcome them, and if not, if Fate always prevailed, why bother making plans, decisions? They would all be pointless. If Fate always prevailed, where was her free will to make her own choices? And what about Sema? Had Fate brought them together - soul mates - only to tear them apart? For what reason? Caipora couldn't make sense of such pointless cruelty.

The fetid smell of the rotting forest grew more sickening by the day and a purple-grey mist permeated the air, bringing with it an uneasy energy. Every now and again, through the corner of her eye, Caipora caught sight of dark human-like figures but when she turned to look they vanished, only to reappear moments later: ghostly, ephemeral shapes silently floating above the ground, never

coming close nor clearly showing themselves. When finally they departed, the trees had changed to a pale purple colour, their trunks and branches smooth, slimy and slippery, forcing the capuchins to travel on the ground, squelching through the stinking sludge with Caipora.

"This isn't fun any more," whimpered the littlest monkey after a time.

"Stop whingeing and be quiet," said the eldest sternly. "We're not on this mission to have fun."

"We don't even have any fruit or nuts to eat any more. I'm getting tired of eating that pudding every night," the littlest one kept on, ignoring the command for silence.

"Be grateful for what you've got!" said another. "And be grateful that you have the privilege of playing a part in saving our forest."

"Yes! You don't hear Caipora complaining, do you?" piped in a third.

"She's got longer legs than I have," the littlest one whimpered.

"Speaking of Caipora, where is she?" the oldest one threw about a puzzled look and caught sight of Caipora some distance behind them - hanging from a tree: feet high off the ground and a slimy branch wrapped around her squeezing the life out of her! The capuchins froze at the sight, unable to comprehend what had happened, then slipping and sliding over the gooey slime they frantically scrambled back to their leader.

"Why are you up there? What happened? How did you get there?" Distressed and bordering on hysteria, they hurled all manner of unhelpful questions at her. When Caipora finally got a word in edge ways, her tight voice was barely audible.

"I.....can't breathe.....machete.....hurry......" The monkeys instantly leapt up the slimy tree trunk - and instantly slid down! Again and again they tried to climb the trunk, but each time hit the ground with a splat in the squelchy sludge.

"We need to make a tower!" shouted the littlest one. "The biggest one at the bottom and the smallest at the top. I'll be able to reach Caipora then and get her machete!" No one argued. They stood on one others shoulders and the littlest one bounded over them to the top and scrambled up Caipora's legs, her machete in his hand in no time.

"Cut the branch......where it comes...... out of the tree," Caipora gasped, her arms trapped across her chest by the vicious strangling branch. The little capuchin hacked at its base but instantly another branch swooped down and coiled tightly around him, squeezing out a terrified scream - but being small and flexible, he slid from its grip and with his arm firmly around Caipora for support, hacked at the attacking branch with all his might. It oozed dark purple blood and fell limply against the tree trunk. He then hacked even more fiercely at the branch squeezing Caipora, finding strength he didn't know he had, inflicting deep wounds into the squidgy flesh. That too began, not to ooze, but to gush torrents of thick purple blood! Slowly its grip on Caipora slackened until at last she slid from its hold and dropped to the ground, the little capuchin coming down with her.

The monkeys crowded round, fussing over their leader, but she was instantly on her feet shouting "Run! Run! Get away from this tree! It could pick us all up with one swoop of another branch and then there won't be anyone to save us!" They ran for their lives and when finally they looked back they saw the littlest monkey still slashing at the tree trunk, blood gushing out in torrents, a rapidly spreading pool of purple staining the ground.

"Enough little one! Enough! Run for your life! Save yourself! Run!" Caipora screamed. Finally the little one turned and hurried towards them. "You were so brave!" said Caipora, crouching down to his level, arm around his shoulder drawing him close. "You saved my life - and risked your own doing it! And then stayed to do more while the rest of us ran!"

"Well, we really did it together," he said meekly, shying away from the praise.

"Yes - but it was your idea, and you took the greatest risk!" said all the capuchins together, talking over one another in praise of the little one. "You were amazing: so fearless, so brave! So strong!"

"Well, it was nothing really," he replied coyly, overwhelmed with all the attention and back-patting, handing Caipora her machete. She slid it into the ground and out again several times to wipe off the purple blood.

The group forged eastward through the late afternoon, the usual torrential downpour splashing the rotting sludge on the forest floor onto Caipora's legs and leaving the monkeys' normally well-groomed hair clogged with stinking muck. The pink evening light turned to mauve and still with nowhere to camp, they were forced to continue through the downpour into the night, dirty, wet, exhausted. When the deafening rain finally ceased, an uncanny misty silence took its place and ghostly translucent shapes again flared up around them, glowing in one place, vanishing, then reappearing in another. They floated silently between the trees in shades of purple, blue and green, some resembling the human form, others soundlessly flapping enormous bat wings or brandished threatening horns on their heads.

When at last the mist cleared, the clouds parted and moonlight filtered through the canopy, the ghostly shapes evaporated. But no sooner had they gone than, with a frenzied screeching, millions of gigantic bats burst through the forest and swooped down on them, tearing the night into chaotic shreds. The monkeys screamed but with nowhere to run or hide they could do no more than cover their faces and duck to avoid them. Despite the intensity of the attack, Caipora noticed that, regardless of how close the bats came they never actually touched her, nor did she feel even the slightest breeze that such violent swooping, almost brushing her skin, would create.

She tried something very daring: as the next bat swooped down on her she didn't duck her head but instead held her arm outstretched, palm facing her attacker. The bat charged straight through it. Again and again Caipora held her hand against the attacking creatures and felt nothing. The bats were illusions! Illusions created to terrify her; to make her give up and run in fright! She turned to her traumatised monkeys. "It's all right! It's all right! You can stop screaming! Stop screaming and look at this!" Caipora shouted above the uproar and the monkeys stared in wide-eyed amazement as the bats flew straight through her hands. "They're not real! They're just illusions! They can't hurt us. The only thing that can hurt us is our own fear! I'm sure the ghostly figures were illusions as well," she said. "We have no reason to be afraid!" And so, exhausted but with nowhere to rest, they forged on through the night, walking through the bats as though they weren't there - which of course, they weren't.

The forest around them was changing: healthy foliage began to clothe the trees, the slime and mould were now sparse and they trod over firmer, drier ground. With bodies aching and in desperate need of sleep, they hoped at last to find a place to rest - but rest was not for them. The Muiraquita stone glowed and heated Caipora's skin but her sleep deprived mind was oblivious to the warning and when in the distance silvery light defined the bloodcurdling shapes of gigantic ghoulish arachnids - a whole army of long prickly legs supporting nightmarish hairy bodies moving slowly towards them - she walked on.

"Don't worry," she calmly reassured the monkeys, "they look terrifying but they're just illusions, like the ghostly shapes and the bats were. They can't hurt us. We can walk straight through them."

The forest teemed with the illusions of gargantuan Brazilian Wandering Spiders - the deadliest in the world - and even though Caipora was positive they couldn't hurt her, the sight sent a shudder through her bones. There was nowhere to go other than straight through them. "They're only illusions," she told herself, clenched her teeth and walked on. Not a sound from the monkeys. They'd scampered high into the trees, wide-eyed and shaking. "Good idea," Caipora said, looking up. "You're better off traveling through the trees anyway, since they're not slippery anymore." Still oblivious to the heat on her chest Caipora turned to walk on but stopped in her tracks: the chilling sound of crunching twigs and rustling leaves made her blood run cold as she watched the solid forms of the approaching spiders now not more than six metres from her. She judged them to be up to her knees in height with a leg span of more than a metre. Massive red-haired fangs and eight gleaming black eyes protruding from each enormous head stared straight at her! They were real and they were very much alive!!

For a moment she froze, surrounded by the monstrous arachnids now only three metres from her. Then her knife flashed in one hand and her machete in the other and the spiders instantly reared up on their four back legs, the front ones clawing at the air. Swaying menacingly from side to side they were almost as tall as Caipora! The moment the first one lurched at her the others followed. In a flash Caipora lunged forward, stabbed the nearest one in the eyes and through the head, then swung around in circles, wielding her blades left and right. Legs flew everywhere as she slashed through them - but there were too many. She cut three of the monstrous creatures down before one climbed onto her back and bit her before she could get it off! The monkeys threw what they could at the horrific things from above but the small branches and bits of bark had no effect. One spider grabbed Caipora's leg and sank its enormous fangs into her flesh several times, injecting the deadly venom into her bloodstream before she could stab it.

All seemed lost when the forest reverberated with ear-piercing buzzing and swarmed with enormous black assassin bugs. Instantly all over the spiders, they pierced their eyes and heads with their long curved beaks and punctured their fat round bodies - from which there spurted copious quantities of spider juice - with paralysing venom and corrosive acid. It was an horrendous sight: the spiders thrashing spiky legs every which way trying to get the assassin bugs off them but the ultra strong grip of the bugs' front legs with their super sticky pads was impossible to dislodge and the bugs were three times their normal size: twice as long as Caipora's fingers - their beaks even longer. The forest reverberated with buzzing, hissing, wheezing and the shrieking of the monkeys in the trees.

The blinded, punctured, leaking spiders thrashed about, bumping into and attacking one another in sightless confusion. The battle seemed interminable but slowly the army of arachnids succumbed to the onslaught, more and more lying limp and paralyzed on the ground, the corrosive acid slowly turning them to slime. Only when the forest floor was covered with their dismembered heads, unattached legs and flattened wrinkled bodies, did the assassin bugs leave the forest.

Silence descended over the gruesome scene. The monkeys stared down from the trees in abject horror, hearts in their mouths and beating faster and louder than native drums in their ears: lying on the ground among the mutilated oozing bodies of the dead spiders was their fearless leader. Although terrified that not all the arachnids might be as dead as they looked, they could not sit and watch Caipora dying from their deadly venom. Armed with solid branches and all the courage they could muster, the capuchins descended to the battlefield, prodding the gory bodies with the branches to ensure they harboured not even the slightest grain of life - but nothing moved. Pushing them aside, they hurried to Caipora whose normally brown face was ashen grey, her legs and most of her body red and swollen; her breath barely there. She had been bitten countless times!

"Caipora, can you hear me?" called the oldest capuchin, voice trembling. No response. "Caipora!" she called again loudly, this time shaking Caipora's shoulder. "Can you hear me?" A faint groan issued from Caipora's mouth but otherwise she didn't move.

"Get the vial! Get the vial!" called one of the capuchins urgently. "Give her the potion!"

The eldest monkey fumbled at Caipora's belt. "There are two vials! Which one do we use?" No one knew. "Caipora! Caipora!" the oldest shouted, vigorously shaking Caipora. "Which vial do we use? Which vial, Caipora?"

Caipora's eyelids trembled but failed to open. "...old.... ol...." fluttered through her lips as softly as the wings of a butterfly and she said no more.

One vial was silver, one gold. "The gold! Use the gold!" the monkeys shouted over one another. "Quickly! Be quick!" But it took the capuchin some time to pull out the stopper.

"Hurry up! What are you doing? Be quick!" Finally, with a slight pop the stopper left the vial.

"Put it to her lips!" one cried out.

"I'll hold her mouth open!" cried another.

The littlest capuchin held Caipora's head up while the eldest poured a good amount of the potion into her mouth. Someone held her mouth closed so that the precious stuff wouldn't run out before Caipora swallowed it. Then they waited and waited.....and waited. The littlest monkey stroked Caipora's head as he held it in his lap, tears falling from his large dark eyes into her hair.

Hours passed before Caipora groaned again. Her eyelids fluttered, half opened. "Everything..... hurts....so much.... hard.... to breathe....." and her eyelids fell shut again. They administered more potion and again waited, unable to do anything other than watch her chest rise an fall. She was alive, but fighting for her life, even with the help of so much potion.

Evening shadows fell into the forest, throwing darkness over the group. Caipora slept. They covered her with her hammock and watched over her until sleep finally got the better of them - the last time they'd slept was almost too long ago to remember. And so the night passed: the troop of sleeping capuchins huddled around the sleeping Caipora.

First light found them still in dreams, but when the rays of the dawning sun slipped through the foliage and stroked their eyelids, they woke to the grisly scene of the previous night. Every gory detail assaulted their eyes: sticky spider juice covering the forest floor together with slimy innards; thousands of disconnected hairy legs; heads that had rolled away from their bodies, horrific red fangs still attached; punctured eyes staring blindly at them. The capuchins shuddered and covered their faces against the waking nightmare.

Caipora stirred. They had not moved from her side all night. Now the eldest took Caipora's hand in hers and the valiant warrior opened her eyes. "How nice to see such friendly faces," she whispered. The monkeys, ecstatic on hearing her voice and seeing her move, vented their pent up emotions in unison. "We've been so worried about you! So terribly worried! We gave you lots of potion from the gold vial but after that there was nothing more we could do. Oh! Thank goodness you're alive!"

"You did well," Caipora praised them. "I would not have lived without the potion. You've saved my life again." She tried to push herself up on her elbows, but her head fell back into the lap of the littlest monkey. "I'm so tired......it's hard to move."

"You need more rest - and energy," the older female advised matter of factly and rummaging through Caipora's bag, pulled out the pudding, broke off small pieces and began feeding them to Caipora.

"You all need food," said Caipora in between mouthfuls.

"Eat as much as you want. It will always grow back. There will always be more." Then she sighed and seemed to fall asleep again, those few words exhausting her. The capuchins, greatly relieved at their leader's recovery, eagerly helped themselves to the never-ending pudding.

"I wish it would change its flavour each time it grew back," said the littlest monkey as he chewed. "I'd like some nutty pudding and I really like strawberry guava as well. The fish we had by the river where the bridge fell down was good too. I sometimes dream about mangoes and avocado and papaya. Maybe we could ask the pudding to......"

"STOP IT! Just STOP it will you? Is there no end to the nonsense you can come up with?" shouted their leader. "Here we all are, with Caipora only just beginning to recover from death's door and you complain about nourishing food that is simply handed to you with no effort on your part whatsoever! Be grateful and be quiet! And for once and for all, stop your endless whingeing!"

Well, that put an end to the little one's hopes and dreams! He quietly picked at the pudding and put the pieces into his mouth without another word.

Many hours passed before Caipora was able to move - the spider venom had paralysed her muscles and without the potion she would have stopped breathing; even with it her body would take a long time to recover. When she was at last able to struggle to her feet she could barely walk but they were eager to get away from the sordid scene around them: not only was it stomach-turning but the dismembered arachnids were now beginning to putrefy and stink.

"One of you take my machete and cut down two straight, sturdy branches for walking sticks. I need something to lean on until I get my strength back," Caipora instructed, breathing heavily from the effort of getting the words out. Instantly a young adult capuchin was up a tree and two good branches fell to the ground where another one cleaned the leaves and twigs from them. "And while you're up there, get a few more branches to push aside these stinking bodies so we can get through this vile mess," she said, again breathing heavily from the effort.

Slowly and carefully they made their way through the ghoulish battlefield, the capuchins pushing aside the rotting spiders with branches while insects crawled over them, feasting on their gory remains. "Insects!" Caipora exclaimed joyfully. "We've not seen insects in a very long time!" Insects heralded a healthier environment but progress towards it was slow and even with the walking sticks Caipora struggled to stay on her feet. Her breathing was laboured but she refused to stop. Late afternoon found them beneath a leafy canopy resonating with bird calls and the chatter of howler monkeys and as they moved on, the understory grew more lush and verdant foliage buzzed with insects. Red-eyed tree frogs observed their passage from low branches as did keel-billed toucans high above. An exceptionally hairy three toed sloth gazed down sleepily at them and poison dart frogs leapt from branch to branch for a better view of the passing group. With the appearance of animal life the capuchins were again on the alert for jaguars and leopards while they harvested much longed-for fruits and nuts.

A giant anteater ambled towards them, the black wet end of his long curved snout skimming the ground as he sniffed for ants in his path and lapped them up with his enormously long and sticky tongue. His tail, as long as his body and equally thick, swept the ground behind him as though to obliterate his trail. He stopped in front of Caipora. "You've done well to get this far," he said in a husky voice, "but don't think your troubles are over," he paused his advice to slurp up an ant. "There's much danger about. Not everything is as it seems."

"Thank you," Caipora said, happy to meet a friendly being at last. "I've just discovered that, in the forest behind us."

"Yes, but there's more to come. Be wary on the water," and with those brief words the anteater moved on, nose to the ground, meticulously sniffing for his food.

"Water! Could that really be the Amazon River?" Caipora exclaimed excitedly. Sure enough, the land soon fell steeply into an aguajale - a low-lying area of flooded land, dense with tall palms. Keen to see what lay beyond it, Caipora mustered what little strength she had and climbed a tree: the view that met her eyes made her heart sing. The aguajale merged into a low lying flooded forest and beyond that, drawing a shimmering line between sky and earth, a great ribbon of copper light stretched from east to west across the horizon: the Amazon River carrying the rays of the evening sun. Caipora had stumbled upon it without really knowing where she was on the map. To have it now in her sights boosted her strength and lifted her spirits; allowed her to put the horrific spider ordeal behind her and focus on crossing the great river.

Dusk stained the sky as they made camp for the night. With Caipora not yet fully recovered from the arachnid venom, the capuchins gathered firewood and foraged for Suri grubs and aguaje fruit. It was all Caipora could do to build the fire, hang her hammock and climb into it. Following her instructions, the capuchins cooked the Suri grubs and fed them to her one by one. Finally they slept - and slept and slept.

The sun was high when Caipora opened her eyes - and felt well at last. Eager to reach the Amazon, they moved on with fresh vigour and by midday, stood at the water's edge. Caipora checked her map and the position of the sun: they had to head north through the aguajale and the flooded forest, cross the great river and follow it north east until it turned directly east. At that point they would leave the river and continue north north east to Japura.

To walk through the aguajale, even in shallow water, was not an option. Progress would not only be slow and difficult but also highly dangerous: they would undoubtedly very quickly become a sumptuous meal for a caiman or anaconda. Water called for a canoe - but to carve one out from a tree would take many days. Caipora opted for a raft. She cut a sturdy straight branch and sent the monkeys, equipped with her machete and knife, to find others just like it - and plenty of them. The resourceful capuchins soon had more than enough for a raft big enough to carry them all. Following further instruction, they shredded bark from aguaje palms into long strips which Caipora wove into ropes and used to tie all the branches together to form the raft. She bound together short thin branches to form a paddle and attached that to a long branch which served as the shaft. Pleased with the results of their efforts, they dragged the raft to the water's edge and set off into the shimmering aguajale.

CHAPTER 10
On The Water

To glide smoothly and silently across the glossy water was sheer bliss - a great reprieve from thrashing through tangled thorny undergrowth, crawling over slimy fallen trees and trudging through stinking bogs! Caipora navigated the raft around the palm trunks in the aguajale, resisting the temptation to stop and gather aguaje berries. Time was precious. She paddled hard through the afternoon light, hoping to find land on which to camp before nightfall. Hours passed and the aguajale merged into low-lying forest - the flood plain of the Amazon River - where tree trunks stood in floodwaters holding their canopies high like mothers with outstretched arms saving their children from drowning. Shorter trees masqueraded as floating bushes or lived completely submerged in a watery world.

The setting sun varnished the polished surface of the water with flaming evening light but still no land came into sight. Caipora searched furtively for a tree from which to hang her hammock and night had almost draped its mantle over the earth before her eyes fell on one that would suffice. She checked for snakes, tied the raft to a low branch and hung her hammock well above the water - out of reach of hungry caimans. The monkeys snuggled in with her and all shared, with much appreciation, the eternal pudding, including the littlest one - even though its flavour had not changed.

No one mentioned the horror of the spider attack but as soon as Caipora closed her eyes the ghastly arachnids assaulted her from the blackness of her eyelids. She opened them instead to the moon-splattered forest resonating with its orchestra of nocturnal recitals and wondered, did Fate organise the attack? But if Fate were on her side and had chosen her for this mission, why had she tried to kill her - and then let the monkeys save her?

"Do you think Fate determines what happens to us?" she addressed the capuchins warming her with their hairy bodies, on the threshold of their dreams. A moment of stunned silence, then a puzzled "What?" from one drowsy voice.

"Do you think Fate brought on the spider attack?"

"What on earth are you talking about?" The oldest stirred sleepily from her comfort and blinked heavy eyelids at the night.

"My mother told me that Fate determines when we live and when we die. She said that Fate gave me my freedom and chose me for this mission."

"What freedom? What *are* you talking about?" And so Caipora related to the eldest capuchin, the only one awake, how she had longed for freedom and how it had come to her.

"And the Mother of the Muiraquita told me that if you truly believe in achieving something, you will achieve it -

through the power of your mind. So then I believed I had killed my tribe through wishing to be free, to live my life away from everyone. But my mother told me Fate was responsible for the massacre, not me. So now I don't understand what Fate does and what my mind can do." For some time, only silence responded through the darkness.

"Why? Why on earth would you want to be alone, away from your own family?" Questions of Fate and the power of Caipora's mind sailed straight through the capuchin's brain without touching it. "If you'd been alone when the spiders attacked you, who would have given you the potion? If you'd been alone when the slimy tree snatched you up, who would have saved you? We capuchins normally live in a much bigger community because greater numbers offer more security and protection from predators. None of us would ever wish to be alone. I think I would die of loneliness if I were all by myself. But Fyglia chose only five of us to help you because ……well, even five of us make a lot of noise sometimes…..alone?…..why would you….?" And sleep muffled her words and snuffed out her thoughts.

Snuggled together with the sleeping capuchins, Caipora wrestled with the problem of how she might have overcome the arachnid attack with the power of her mind - but her mind offered no solution. And there would be more attacks - more harm in her way. How could she use her mind to avoid or overcome them? Was she to simply steel her mind with the words "I will overcome" everything that lay in store for her? Was it a general belief she needed? A general vizualisation of herself winning battles and onslaughts? Then it flashed into her mind: she needed to visualize herself succeeding! She needed to channel the courage and strength her mother had imparted to her to see herself capturing the Toad and freeing Verita! Believe it, see it and it will happen! As long as she visualised herself achieving her goal, *believed* she would achieve it, she *would* overcome *whatever* challenges Fate put in her path. With that resolve Caipora closed her eyes, secure in the knowledge that she would succeed.

Daybreak welcomed them with thundering clouds, eating their pudding with rain-wet fingers as water streamed through the canopy - and so it continued for countless days as they paddled through the half submerged forest under deluging skies that hid any hint of the sun and where north might lie, leaving Caipora guessing at its direction.

At last they were met with a morning of sunshine dazzling against sapphire blue and they set out with great hopes of reaching the flooded banks of the Amazon itself that day. The forest brimmed with life: small turtles lined up on floating logs, bathed in the warmth of the sun while butterflies flitted around them sipping their salty eye and nostril fluids, settling on their backs when they'd had their fill; lizards clung to gnarled and twisted vines, hoping for tasty morsels to fly by; spiders sat patiently in their webs, waiting to trap their food. Caipora's skin crawled at the sight of them. Shuddering, she turned her head away.

It was mid afternoon when the low lying forest abruptly ended and at last the vast expanse of the Amazon stretched before them. They had to follow the mighty river in its north easterly direction until it turned directly east, then leave it and continue north north east. Caipora kept the raft close to the edge of the forest but far enough into the river to use the current to carry them swiftly, with no effort on her part. All she had to do was steer.

They'd traveled at a good pace for some hours when the Muiraquita stone turned hot on Caipora's chest. Danger was near - but there was no time to prepare. All at once the water was alive with thrashing fish jumping in every direction - even onto the raft! And not just ordinary fish, but huge flesh-eating piranhas! The monkeys leapt about screaming while Caipora leapt about whacking the piranhas with her paddle and flicking them back into the water before they could get hold of someone's feet. Once these creatures got their teeth into you it was impossible to get them off and you'd be devoured within moments! But the more Caipora knocked them off the more they jumped onto the raft again. On and on the horror went! Then, just as suddenly as it had started, it stopped. She looked around but saw nothing - until the monkeys began screaming again and her eyes fell upon the menacing head of an enormous black caiman rapidly heading towards them.

He would barely feel her arrows through his thick skin. Instead, Caipora's fingers gripped her machete and when the fearsome black reptile was at the edge of the raft, his snout butting onto it, his menacing eyes staring into hers, she wielded her gleaming blade and the crocodile sank into the soothing cool depths of the water and disappeared.

"That Toad is really working hard to stop us," Caipora said, more to herself than to the capuchins. "He's organised all the animals that can harm us to attack us. The anteater was right. I wonder what more there is to come!"

"I'm scared," said the littlest monkey.

"I know you're feeling scared, but I will always do my best to protect you," Caipora reassured the little creature, stroking his head.

"But I'm supposed to be protecting and helping you!" he replied, stifling a little sob.

"You *have* helped me: you saved my life - and more than once!" Caipora wrapped her arm around him and drew him close. He snuggled into her side.

"We will all do what we can to the best of our abilities," the oldest capuchin spoke, stalwart and strong, "and we will not allow these evil creatures get the better of us."

"Good! That's what I like to hear!" said Caipora, paddle in hand again. Two more days of paddling took them to the point where the Amazon River turned directly east. There they crossed it to its northern bank without incident and headed north north east.

CHAPTER 11
The Japura River

A week of hard paddling through the still and heavy water of the flooded forest finally brought them to the Japura River. Caelia had described it as fast and dangerous, but it was far more than that. Broken by rapids and cataracts, it raged by at terrific speed, roaring like a mortally wounded jaguar vowing retribution against his assailant in his next life. Attempting to cross the river in the raft would be madness: it would be flipped in a moment. They needed a canoe and even with that the crossing would present a formidable challenge - but she *would* do it! She reckoned that if she were more or less on track with her intended route, the town of Japura would be only a short distance downstream to the east - and full of canoes. Believing she *was* on track, she followed the raging river from the safety of the calm waters of the forest and by the next afternoon, ran onto dry land. Abandoning the raft, the monkeys took to the trees while Caipora made her way through the undergrowth and when the sounds of shouting, calling, laughing, caught her ear, she dropped to her knees, creeping cautiously towards the voices until she came to the edge of the town bustling with people working around a great number of boats moored in a small harbour - dugout canoes and other boats which left her open-mouthed and goggle-eyed as they purred loudly alongside the riverbank, smoke billowing from their rear ends and a great white tail of frothy water streaking out behind them.

Caelia had described the town as a gigantic village where houses were made not of grass or reeds but of smooth stone or wood and whose inhabitants looked much like her but covered themselves with white people's clothing. It was as Caelia had said. Caipora watched men pushing wooden carts laden with boxes and crates and unloading their cargo onto the boats. Others hauled bulging sacks from different boats and threw them into carts pulled by mules. But what really amazed Caipora were the large things made of a strange shiny substance which moved along on four round black turning legs. Their colours varied but always the front half resembled a tiny hut with windows all around and doors on both sides and at the rear was a large cart into which people piled all kinds of boxes and bags and crates. When they had loaded their cargo they opened a door, climbed in, sat down and took hold of a circular object in front of them, resembling a smooth twine coiled into a loop which held its shape - on one side of the hut only - and moved off with a loud purring noise exactly as the strange boats made. Sometimes a second person climbed in through the other door. It was beyond all comprehension!

A large board displaying the word "Japura" caught Caipora's attention. She checked her map: yes, it was the same! They were in the right place! The sun dipped into the watery horizon, a flaming circle of red; the riverbank far too busy and crowded for borrowing a canoe. They'd spend the night in the trees on the edge of the town, rest well and make their move in the morning. But rest did not come to Caipora. Horrific images hurtled across the black of her eyelids: gigantic caimans snapped the canoe in half; waterfalls hurled her into bottomless churning abysses; deadly snakes invaded the canoe, sinking their venomous fangs into her flesh. Through the darkness, fear crept in and took hold of Caipora's mind, sucked away her confidence, ate her belief in her abilities. Filled her mind with fear. Time and time again she woke, gasping for air through nightmares of plummeting into the savage river, attacked by piranhas and crocodiles from all sides.

Then in the dark fear-filled stillness just before daybreak, the voices of her elders echoed through her memory: "Courage is not the absence of fear. It is the mastery of it." She held the words in her mind, turning them over and over, probing their meaning: how was she to master this poisonous fear which had locked her body and mind in its grip? Again the voice of the Mother of the Muiraquita spoke to her: "Visualize your objective. Believe it will happened and it will. Use the power of your mind to believe in yourself." But how could she make herself believe and how could she she unlock the power of her mind?

Caipora opened her eyes to the stars peering through the canopy and her memory hummed with the words of her elders: "We are all one entity," they said. "We are part of the universe: its limitless power and knowledge is within us all to use - if we know how to connect to it." She knew at the time that these were valuable words, meaningful words, and now she sensed they held the key to the power of her mind. But how to connect to this power of the universe? She surrendered herself to the vast emptiness of the black velvet sky and allowed her spirit to fly among the stars, absorbed their white light until she felt herself glow with their incandescence. And there rose within her an overwhelming force which spread to every fibre of her being and lodged itself in her mind: the same force she had felt in her mother before she dissolved and disappeared - but now Caipora had found her own. And now she knew she could do it. She knew it and believed it: she *would* get across the river.

***

The fear still clung to her thoughts when first light washed away the stars but now Caipora was stronger than the fear. Through the cool still grey of the morning, Caipora and the capuchins crept stealthily towards the small harbour where a multitude of moored boats flocked the silvery riverbank. Good fortune had placed an excellent canoe - no holes, even a paddle - only a few paces from the shelter of the forest. Unaware of the heat of the glowing Muiraquita Stone caught up in her quiver, Caipora and the monkeys climbed soundlessly into the canoe. A short distance from the bank the river tore by at terrifying speed, throwing up standing waves, vicious whirlpools and roaring like a wounded demon. The monkeys huddled together in a trembling heap, gripping firmly onto one another wherever a handhold allowed.

"Don't worry, we'll make it. We will be all right!" Caipora spoke confidently with complete belief in her words. Frightened, yes, but gritting her teeth she faced the ferocious river upstream and angling the canoe at forty five degrees to the raging current she paddled into it, then held the paddle firmly in place at the rear of the boat to maintain its angle so that the water would do all the work and carry them across without taking them downstream. The current instantly powered them into the middle of the river just as she'd planned but all at once things began to go awry: alarmingly, the canoe swung itself around to face downstream and refused to move towards the opposite bank regardless of Caipora's efforts to take it there. Now firmly in the grip of the racing current, they flew downstream at a meteoric pace past the town of Japura and were well off their course in no time. Huge boulders and a massive rapid loomed in front of them and still the canoe would not yield to Caipora's ruddering. Instead, it defiantly held its course and headed straight for the boulders!

"Hold on as tight as you can!" she shouted to the monkeys who immediately grabbed hold of each other with all the strength they could muster. "No! No!" screamed Caipora. "Hold onto the sides of the canoe!"

They hit a huge boulder head on. The front of the canoe flew up but Caipora instantly leaned forward to stop the boat from flipping and by some miracle they landed, without capsizing, downstream of the drop where the rapid raged on. Smaller rocks were everywhere, but mostly underwater and they bounced over them, sheer luck keeping them upright.

Captured and imprisoned by their boat they could do nothing other than hang onto its sides as the violent river twisted and turned and threw them around bends and over rapids again and again, water whipping their faces as their canoe plunged nose first over massive drops. Caipora gave up trying to steer the boat towards the bank and focused all her efforts on keeping it upright. Flying past a town on the left bank, she caught sight of a sign displaying the word "Maraa" and soon after that the river turned south east - the opposite direction to which they should have been heading. Still the current raged on. Again more boulders loomed ahead but this time the river beyond them was at a much lower level: they were heading for a waterfall!

"Hold on! Hold on! Don't let go!" Caipora screamed over the roar of the water at the monkeys who shrieked as the canoe dropped down the five metre fall, flipped and propelled its occupants into the air. Caipora plunged down through the foaming white water. Previous experience told her not to waste energy struggling to reach the surface. Instead, she dived down until her fingers scraped the gravelly bottom where the water was solid and she swam away from the waterfall, finally bobbing up at the surface, gasping for air - still in the grip the current! The capuchins were nowhere to be seen. Angling her body just as she'd angled the canoe Caipora faced upstream and swam towards the right bank - but not as fast as the current was hurtling her onto a massive cataract littered with jagged rocks that would cut her to pieces.

Silently gliding out of nowhere, a huge shadow cloaked her, something wrapped itself around her torso and she was instantly high above the river, heading towards a grassy bank by the water's edge onto which she was gently deposited. "Wait here," her rescuer said. Only then could she look up to see the enormous condor flying downstream. Gasping to catch her breath, Caipora struggled to understand what had happened. How had the canoe defied her ruddering? Where had the gigantic condor come from? This was not even his territory!

The words of the anteater came to mind: more evil to come, he'd said, and warned her to be wary by the water. Yes, there was definitely something sinister about that canoe. The sound of flapping wings stole her attention. The approaching condor filled the sky, this time carrying a capuchin in each enormous claw. Flying low past Caipora, he gently dropped the monkeys next to her and flew on without stopping.

"I'll be back," he said, and was gone. The two wet, bedraggled capuchins huddled beside Caipora without a word - not even looking at her. Traumatised and trembling, they simply stared into the space in front of them. Fortunately, capuchins can swim or they would not have stayed afloat long enough to have been rescued. Caipora wrapped them in her arms, stroking their wet hair, comforting them. She'd never seen their little old men's faces so terrified. "You're safe now. We're alright now. Everything will be fine. The condor will find the rest of our troop and bring them back. I know he will." And there he was, blotting out the sunlight with his enormous wing span, the three remaining monkeys in his claws. He set them down as he had the others, without stopping: there was nowhere for him to land - he was simply far too big.

"Be careful in the dark!" he called as he surged up and away. Caipora soothed and reassured the newly arrived, terrified capuchins. "We're all back together again. Everything is going to be alright. We're going to be just fine. Let's eat and rest before we move on, shall we?" Caipora handed out pieces of the pudding to the terror-stricken monkeys who took their food without glancing at it, staring blankly and silently into the space before their eyes.

A family of capybaras meandered into the clearing to graze on the succulent grass by the water's edge. "You must be the girl trying to save the forest," said one, seemingly unsurprised to see a girl with five wet monkeys sitting by the bank. "How's it going?"

"It's hard work," replied Caipora.

"Yes, I can imagine," continued the capybara. "I've heard there's worse to come. Stay away from strangers," she warned and suddenly, in a flurry of flying grassy tufts, the capybaras were on their heels and back in the shadows of the forest as swiftly as their short little legs could carry them, leaving Caipora and the monkeys facing a caiman coming straight at them from the water. In a flash they were on their feet and into the forest even faster than the capybaras!

The current had swept them downstream well beyond Japura, the point from which they were meant to travel directly north to the Rio Negro (the Black River) and cross that to arrive at the town of Sao Gabriel da Cachoeira. From there they were to head north east to Pico da Neblina. Such had been Caelia's instructions - but Caipora was now off course. They'd been swept past the town Maraa on the northern bank of the river. Caipora checked her map - and there it was. Now she knew where they were - a little east of Maraa. As long as she knew where she was on the map, she was not lost.

A good distance north east of Maraa, on the northern bank of the Rio Negro, lay another town marked on Caipora's map: Santa Isabel do Rio Negro. They'd make their way there and take their bearings for Pico da Neblina from that point. That would now be the shorter route, although they'd have to travel through Yonukari territory, against which Caelia had warned. Caipora took her bearings for a north easterly direction from the sun and set out for Santa Isabel do Rio Negro.

They now traveled through a healthy, verdant forest rich in every imaginable fruit. Animals also abounded: a jaguar dropped a growl from a tree high above, drawing jittery exclamations from the capuchins; colourful birds zipped through the canopy and the forest floor was lively with rodents, anteaters, tapirs, small reptiles and innumerable insects.

That night, as they lay tucked into their various sleeping nooks, the littlest monkey began at last to put into words the trauma they had endured. "When the boat flipped us out and we flew through the air - way, way past the waterfall - and finally fell into the water, I went down and down and down!"

"So did I!" chipped in another voice. "Was that you I bumped into on the way down?"

"No! That was me! You hit me hard on the head, as if things weren't bad enough already!" complained another voice.

"I couldn't breathe for such a long time. I really thought I was going to die!" said the older female.

"We all thought we were going to die!"

"When I saw that gigantic bird coming towards me I thought I was dead. I thought he was going to tear me into pieces and eat me then and there!" the littlest one cried.

"That bird was big enough to eat you whole without tearing you up at all!"

"My heart stopped beating when he picked me up, it really did!" The monkeys went on and on, sharing their terrifying experiences while Caipora reassured them that they were now safe and all would be well.

"But we don't know that, do we? We don't know that all will be well in the future," cried the littlest one again.

"No, it's true, we don't. But we have to stay positive and simply forge on. We have no choice," replied the oldest capuchin and with those words silence finally fell over the group and sleep mercifully blotted out their horrific memories. Only once did the littlest one wake up screaming but immediately comforted by the others, quickly fell into the oblivion of sleep again.

But Caipora's mind still grappled with the river crossing. There was no question the canoe had been an evil entity. Was it Boiuna? But why would Fate allow Boiuna to try to kill her when Fate herself had chosen her to free Verita? Could it be that Boiuna and Fate were equally powerful and fought over what happened to her? Surely not! Too many questions without any answers. Nothing made sense. But what *was* true was that she *did* reach the northern bank of the river - not the way she had planned, but she had truly believed she would and she did! Could it be that the power of Caipora's mind - the power of the universe to which she had connected - was greater than that of both Fate and Boiuna?

CHAPTER 12
The Meeting of the Three Evils

For two weeks they walked north east through daily downpours and storms towards the Rio Negro. All the horrors the Toad had in store for them seemed far behind until one evening, while looking for a place to spend the night, they came across something unexpected.

"Shhhhh! Don't move! There's someone up ahead!" Caipora whispered furtively. The capuchins stopped in their tracks, eyes fixed on fragments of firelight flickering through the foliage. Caipora held her breath, listening for sounds. Nothing - until branches cracked and a deep gravelly voice spoke. "Now that should be enough wood to keep the fire going for a while."

Other voices joined in, but more quietly, the words unclear. "Wait here and don't move. I'm going to see what I can see," she instructed her troop and soundlessly crept closer until she could not only hear what was being said but also see who was saying it. What met her eyes sent shudders through to her bones and her hand flew over her mouth to stifle a gasp.

Sitting in the orange glow of the fire were two horrific creatures and a woman. Red slanting eyes glowed like coals on the face of the nearest creature and a lip-less mouth sneered under a huge hooked nose. Two curved horns protruded from his head and long pointy ears stuck out from either side of it. The rest of his body was human-like except for the legs which appeared to belong to the hind quarters of a large wolf, but bearing hooves. The arms, convoluted with muscles, ended in five knobbly fingers from the tips of which there curved long sharp claws ready to snatch at anything within reach. Rough red scales covered his entire body and two enormous folded black wings bulged from his back. A long serpentine tail protruded from his rear and at its tip a spiked arrowhead flicked proportionately with the agitation in his speech. Caipora had heard her people describe this creature so many times that she knew instantly she was looking at Jurupari - the god of darkness and evil!

She retched at the sight of the abomination sitting next to him. Grey rotting flesh hanging in tatters from his torso opened windows to a cracked and moldy rib cage. One misshapen nostril still clung to the base of the cavity which the nose had once filled. The skull, scattered with a patchwork of putrid flesh, housed a pair of black holes which had, a thousand years ago, held seeing eyes, and a few black and yellow rotting teeth lurked inside a gaping dribbling cavern that was the mouth: it was none other than the zombie Corpo Seco!

The woman was hideous! As though suffering the aftermath of electrocution, long frizzy strands of red hair sprang from her scalp in all directions and red bloodshot eyes leapt restlessly from side to side in deep black sockets. Purple tattoos on her wrinkled greenish skin quivered grotesquely as she moved the long black shiny claws on the tips of her fingers which looked as though they itched to dig into something - anything. A thin sharp nose distended by a huge bump reached down over a pair of wrinkled purple lips through which a pointy black tongue flicked in and out and cracks rather than wrinkles serrated her narrow green face, frequently punctuated by black hairy moles and ending in a chin so long and pointy that it curled up at the end. A mangy tattered black shroud hung over her thin bony body.

"That girl is a real nuisance....." whined Corpo Seco, lisping through his almost toothless mouth. "How could we have lost sight of her? Where could she possibly have got to?"

"She should have been stopped long ago by all we've put in her way!" the woman complained agitatedly, the breath carried by her menacing voice alarming the flames into jumpy agitation. "It's ridiculous that she's been able to survive it all! It's just not right! I put a great deal of effort into chasing her down that river but those blasted dolphins got the better of me! And then all the evil I put into the forests after that; the time and energy it took to organise the wandering spiders - and it's all come to nothing! I still don't know where those assassin bugs came from! And now we don't even know where she is!"

"I have to admit I did relax a bit when the Mohana got hold of her. I really thought she'd be there forever - but no! That Fairy Godmother had to stick her nose in there and get her out!" the disgruntled Corpo Seco savagely poked the fire from a distance with a very long stick - too close and he would quickly sizzle. "And now we have so much more work to do!"

"I really thought I'd put an end to her when I changed into a canoe and tipped her out into the raging Japura River

- but that wretched condor turned up out of nowhere! That's not even his territory! That's just not fair play!" squawked the bony green woman, wringing her cracked hands and grinding her sparse teeth.

"It's just not right! And when she can't cope on her own that Fairy Godmother of hers always comes to the rescue," moaned the Corpo Seco. "The Toad was right: she's the real problem!"

"Aarh! Aarh! Aarh! Well, not any more! Just as the Toad ordered, I've put an end to her, haven't I?" laughed the grotesque and ghastly Jurupari. "I haven't just been on holiday you know!"

"Well in truth, you've been gone such a long time that I was beginning to think you'd abandoned the project," the woman croaked. "Do you mean to say you caught her? That I didn't go to all the trouble of making that second cage for nothing? Where did you put her?" she cackled excitedly, wringing her bony green hands.

"Yes! I did! I caught her! I got her as she was on her way to stop the girl from getting into your canoe. I flew her up to Pico right away and put her in the same place as that Goddess of Good. No one will ever find them there. They'll starve to death or die of cold or lack of air after a few months," exuded Jurupari gleefully.

"Hee! Hee! Hee! That *is* excellent news!" the green woman clapped her clawed hands and bouncing and shrieking with excitement, fell off the log she was sitting on, almost rolling into the fire. "Our job will be so much easier now! Hee! Hee! Hee!" she shrieked on as she gathered up her shroud and stamped on its smoking edges with her cracked green feet to put out the embers that were caught there.

"Once we find her again, that is," Corpo Seco

droned gloomily.

Caipora was aghast at what she was seeing and hearing. If the woman had changed herself into the canoe, she must be Boiuna! Now Caipora understood just what she was up against.

"It's a real pity we can't put a spell on her. I've tried, but it just rolls off like water off a duck's back! She doesn't even notice!" complained Jurupari.

"Never mind. Never mind. An excellent plan just sprang into my mind! It can't go wrong!" said the woman leaning her cracked face into the fire, the skin on her hands crinkling into small sharp-edged folds as she energetically rubbed them together. "We'll get her for sure with this one." The red flames danced in the mirrors of her inky black eyes as she leaned even closer to the fire and its spattering sparks - and all at once her long frizzy hair burst into a sizzling frenzy of flames! The other two instantly leapt up and began to smack her about the head to put them out while she screamed and wailed "Oh my hair! My beautiful beautiful hair! It's ruined now! It's ruined!"

"It'll grow back," her two vile companions reassured her. "Now settle down Boiuna, and tell us your plan!" Caipora was right! It *was* Boiuna - changed into a woman - the most hideous woman one could ever imagine! Boiuna pulled herself together, ran consoling fingers through the sizzled remnants of her hair and spoke in a hushed voice, as if afraid the trees might hear her plan and pass it on. Caipora was too far away to make sense of the whispers.

"Yes! Yes! Fantastic! It can't fail! We'll finally have her!" the other two shouted in gleeful exuberance, leaping about and tripping over fallen logs in unbridled enthusiasm.

"Well, if it does fail, I'll just jump out in front of her and scare her to death!" said Corpo Seco. "It'll be so quick there won't even be time for potions or anything else to help her!"

"Yes, well, it would be about time you did something to help! All you do is sit around whining and complaining! You've never yet had even one idea to contribute! I know you're a bit limited physically, what with all your bits and pieces always at risk of dropping off and you can't fly or doing anything else particularly useful - really, all you can do is stand there and look horrific - with no effort on your part whatsoever! No wonder the Toad threatened to fire you!"

Corpo Seco sat stunned at this barrage of abuse. "That kind of language is completely unwarranted," he said quietly, defensively, trying to hide his pain at being made to feel so inadequate. "I do my best you know. Not all of us are endowed with scaly wings and vicious claws. Not all of us can change into whatever we like." Having said that, he became surprisingly assertive, standing up and waving his arms about, bits of rotting flesh flying off and smacking Boiuna in the face. "The fact is, I used to do unbelievably vile and abominable things to people - far far worse than what you're capable of! Far worse than you could even begin to imagine! And have I been rewarded for my efforts?"

He slobbered foaming saliva as he spat out these pain-filled, resentful words. Then throwing himself dramatically upon a tree, he thumped his head against its trunk time and time again. "Oh no! No No! No rewards for me! No! Instead, I'm being punished for all eternity for being so good at what I did - even your boss in hell wouldn't let me go there because I was too evil! But you and Boiuna are praised for your meagre efforts and will live in the Toad's castle! Do you call that fair? Do you? Do you? Do youoooooo.........?" His shrill voice stretched thin as a thread until it finally broke into a heartfelt sob.

"Calm down! Calm down before you completely fall to

pieces! We know you've had a hard life - death - whatever it is, with all your physical limitations. Let's focus on the task at hand," said the cracked tattooed green woman in an effort to restore peace around the fire. "Pico da Neblina is north west of here. That's where the girl will be heading. At first light, we too will set off in that direction and keep a close eye out for her. When we find her, I'll put my plan into action," she said, grinning a hideous grin, her head nodding like a cork in bubbling water.

Without a sound, Caipora crept back to her waiting capuchins. "We can't stay here," she whispered. "There are three evil spirits over there, plotting to capture me. We have to backtrack - not a sound, mind you - and get some distance between them and us. We can't get far in the dark tonight and they'd be sure to hear us moving about so we'll sleep high in the trees, well out of sight from the ground."

CHAPTER 13
Onward to the Rio Negro

Nightmares of capture tortured Caipora's sleep that night. She woke with every creak in every tree, muscles tensed, fearing the evil creatures were climbing up to get her, imagining the worst possible horrors that Boiuna could bring upon her! Daylight found the monkeys chattering happily, indulging in abundant forest fruit and offering it to her. Juice trickled down her chin as she lay in her hammock, eating instead of getting up and moving on. But she was burdened with guilt. Her thoughts were with Fyglia and the suffering she must be enduring: it was through protecting her that she had been captured.

"What's happening? Are we having a rest day?" one of the monkeys eventually inquired cheerily.

"What a good idea!" exclaimed the littlest one. "I've been wanting to practice some new swinging tricks for a long time but we've just been too busy! I could do that today!"

"Can I do them with you?" asked an eager young female.

"Sure you can. In fact, some of them need two of us. It'll be great fun!"

"Sorry to spoil your plans, but no, we're not having a rest day," Caipora interrupted. "I'm waiting so that the evil creatures can get ahead of us. They started out at first light this morning, heading north west. They believe we're traveling in that direction and that we're ahead of them. You can practice your tricks for an hour or so, but then we'll be moving on - but we'll be heading north east."

They set out late in the morning and for several days their progress was without incident. Then early one afternoon they found themselves in a small clearing unusually thick with long hanging vines. The capuchins, who'd been traveling through the trees, couldn't resist the fun of sliding down them.

"Well, since you're all on the ground now, why don't we stop here and have some lunch before you climb up again?" Caipora suggested.

"Has the pudding changed its flavour yet?" the littlest one dared to ask.

"We won't know until we try it, will we?" Caipora replied. "But you can always find your own lunch if you don't like it." The capuchins entered into a lively discussion about what flavour they'd like but as Caipora began to unwrap the pudding, the Muiraquita Stone suddenly glowed red and hot on her skin. Her eyes flashed around at the trees and undergrowth, seeking signs of danger but could find nothing threatening anywhere. It was odd that the stone should glow red when no threat was evident, but having searched again and again Caipora finally sat down with the monkeys to indulge in much needed food. The Muiraquita Stone glowed as they ate - and the long vines began slowly, imperceptibly, to twist themselves around one another. By the time Caipora became aware of what was happening, she and the capuchins were trapped in a cage of vines from which sharp thorns, long enough to pierce their bodies, were growing towards them, their menacing bright purple tips clearly poisonous. The cage was rapidly closing in around them and hacking through it with a machete would be impossible: her arms would be ripped to shreds! The evil things not only creaked as they grew, but hissed and snarled as they came closer and closer to Caipora and the monkeys.

There was no escape! The capuchins even stopped screaming and merely whimpered in terror as they clung helplessly to one another around Caipora's legs while she desperately searched for a way out. But there was nothing. She looked up. High above the ground was a gap where the vines had not yet knitted themselves together, but there was no way of getting there - and the gap was closing fast. The end had come. Caipora stood bravely surrendering to her fate when a voice spoke in her head.

"You can fly! Use the silver vial! Use the silver vial!"

"Yes.....The silver vial...." Caipora uttered the words to herself.

"You can fly!" the voice said again.

"I can fly!" Caipora's voice surged with electrifying energy, defying the deadly intentions of the poisonous thorns. The vial was instantly in her hands, the drops on her tongue and Ravan's words in her mind: "Just shut your eyes and see yourself doing what you want, and it will happen."

"Right! All of you climb onto me and hold on tight!" Caipora ordered the stunned monkeys who obeyed without question, leaping onto her back and shoulders while the littlest one threw himself around her neck. "Hold on with everything you've got," she instructed in a calm but determined voice, "and don't let go until I tell you." Their grips tighten on her bare flesh so much so that it hurt - a lot!

She looked up. The opening was now very small and still closing. She closed her eyes and saw herself flying through it - and instantly shot up and through the hole like a bolt of lightning with an audible 'whoosh', with all the monkeys attached to her. When she opened her eyes again she looked down on silvery rivers winding their way through a sea of green and all around, the hazy horizon drew an arc where it melted into the blue of the sky. She was flying! Serenely gliding through the cool clear silent air! Then the monkeys opened *their* eyes and ear piercing screams shattered the ethereal tranquility.

"Ouch!" Caipora cried out as they dug their nails deeper into her skin. She almost shouted 'Let go!' but bit her tongue in time: that might have ended disastrously! "It's alright. You're quite safe," she reassured them, but to no avail: the capuchins' screaming escalated to ear-piercing shrieking and unmitigated hysteria.

"We're not meant to be up here, we're really not!" screeched the littlest one in high-pitched terror.

"Have you noticed we don't have any wings?" a stress-filled wail came from another.

"Sush!" Let me concentrate!" Caipora remonstrated and focused on the scene below. To the north a long wide river ran from west to east. It had to be the Rio Negro, she was sure of it! It was called the black river because of its dark water - and there it was, very black indeed. North of the Rio Negro and a little to the west, distant peaks of steeply rising mountains crowded the horizon. The most distant reached further into the sky than the rest. It had to be Pico da Neblina! And somewhere to the south of it was the Toad in his Stinky Lake! The unexpected view of her destination sent a tremendous thrill through Caipora and imbibed her with the belief that nothing was impossible!

Not far ahead a substantial river flowed north by north east into the Rio Negro. At that point, two very large islands took up most of the black river which ran divided around them. On the north bank was a large village - a town. Picturing her map, Caipora believed it to be the one they were aiming for: Santa Isabel do Rio Negro. The idea of flying all the way there greatly excited her but she had no idea how long the power of the potion would last and falling out of the sky was an experience she could do without. She decided to land in the river that flowed into the Rio Negro. She'd build another raft, paddle downstream and make her way around the islands to the north bank of the Rio Negro, to Santa Isabel. From there she'd take her bearings and head north west in search of Stinky Lake. It all seemed straightforward and the sight of Pico da Neblina filled her with joy and pumped new energy into her veins.

"I think I've found a place to land," she called to the monkeys.

"You *think*? You *think* so do you? Tell us when you *know* you've found one, will you? My arms are killing me!" a whiny panic-driven voice responded.

"Oh for goodness sake! Can you stop all your whingeing and complaining for just one moment? Do you think I'm having a great time? Have a look at my skin where your nails have dug in! Is it bleeding yet?" Caipora scolded.

A quiet 'oops' or two and a communal 'sorry' came from the group, then silence. But Caipora was, in fact, having a very good time indeed! She'd often wondered what it would be like to fly like a bird - and here she was! Fantastic!

Suddenly an explosion of shrill shrieking decimated the silence and nails like needles dug even further into her flesh. A vulture was flying beside them! Its splendid beak - designed for shredding flesh - was level with her face and its cream-coloured body, as long as hers, held its course parallel and close. Never before had she been so close to the brilliant feathers festooning the heads and necks of these phenomenal birds - nor had the monkeys ever before been so close to the flesh shredding beak!

"Stop that racket," the vulture squawked sharply at the capuchins, "or I really will have to eat you!" Well that shut them up instantly and Caipora's body visibly shook from their trembling. Having effectively dealt with the screaming, the vulture turned her attention to Caipora.

"I'm here to tell you that Jurupari, Corpo Seco and Boiuna are no longer traveling north west. They believed you were heading in that direction but when they couldn't find you anywhere, Boiuna changed into a bird and scouted the forest for you. Someone told her you'd been seen traveling north by north east, so they're now heading for Santa Isabel do Rio Negro, believing they'll find you there. I suggest you get yourself to the Rio Negro, give Santa Isabel a miss for now, and head directly east and downstream to Barcelos. It's an easy two day trip - the current will carry you if you have a boat. You'll be safe in Barcelos. No one will hurt you there. I can't vouch for the monkeys, though," and the sideways glance she cast at the capuchins sent a shudder through their already shaking bones. "There's a multitude of small islands on the Rio Negro," the vulture continued, "and it's not hard to lose your bearings, but if you stick to the right bank all the way, you can't go wrong. You should rest in Barcelos for two or three days at least, to let the evil spirits get ahead of you. After they get to Santa Isabel they'll head towards Pico da Neblina in pursuit of you - but you'll be in Barcelos. You can get a riverboat there to take you upstream to Santa Isabel. By the time you get there the evil creatures will have moved on, thinking you're ahead of them and on your way to Pico. Good luck!"

Before Caipora could thank her, the King Vulture tilted her wings and soared away - much to the monkeys' relief - and Caipora set her sights on the river that emptied into the Rio Negro. She simply saw herself descending, and it happened. Gliding low over the water, searching for place to land, she rounded a bend and almost flew into a tiny village on the water's edge! Shocked and flustered, she lost her focus and plunged into the river! Much splashing and chaos ensued before they climbed out onto the bank. "I hope no one saw us," Caipora whispered, "but even if they didn't, I'm sure they will have heard the splash and will be scouring the water and forest for us. We'd best get up into the trees and hide and please, do be *very quiet!*"

Soon enough excited voices filtered through the forest as a group of Indians searched for the cause of the great splash. "Higher, climb higher!" urged Caipora in a whisper. "Get completely out of sight!" They scrambled up to the very highest branches and sat stock-still and silent, barely breathing for fear of being heard while men carrying spears and blow guns which could easily fly through the trees thrashed their way through the undergrowth below - but passed by without looking up. Caipora and the capuchins stayed put until well after dark lest the Indians return to their village along the same route - but they were not seen again. Meanwhile, the capuchins tended to the painful wounds they had inflicted on Caipora's body, sparingly spreading the healing potion over the deep punctures in her skin.

Caipora had intended to build another raft to get them to the Rio Negro and beyond but, on seeing the many canoes tied to the riverbank, borrowing one seemed like a good idea - so long as it wasn't Boiuna again! This time she'd pay close attention to her Muiraquita Stone! When all was quiet and not even the flicker of a flame glimmered in the village, Caipora whispered her instructions to the monkeys: "I'm going to swim to the far end of the village and untie a canoe. I want you to follow me downriver through the trees and wait for me there."

She slid into the black water where the gentle current carried her soundlessly past the stilts of the huts, past canoes tethered to ladders leading up to closed doors, past dark windows through which reverberated muted rumblings of snoring and deep sleep. When she came to the last canoe at the far end of the village, Caipora first checked the Muiraquita Stone. It was green - the boat was good. No holes and a paddle. She untied it, guided it downstream and out of sight of the village, then steered it into the bank and climbed in. The capuchins dropped from the trees like coconuts and climbed into the waiting canoe as quietly as mice. They paddled away through the moonless night - but to be out after sunset, particularly on the water, was never a good idea: a slapping splash behind them swung Caipora around, eyes scouring the water's surface for the snout of a caiman but the obscure blackness revealed nothing. It had been a caiman for sure and Caipora paddled harder and faster not only to put a good distance between herself and the village but hopefully to foil the caiman's plans as well. When a small sandy beach came into view she ran the canoe aground and secured it to a nearby tree - just as another splash sounded in the water! Like lightning the monkeys were up the trees and Caipora right behind them.

They camped in a small clearing a good distance from the river and when the capuchins had settled for the night, Caipora made one last foray to find a solid log that would burn until daylight. Some distance from the camp she walked into a thick uneasy darkness and suddenly the Muiraquita Stone burned her chest. Her hand flew to her machete as she peered into the blackness beyond the glow of the Stone where an overgrown path crept up a slight incline. She took two steps towards it and stopped in her tracks. Not more than six paces ahead, awash with the red light of the Stone, stood the eerie figure of a man with long shaggy hair and strange bedraggled clothing, his back towards her.

Terror anchored her feet to the ground. Was it the Mohana again in a different disguise? Why did he not move? Then all of a sudden the figure dropped vertically into the ground and disappeared! Caipora jumped back! Only the hideous head remained on the path, turning its malevolent eyes on her while its grisly toothless mouth grinned a spine-chilling grin. In an instant the gruesome thing sprang to life, bouncing and rolling down the slope towards her! The horrendous Cabeca Satanica! Satan's head! Coming straight at her! Horror stories about it were endless: should the Cabeca just touch you as it bounces along, you will be very quickly dead, her elders had warned repeatedly. Caipora stood immobilsed, mind and body frozen through fear, powerless as the ghoulish thing bounced closer and closer and was almost upon her when there sprang from behind a tree a small boy with backwards facing feet and flaming red hair! With one great leap, he kicked the head so hard that it flew up through the canopy and didn't come down again! He cast a quick glance and smile at Caipora and vanished into thin air right before her eyes! He didn't need to say anything.

Caipora knew who he was: Curupira, the protector of the jungle and its creatures.

When at last life flowed through her limbs again, she made her way back to camp, curled up in her hammock, closed her eyes and tried to block the ghastly image of the Cabeca Satanica from her mind. She would not mention it to the capuchins. They'd had their fair share of terror.

A sapphire sky heralded the new day as their canoe slid through the silky waters of a river which was at times so narrow that the canopy closed in overhead. Green iguanas imbibing the sun stretched themselves along the lower branches of trees while tegu lizards watched their passing from above. A hoatzin bird, panicked by their presence, did what it always does when faced with danger and dropped from its tree into the water right in front of them. Its blue face wearing a much alarmed expression, it scurried away, half swimming, half running across the water's surface, frantically flapping its reddish brown wings in its haste to escape the canoe. It was not a good flyer and its startling spiky crest quickly vanished into the undergrowth of the bank as though it were part of it.

The sun was well to the west when a second village appeared around a bend. Like long legged insects afraid of getting wet, the huts sat above the water on tall stilt legs, appearing to balance precariously on their wobbly reflections. Caipora deftly pulled into the bank, dragged the canoe out of sight and hiding high in the trees, they watched the Indians at work.

Like the open beaks of young birds calling for their mothers' return, ladders reached down to the river from holes in the undersides of the huts. Returning from fishing and foraging, the Indians tethered their canoes to them and, hauling their cargo up the ladder, fed the hut with the fish and food they'd gathered in the forest. The smiling faces of young children peered from the shadowy windows of a nearby hut as they watched their father sling a tapir across his shoulders and, grunting heavily, struggle from his boat and up the ladder with their dinner.

Birds flapped their wings across the evening sky and when the windows of the huts surrendered their last glimmers of light to the blackness of night and the only sound was the murmur of the jungle's nightly verses, the black water silently carried Caipora and the capuchins past the village.

PART FOUR

To Santa Isabel Do Rio Negro & Beyond

CHAPTER 14
On the Rio Negro to Barcelos

Once on the Rio Negro, Caipora and the capuchins rapidly made their way downstream on the fast moving current, just as the vulture had promised, but navigation became tricky on the second day when the wide river divided into a multitude of smaller ones which snaked around endless little islands that sat like tiny forests in the black water. Remembering the vulture's words, Caipora stayed by the right bank of the main channel to ensure she didn't stray off course.

On the evening of the second day, Barcelos came into view. Far bigger than Japura, it called attention to itself through a tall white tower standing back from a port crammed with a multitude of boats, large and small. Hiding behind foliage on the edge of the town, Caipora and the capuchins watched the hustle and bustle of people moving cargo to and from gargantuan boats. She had heard of riverboats but never before seen one as the river that ran past her village was too small to carry them. Stunned by their size, she was at a loss to understand how they stayed afloat with the weight of all that was being loaded into them. People heaved cargo back and forth across planks that provided a bridge from the riverboats to the land. They loaded boxes and crates bulging with chickens into carts or threw them onto one of the strange things Caipora had seen in Japura: the tiny shiny huts with doors and windows on four black turning legs, purring loudly as they moved along, their flat back parts piled high with all manner of things. Always, a man sat in the front holding onto a circular tube. Sometimes these moving huts would bleat loudly as if crying out in pain. Caipora jumped every time.

Other things also left her gob-smacked: people sitting on top of thin structures consisting of two large narrow wheels joined by a bar while they held onto a horizontal bar in front of them, moving their legs up and down as the object moved forward. Some of these things had a basket above the front wheel and others pulled a small wagon behind them, both laden with bags and other bits and pieces. To the girl from a remote village in the jungle, they were incomprehensible.

Fascinated as she was by the mind-boggling sights, Caipora turned her attention to getting to Santa Isabel do Rio Negro. She'd heard her people say that you had to trade something called money to travel on big boats: circular flat metal objects and also coloured pieces of paper with pictures on them. If you had enough, you could give them to the owner of the boat and he would take you to where you wanted to go. But Caipora didn't have any of these objects. In fact, she had nothing to trade at all. How would she get on the boat? Not only that, but she also had to take the capuchins with her!

She pondered the dilemma. Perhaps she could sneak on somehow without trading - but of course she'd be seen, especially with all the monkeys! Then bing! It came to her all at once - a great idea in the blink of an eye! She'd use her wand to make herself invisible! But could it make the monkeys invisible as well? Perhaps, but first, she had to find out when a boat for Santa Isabel would be leaving.

"Wait here. I'll be back," she instructed the monkeys. With the light seeping from the sky the mass of cargo shifters, like birds flying to their roosts, were rapidly departing from the port. There was no time to lose. Trusting the vulture's assurance that no one here would harm her, Caipora made her way towards the riverboats, cautiously passing groups of people who, surprisingly, paid her no attention and if they did, it was with a slight nod and a benign smile. Most looked much like her - except that they wore white people's clothing. Caipora ventured up to a man loading his cart and asked him when the next boat for Santa Isabel was departing.

"You just missed one," he said. "The next one leaves tomorrow afternoon at five o'clock. This boat right here," he said, pointing to the one nearest him. That she understood him and he her, was no longer surprising. Caipora hurried back to her troop.

"Come down at once! I have exciting news!" she called to her capuchins in the trees. "There's a boat leaving tomorrow afternoon at five o'clock. I don't know when that is, other than that it's in the afternoon, as I don't know what 'o'clock' means, but I expect it will be before dark," she said. "We did have one problem," she continued, "and that was how to get on the boat without any money - but I've solved that! I'm going to make us all invisible!"

Caipora whipped out her wand. "Everyone stand in a circle and join hands," she instructed enthusiastically. "May your power burn bright, beacon of light! May your power burn bright and make us out of sight!" she commanded the wand, drawing a circle with it and then quickly grabbing the hand of the monkey next to her. A moment later they could still feel each others' hands but could no longer see one another!

"It worked! It worked!" Caipora shouted jubilantly. The monkeys were dumbfounded. Where was everyone? What happened? Then as soon as they let go of each others hands chaos broke out: they bumped into one another, knocking heads and tripping up in every direction. This was a problem. While it was a great success in that they were invisible, clearly, they still needed to see one another. A further problem was Caipora's equipment - it too was still visible, appearing to float mysteriously in the air. She re-thought her command to the wand.

"I need to make an adjustment. Everyone back in a circle and holding hands again!" This was more easily said than done as they couldn't see one another. After much bumping, thumping, falling over and many fingers poked into many eyes, every hand finally held another hand.

"May your power burn bright, beacon of light! May your power burn bright and make us and what we carry out of sight to everyone but ourselves." This time they could see each other, but they could also see through each other - although only in a hazy kind of way, as though each was wrapped in a cloud of mist.

"Good enough," said Caipora and instructed her troop about boarding the boat. "We need to be there well before dark, before people start arriving. If we wait until it gets crowded you could easily be stepped on or have a heavy bag dropped on you, or be kicked and pushed about and badly hurt. I won't get stepped on but I could certainly get hurt as well," she explained. "If we get there early, while the boat is still empty, we can look around for a safe place where we'll be out of the way."

***

As the smoldering light of the sinking sun slipped across the river, instead of going to sleep, the town woke up! Lustrous white lights beamed from the tops of tall posts lining the riverbank, illuminating the boats crowding the port. No flames; no smoke; no flickering - and no one to light them! Incomprehensible! Nor did silence blanket the town after dark: laughter, shouting, music and singing all resounded through the air. Instructing them to lie low, Caipora left the monkeys to investigate more closely the wondrous lights and the festivities in the town. Leaving her equipment behind so as not to appear threatening, she walked along the riverbank carrying nothing. Opposite the harbour stood houses whose windows glowed warm and golden without the flicker of flames. Cautiously creeping up to one, she peered into a room empty of people, no fire, no smell of smoke - only a luminous round glowing object hanging from the ceiling by a cord. It hurt her eyes to look at it. There was no explanation other than magic!

Beyond the port, a street on the right lined with posts which appeared to have speared gigantic iridescent stars lead away from the river to a bustling hub of people laughing, talking, eating, drinking and dancing to the rhythm of extraordinary music, beautiful and completely foreign to her.

In the cool of the evening, men, women and children sat outside on strange white objects with four legs, resting their backs against a flat vertical part. Their food and shiny transparent drinking vessels were on a white object in front of them - a flat surface with four legs, but no back support. These strange white objects were in one piece with smooth rounded corners. When their drinking vessels were empty, people went inside a house and came out again with full ones. Caipora watched through a glowing window as they traded the thing called money for their drinks and food. Sometimes the liquid was almost black, sometimes orange, but most often it was a deep golden colour topped with white foam.

Filled with wonder and amazement, Caipora slowly walked down the street. Everyone wore white man's clothing. She wore only a loin cloth. People glanced at her at times, but no one asked what she was doing there. The music grew more intense and she made her way along the verge of the dancing crowd, searching for its source but surprisingly, could see no one playing an instrument of any kind. She stood and watched as the beat reverberated in her chest, her feet moving shyly to the rhythm.

Suddenly, Sema was in front of her! His back to her. So close she could touch him!

Her heart stopped. Her breathing stopped. The world stopped. The music stopped. Only he kept moving to the beat of the drums she heard no more: skin dark and gleaming; hair black and shining; arms holding close a girl who looked with love into his eyes! She felt sick and dizzy. He turned just as she fell, and caught her in his arms.

When she opened her eyes and looked into his face, it was not Sema's face. A small group of people gathered around and sat her, weak and trembling, on a white thing with a back support and the boy she'd thought was Sema held a drink to her lips. It was sweet and dark and quickly revived her. He offered her food, but she couldn't eat.

Once recovered, she thanked the people who'd helped her

and walked back to the river. Behind her, the laughter and music died down. One by one the magic lights in the windows disappeared and the streets lay empty and silent. Only the tall posts holding the captured stars against the velvet sky stood sentinel over the town.

That night Caipora cried through her dreams. She relived the day her life changed: the day when Sema's penetrating gaze made her heart skip a beat and sent a bolt of fire through her body; the day they changed from being devoted caring friends to falling in love, unable to repress the fervor each felt for the other, the intense desire to be together. To be close.

Memories of their love crowded her mind: the day he'd run, carrying her all the way back to the village after she'd been bitten by a scorpion, to get medicine for the venomous bite, and how he'd sat by her hammock singing to her as she lay recovering. How he'd smiled, eyes twinkling, presenting her with feather necklaces and headbands he'd made for her; how he gave her the biggest fish they'd caught for her family's dinner; how he'd jumped in front of her when a puma threatened them.

Her heart both ached and glowed with recollections of days swimming in the stream: water glittering on his gleaming brown skin, streaming through his black hair. He would disappear under the water, then grab her legs as if he were a caiman. She would scream in fright and he would surface, laughing, putting his strong arms around her, kissing her neck and face; holding her tight, and she would tickle him mercilessly until he dived under the water to get away.

CHAPTER 15
On the Boat to Santa Isabel do Rio Negro

The yellow sun was high and warm when Caipora and her troop arrived at the wharf. She had intended to be first on board but already men were loading cargo into the boat and she admonished herself for spending so much time foraging for Suri grubs and other delicious morsels. Now they would have to deal with people.

Invisible, they stood a safe distance from the men carrying heavy loads across the plank joining the landing to the boat, waiting for a chance to get on board without bumping into anyone. "Wait for my signal, then we'll all go at once. Stick close together and follow my lead," Caipora instructed. The boat had only two decks: the lower one where passengers hung their hammocks and slept and an upper deck which was also the roof. Below the passenger deck was the cargo hold. The men carrying their loads disappeared into this through a dark hole - not a good place to hide.

Caipora moved closer to the boat to get a better look. Without hammocks hanging from the ceiling, the lower deck was a vast empty space but once crowded with passengers and baggage, it would be a dangerous place offering no safe nook in which they might shelter. Narrow steps at the far end of the boat led to the top deck. Hopefully they would find refuge there. As they watched and waited, the men gathered in a small building across the street. Caipora had no idea how long they'd be there but knew this was their chance.

"Let's go!" she called, and ran for the plank, the monkeys right behind her. Inside, they thumped across the wooden floor boards towards the stairs at the far end of the boat.

"What's that noise?" a gruff bellowing voice demanded. "Who's there?" it thundered angrily as a man with a drooping black moustache and darting little eyes emerged from the blackness of the cargo hold. Clearly, not all the men had left the boat! The man stopped a short distance from them. Caipora froze, as did the monkeys behind her. She put a finger to her lips, signaling her troop to be quiet. Although they could not be seen, they could still be heard! It was strange to stare at a man who was staring straight back at you - and straight through you, without seeing you! They stood motionless, barely breathing. Finally, seeing nothing and hearing nothing more, the man turned his darting little eyes to a pile of crates and went back work.

"All right. Let's go - very quietly," whispered Caipora. As they tip-toed towards the stairs a crate smashed onto the deck with a shattering explosion! The monkeys shrieked and ran in confused panic for the stairs knocking over a stack of tins which came crashing down and rolled thunderously towards the man's feet. This time he didn't ask who was there. Like lightning he bolted screaming from the boat, almost falling off the plank in his panic to get away.

Caipora and the capuchins sprinted to the top deck. White chairs like those in the town stood stacked along one side and on the bow of the boat a small cabin promised the possibility of a safe refuge. Its door squealed a long and painful creak as it opened onto a storage room crowded with boxes, baskets and half-empty bags of stuff as well as coiled ropes, hammocks, tools and containers that rattled - the perfect haven and just big enough for Caipora to hang her hammock along one wall. The baskets and bags, nooks and crannies, would make excellent beds for the capuchins. They would all be cosy and dry.

Their quarters for the night established, they stood at the railing and watched the moustached man, who'd run from the boat in terror, come out from the building across the street with his friends. In a frenzied state, arms madly flailing about and face horror-stricken, he was relating to them his spine-chilling experience with the ghosts on the boat. His friends laughed as they crossed the plank while the petrified little man stood trembling on the landing, warning them not to go in.

"There's nothing here, Jose. You can't stay out there all day! There's work to be done! Are you a man or a mouse?" they ridiculed him. Clearly petrified, Jose tremulously made his way across the plank, casting wide and fearful eyes in every direction, taking two steps forward and one back and eventually, reluctantly joined his friends in loading the cargo onto the boat.

From the top deck, away from the hustle and bustle, Caipora and the capuchins watched passengers arriving with rolled up hammocks and bags of belongings and men heaving enormous bunches of bananas onto their backs and loading them onto the boat. Others carted weighty boxes of avocados, potatoes, bags of rice, flour and many other goods. Chickens squawked as they bounced about in crates passed roughly from one handler to another. Squealing pigs, feet tied to a sturdy stick, jolted upside down between the shoulders of pairs of men on their way to the cargo hold. The boat thrummed with vigorous activity and the noise level rose to a loud drumming as the deck below filled with passengers - but no one came to the roof of the boat.

Finally the chaos subsided and as the sun slid like molten gold into the watery horizon, a welcome serenity settled over the gently swinging hammocks. With dusk, there resonated through the quietude of the mauve evening a deep rumbling and the boards under Caipora's feet began to tremble. The rumbling issued from the back of the boat and she hurried there to find the cause of it. At the rear, foaming white water churned and billowed in every direction as the riverboat moved forward, but it was impossible to see what was making the noise or doing the churning.

Tethered by a length of rope to the riverboat, a small canoe bounced energetically in the frothing wake which stretched out behind the boat to a thin white thread as Barcelos blurred into the purpling distance.

The boat wound its way around countless islands where caimans slid over grassy banks to splash into the black river while monkeys scampered higher into the trees as they approached. Immersed in tall grasses, a jaguar watched stealthily from a nearby shore, and far away, floating on the water against a dusk-stained sky, the town of Barcelos sparkled in all its magical lights and, when the last glow of day had dissolved into the blackness, the night sky fell into the river where its stars danced with the sliver of a moon on the rippling surface of the water.

Caipora brimmed with excitement. She had never before been on a boat bigger than a canoe and wondered how the man steering the boat could find his way through this maze of islands in the dark: only one magical light on the bow of the boat illuminated his way as the engine purred on and on without changing its tune.

Time passed and drew a shroud of silence over the passengers below, allowing only the chorus of snores to filter through to the top deck. Caipora and the capuchins settled themselves into the nooks and crannies of their cabin, closed the door and allowed the purring and snoring to lull them to sleep. But sleep avoided Caipora and a painful loneliness, quite foreign to her, filled its place.

Images of the people in Barcelos the previous night danced before her eyes: the love between the families, the laughter of the children, the togetherness of the people of the town. She had once had all that. Now she had nothing. A deep pang of pain shot through her as she re-lived the moment when she thought Sema was standing in front of her. When sleep finally came, it came to eyes brimming with tears.

***

Light had barely brushed the sky when Caipora and her troop woke to lively voices from the deck below. Soon footsteps slapped their way across the top deck and were quickly at the cabin door behind which they huddled. Suddenly the door flew open and Jose, who, the previous afternoon, had charged from the boat screaming hysterically about ghosts, stood for a moment in the doorway, then stepped in and lunged forward with an extended arm to grab hold of a rolled-up hammock - on which sat an invisible capuchin! The monkey, completely taken by surprise, failed to jump out of the way in time.

Instead of grabbing hold of the hammock, the man's fingers closed firmly around something soft, warm and hairy - something he couldn't see! He shrieked and leapt backwards out the door, aghast and petrified, flinging the warm hairy thing back inside. The unfortunate capuchin landed against a wooden box, hit his head on the edge and screamed in pain, causing the cabin to explode with the hysterical howls of terrified monkeys scuttling about in a clamorous riot and sending the stuff around them flying in all directions.

What Jose saw was everything in the cabin jumping and clattering about without anyone there to move it! This and the screams of the invisible monkeys sent him hurtling down the steps to the bottom deck, frantically yelling "Help! Ghosts! Evil spirits! Help! Help!" in a high-pitched, terrified voice.

Caipora thought it best that they get out of their hideaway before Jose came back with men who might be braver than he was. There was no place on the top deck where they could be safely out of the way other than the roof of the cabin in which they'd slept. No sooner were they perched there than a group of men appeared and headed straight for the cabin.

As they came closer their steps slowed until about four metres from the door they stopped and began to argue in whispers among themselves. It was clear they were working out a plan of approach, that is, who should open the door. Unable to agree, they pushed one reticent man forward, nudging him closer and closer until, when almost at the door, he turned and bolted, cowering and hiding behind the group. The men then pushed another reluctant man forward to follow in the footsteps of the first, then another, and so it went on. And on.

At last one brave man came forward of his own volition and stood in front of the door. He stood there for some time, gulping in deep breaths until he was huffing and puffing, pushing out his chest and beating it as a gorilla does when making his power known. At last he worked himself up into such a frenzied state of bravery that he suddenly charged at the door with a great roar and grabbed it with such astonishing force that he ripped it clean off its hinges and stood holding it in one hand!

At this ferocious, frightening explosion of energy, the men all jumped and fell into a terrified heap, burying their faces in their hands and hiding behind one another as best they could. The hero holding the door stood staring at the space in the cabin. A moment passed before he dropped the door, stepped forward and reached in to pull out a rolled-up hammock. Then he turned to look at the whimpering heap that was his friends.

"Is this what you wanted Jose?"

With these words, he threw the hammock at poor Jose who seemed to have shrunk to almost half his size from sheer fright and was just getting up on his wobbly legs from the middle of his trembling heap of friends when the rolled up hammock hit him in the face and knocked him over backwards. The others, having forgotten their own terror of a moment ago, laughed loudly at poor Jose who pulled himself up to a sitting position and sat hugging his hammock as though it were his only comfort in life. The laughter and the men disappeared below deck and Jose looked up to find himself alone. A black rat leapt from a fold in his hammock, scurried over his knees and under his legs. Jose yelped, sprang to his feet and scrambled across the deck as fast as his trembling legs could carry him, whimpering, stumbling and almost falling down the stairs in his hurry to get away from the haunted cabin - and the black rat. Caipora's heart went out to him: no one believed him.

Slowly and deliciously, cooking smells began to permeate the air on the top deck as it gradually filled with people carrying aromatic food. They took the chairs stacked against the railing and made themselves comfortable in the sunshine. Someone set a smallish black box on the deck, poked it with a finger and all at once music poured out of it! Another finger poked it again and again and the music grew louder and louder - and now Caipora understood where, two nights ago, the music in the town had come from - although how it actually happened left her wonder-struck and marveling at the mind-boggling magic these people had at their fingertips.

The atmosphere rapidly turned festive and just as in Barcelos, people ate, drank, danced and sang along to the words pulsating from the black box. Of course her tribe had danced and sung, but not like this - and never to such exotic sounds as these! Hours passed before fatigue crept into the leaping legs and flailing arms of the dancers and led them downstairs to their hammocks: it was siesta time.

The riverboat chugged relentlessly through the black water of the Rio Negro, passing countless small villages where young children fishing from canoes waved and laughed as their tiny boats rocked alarmingly in the wash that followed. A small motorboat carrying four older children cut out sharply from the bank and pulled up beside the riverboat where a tall girl threw a rope up to the passengers who caught and secured it to the railing. While the riverboat pulled the small tethered boat along with it, three of the children climbed up and down ropes, carrying fresh fruit and smoked and salted fish to passengers waiting on the deck, in exchange for money, while the fourth child stayed in the boat manning the rudder.

***

At midday the riverboat pulled into the bank at a sizable town and sent Caipora into a flutter of excitement. On the landing was a sign with words matching those on her map - Santa Isabel do Rio Negro! It was smaller than Barcelos and had no white tower, but here too, the people were dark-skinned like herself and wore white people's clothing. Caipora wondered why they lived in a town rather than the beautiful jungle.

A plank slapped down between the boat and the landing. Caipora and the capuchins watched from above as passengers shuffled their way off the boat with bags and other paraphernalia and men lifted crates and boxes onto waiting carts. Many carried baskets of fresh fruit and vegetables which they sold to locals waiting on the riverbank.

It was clear that getting off the boat would be tricky as the traffic on the plank was heavy with people constantly coming and going. Caipora watched carefully and when the hustle and bustle had eased, she instructed her troop to wait at the top of the steps while she crept to the lower deck to assess the situation. There, new arrivals hung their hammocks in the empty spaces left by those who'd gone while others remained resting in theirs, swinging soothingly in the midst of the surrounding chaos. Many simply stood at the railing observing the hectic activities onshore. All in all, there were still lots of people milling about, going nowhere, leaving Caipora and her troop no choice but to cautiously make their way through the thicket of passengers to the gateway from which the plank led to the shore. She motioned for her troop to come down.

"We have to stick close together. Watch me for signals and stay out of the way of everyone," she instructed at the bottom of the steps. They carefully made their way through the jumble of hammocks, people and bags, ducking this way and that to avoid bumping into men carrying crates and coming straight at them, or children chasing one another every which way. Somehow they managed to get to the gateway without any collisions. A stream of men carrying a load of cargo was making its way onto the boat. Caipora planned to make a dash for it as soon as they were on board - but once on the boat, the men left their cargo right in front of the gateway and stood there talking, laughing - blocking the way! Caipora waited nervously for them to move - the plank was finally free but its access was blocked! Suddenly the whistle blew and the engine started with a thunderous rumble! Without warning, the men closed the gateway and others on the landing pulled the plank away from the boat!

Aghast at the boat moving away from the bank and forgetting the need to be quiet, Caipora shouted to her troop, "We have to get off! Jump! Jump! There's no other way! Get onto the railing and jump! Jump!" The startled monkeys were at once on the railing and jumping into the water without questioning their leader - all except the littlest one who seemed to have frozen from fright.

"Don't wait for anything! Just jump!" Caipora screamed at him. Still he didn't move. The next moment he found himself securely under her arm and flying over the railing. They hit the water with a resounding splash, leaving the people on the boat shouting, arguing and blaming one another for the pushing and shoving which had suddenly and violently erupted out of nowhere. Others, hearing the splashing in the water together with Caipora's alarming commands to jump, panicked and began shouting 'jump' themselves. Confused and frightened, they screamed and pushed and shoved to get to the railing and throw themselves overboard, believing the boat was sinking and they were about to die. It was clear also to those on shore, that something was terribly wrong and they too, panicked and ran about in circles shouting for help.

Meanwhile, Caipora and the monkeys scrambled out of the water onto the landing and charged through the crowd with great alacrity. With all the chaos and hysteria around them no one noticed the footprints and puddles left on the ground by the wet and invisible group of escaping stowaways. They fled along the riverbank leaving the screaming, frenzied crowd behind them. When finally they looked back, the boat, a long way from shore, was returning to pick up the passengers who now stood dripping on the landing, completely confused about everything.

Caipora checked the position of the sun. They were to head north west through mountainous territory towards Pico da Neblina - the last leg of her journey. Somewhere between Santa Isabel and Pico, the evil Toad squatted in his Stinky Lake. She was very close now to accomplishing her mission: capturing the Toad and putting him out of action and finding and freeing Verita and Fyglia. She'd not yet given any thought to how she would achieve this, but was confident that something would come to mind.

CHAPTER 16
Jurupari, Corpo Seco and Boiuna: the Plan

On the branch of a tree not too high off the ground sat a hairy three toed sloth. He'd come down from the canopy for his toilet needs, which he did every eight days or so and was resting a while before climbing higher. As his languorous body slowly stretched upwards to grab hold of another branch, two very ugly creatures and a grotesque green woman approached the clearing at the base of his tree carrying wood they had gathered for a fire. The creature with two horns was grinding his teeth and rumbling and mumbling to himself like a restless volcano and every so often bursts of steam shot from his ears.

Now, as they all sat around the leaping flames, he finally erupted. "How could we have lost her?" he roared. "She was headed for Santa Isabel! We went in exactly that direction and even split up so we could cover more ground! Where on earth did she go? Did she disappear into thin air?" he spat the words out onto the fire where they hissed and were consumed by the flames.

"Maybe she got lost. Maybe she's still there, somewhere between Maraa and Santa Isabel," Corpo Seco whimpered. He was tired and had seemingly lost interest in the whole business.

"Or better still," spoke the woman, sprightly at the thought which had sprung to her mind, "maybe she's been captured by local Indians along the way!"

"That would be excellent, but we don't know that and we can't depend on that!" fumed Jurupari.

"Until we know where she is, we can't do anything to stop her," the rotting Corpo Seco moaned glumly, sitting slumped on a log.

"Brilliant! Yet another of your excellent contributions to this exercise! That kind of thinking is exactly what you need to get the Toad to build you your own swimming pool! If anything could do it, that would be it!" the horned being snarled sarcastically at the rotting creature.

"Leave me alone! I'm doing what I can! I'm not as strong as you," whined Corpo.

"Oh you poor thing! Clearly, you'd better talk to the Toad about the special care you'll need once you retire to his castle: the nurse, the soft pillows. What about your diet? Any special needs there?" the snarling Jurupari continued mockingly.

"Oh, that's a good idea!" Corpo looked up, momentarily cheered by the suggestion, Jurupari's derision flying in through one hole in his head and out another, but he quickly succumbed to gloom again. "To tell you the truth, I don't really eat anymore - there's no point: it just falls straight through me. Still, it would be nice to taste something delicious - I just don't know how good my tongue is, how many taste buds I have left.......or in what condition they are......."

"Well don't worry about that! I'm sure the Toad would be delighted to organise a new tongue for you!" Jurupari continued his ridicule.

"Do you really think so? That would be fantastic! Perhaps he could get me a whole new set of body parts!" Corpo naively roused himself almost to a level of joy.

"We can only hope! I suggest you inform him that what you most urgently need is a brain: your mouth seems to work quite well but appears unattached to a brain. Clearly, that has completely rotted away despite the other remnants of yourself still clinging to your bones" the devil mercilessly insulted the rotting Corpo, who remained simple-mindedly oblivious to the contempt thrown at him.

Accepting without question the devil's words, the gullible Corpo was much buoyed by the hope of a completely new body and - dare he dream it - a new life? "I'd look so much better with a new nose; a nice set of teeth - then I'd be much more likely to smile......"

"What on earth have you got to smile about?" interrupted Jurupari, astonished at the thought and recoiling at the image.

"That's a good question, true - but if I had new teeth, I'd be able to chew things!" Corpo embraced the thought.

"You just said that food falls straight through you!" Boiuna chipped in at last, exasperated at this pointless and ludicrous conversation.

"I wonder when we'll see him again," Corpo continued, staring into the space in front of his eyes as if transfixed by a beautiful vision of his new self. "I'd like to discuss these requests with him as soon as possible, so that he might start working on them right away."

"Absolutely! He has nothing better to do, I'm sure - at

least nothing nearly as important as new body parts for you, all ready for you as soon as you move into his castle!" the devil went on, relishing Corpo's simplistic belief in the feigned possibilities he presented.

"Yes! Yes!" shouted Corpo, his glee almost animating him to a semblance of life.

"Oh! But wait - what did he say at our last meeting about firing you?" Jurupari's lips twisted into a malicious sneer as the evil words slid through them. Corpo lifted his head and stared at the scaly devil, his dilapidated face painfully twitching with the brutality of the caustic words that shattered his newfound hopes and dreams and sent them flying to the edge of oblivion.

"Let's get back to matters at hand shall we?" interjected Boiuna, fed up with the nonsense of her comrades. "I've just had an excellent idea. I'll change into a bird and fly around looking for her. I'll ask the other birds to search for her too, tell them I've got important news for her. They won't know I'm not really one of them. With their help I'm sure to find her. Then I'll change into a little girl and put my plan into action. It will work beautifully!"

The three toed sloth, who'd heard of the girl who was trying the save the forest, had been listening very carefully.

CHAPTER 17
Towards the Mountains

From Santa Isabel, Caipora and her troop traveled north west through a green and healthy forest abundant in both food and life, without a whiff of evil anywhere, but on the fifth day they found themselves standing before a vast area of barren land - the scene of a massacre: the forest had been decimated and the earth lay strewn with remnants of its broken limbs and thousands of stumps. Some sat like squat decapitated bodies in the ground, roots still gripping the soil that provided life. Others, torn from their life-giving source, lay on their sides, roots grasping at thin air, at the mercy of the sun. Away in the dusty brown distance, on the far side of the ravaged and scarred earth, huge trucks roared and groaned under the weight of tree trunks piled high onto their backs as they slowly crept past yet uncut forest where the still living trees stood sentinel to their slaughtered comrades passing by.

The maimed and barren land, the raw gaping wound

stretching far and wide, struck horror into Caipora's heart. "So here," she said to herself, "where the locals haven't heard about the man who wouldn't pay, but changed instead into a fire-breathing dragon, the Toad has finally found men to do the logging - the slaughtering!" Anger flamed within her: he would pay for this - and far more than he was paying the men doing his dirty work!

For two days they walked along the verge of the ravaged forest, so vast was the area. On the third day, hazy mountains reaching out of the verdant horizon, perforated the blue of the sky. Caipora's map showed a vast range of mountains a good distance to the north west of Santa Isabel and she believed she was looking at them now. The map also showed a great valley beyond them, to the north of which Pico da Neblina towered above all else. Caelia believed the Toad lived somewhere in the mountains south of Pico - the mountains now visible on the horizon. So close now! A shiver ran through Caipora. But according to the map, they were now also in Yonukari territory, against which Caelia had advised. Well, too late now. Unforeseen circumstances had brought them here and she would have to be very careful.

That evening, Caipora considered her situation. She was close to the Toad now and the very thought of the slimy stinking creature left her shuddering. She wrapped her fingers around her vials of potion and reassured herself that she would survive both the Toad and the poisonous stench surrounding him. As she contemplated the task before her, a three toed sloth slowly made his lazy way down from the leafy treetop and sat himself comfortably on a branch above her.

"Excuse me," his soft furry voice fluttered down to her. Caipora's eyes sprang open. "Am I right in thinking you're the girl who's going to save the forest from the evil Toad?"

The astonished Caipora stared at the sloth for some moments before gathering her wits. "Yes. Yes, that's right," she replied.

"I think you should know that there are three evil creatures planning to capture and harm you. Beware of a little girl."

"Thank you. Thank you very much," Caipora said as the sloth began to slowly haul himself back up the tree. "Can you tell me when or where?"

"That's...... all......I know," he sleepily dragged out his words. "I wish...... I knew...... more.....but...... I don't." It took some time, but finally he merged with the shadows of the canopy.

The evil creatures could be none other than Jurupari, Corpo Seco and Boiuna. Had they discovered her whereabouts? The King Vulture had advised her to stay in Barcelos for at least two days to let them get ahead of her but she had barely stayed one. That night Caipora woke to every creak of a branch and every crack of a twig. The following morning she was on the alert for anything unexpected but they walked many more days without incident before finally arriving at the base of the mountain range. Climbing them all, looking for Stinky Lake, would take weeks. It occurred to Caipora that perhaps the Muiraquita Stone might help her. As she rubbed it, asking it to point her to Stinky Lake Mountain, it warmed and glowed red. Believing it was giving her an answer Caipora focused on tuning in to the voice that often spoke to her when she needed help. But instead, the alarming cries of a distressed child snatched her attention. Astounded by the sound, she slashed her way through the undergrowth in the direction of the sobbing and found, sitting on the bank of a small river, a young girl much like Caipora herself but not more than five years old, head buried in her hands, crying as though her heart would break. Astonished at the sight, Caipora hurried to comfort her. Between heart wrenching sobs the girl told how her family had been destroyed by a fierce tribe, leaving her all alone in the world with nowhere safe to go. Caipora's heart went out to her. She sat beside the child and put her arms around her.

"I know how terrible that is and how hard it is to be all alone. Don't be sad. I'll take care of you. I'll look after you," she promised.

"Thank you so much," sobbed the girl as she put her arms around Caipora, kissed her cheek - and instantly turned into a mighty anaconda, already coiled around Caipora's body! The monkeys watching from the trees shrieked and threw whatever they could find at the enormous reptile - but to no avail. They leapt to the ground and began to bite it - but it didn't even notice.

Caipora was blue and unconscious when a group of Indians charged out of the forest and drove their spears into the serpent. The anaconda loosened its grip and the capuchins watched in dismay as the Indians snatched their leader from the reptile's coils and carried her away. They ran after them screaming in protest but when a few of the men turned with raised spears, they scurried into the trees.

The moment the Indians were out of sight, Jurupari and Corpo Seco crept from the undergrowth. The Yonukari were fierce and unafraid of anything. Rather than fleeing at the sight of the evil spirits, they would have riddled their bodies with spears without a second thought. Corpo Seco would have fallen to bits - a lot of trouble to put himself back together - and Jurupari would be scarred with unsightly dents in his scales. Better to stay put and hide.

The anaconda had now disappeared and in its place sat

Boiuna, soothing her wounds in the cool water. The spears had dug deep and the annoying bites from the monkeys were stinging. "How is it that something always saves her? This time it wasn't her Fairy Godmother or her monkeys or a gigantic condor! No! The Yonukari just happened to be in the wrong place at the wrong time!" complained a furious and frustrated Jurupari, steam spouting vigorously from his ears yet again.

Corpo Seco was seething and frothing at the mouth, which, just when you thought he couldn't look more hideous, made his appearance such that even Boiuna averted her eyes! "Well at least we now know where she is. It won't be hard to find that Yonukari village. We can creep in there and get her out while everyone's sleeping," Corpo slobbered through his froth and foam.

"Why not just leave her there?" said Boiuna, now completely immersed in the soothing water. "The Yonukari aren't going to let her go. They're going to keep her captive - if she survives - and force her to marry one of their men."

"You're right," said Jurupari. "That girl is well and truly a Yonukari prisoner. She won't be going anywhere, that's for sure! I think we can safely say that we've finally achieved our objective: she's out of action! I say we leave her there - dead or alive - and celebrate our victory with a well deserved rest! I haven't worked this hard since I can remember!"

With that they made themselves comfortable around a blazing fire, secure and relieved in the knowledge that Caipora had been disposed of and would no longer be a threat to the Toad or to their place in his castle. It was time to focus on the luxuries they would soon enjoy!

CHAPTER 18
The Yonukari

In a thick forest somewhere south of Pico da Neblina, a huge oval structure with a shabono (a thatched palm roof) encircled a spacious clearing. The roof on the outer side of the shabono almost touched the ground but the inner side facing the central area, was supported high off the ground by sturdy poles. More poles under the enormous roof divided the interior into nanos, (separate dwellings) in each of which a fire glowed day and night.

A large number of Yonukari men and women, young and old, squatted in one of the nanos, elbows on their knees, whispering and murmuring, the afternoon light bouncing off their dark gleaming skins. Most wore loin cloths but some, not even those. Thick clumps of hair sat like halved black coconuts on the heads of the men, almost touching the eyebrows but leaving the ears exposed. The women's hair, cut straight across the forehead, fell thickly over their ears and shoulders.

The Shaman, face blackened with charcoal and three short sticks protruding from his chin, danced about energetically, upper arms garnered with long red plumes and a necklace of beads and feathers bustling about his neck to the beat of several drums. One hand shook a rattle while his deep rasping voice ground out a chant, shouting out the same words over and over again. The more frenzied his dance grew, the greater the volume of his chant until, seemingly engorged with rage, he bellowed and blasted the onlookers with a squall of fiery words, whooping and roaring until he fell into a paroxysm of violent coughing. The silent onlookers watched intently until, at his direction, they launched into a chorus of mournful moaning, groaning and wailing as if tormented by great pain while the Shaman continued to roar as though his insides were being ripped out.

In the midst of this tempestuous agitation, Caipora lay on the floor on a grass mat, eyes shut, body motionless. As the Shaman hopped and stomped around her, coughing, chanting, roaring and moaning, he would bend over her from time to time to shake the rattle in her face and along the length of her body. Then he would kneel beside her and put a small bowl against her lips to pour a little of the liquid it contained into her mouth before hopping and stomping around her again, chanting, shouting, coughing and rattling, again and again and again.

Moonlight had splattered the village with silver when Caipora's eyelids fluttered for a moment, then closed again. A shout immediately issued from the Shaman's lips and silence fell with a thud. He called for water and a woman bearing a small vessel hurried to Caipora and, supporting her head, held the bowl to her lips. Caipora's eyelids opened and she took a small mouthful.

"You must rest now," the Shaman's gravelly voice directed as he picked her up and carried her to a hammock at the back of the nano. Caipora grimaced as searing pain cut through her ribs. "Take care of her," he instructed the woman. "Do not allow her to walk." The woman nodded. The Indians followed the Shaman from the nano and left Caipora alone with only the woman tending her.

***

Through her kiss, the crying girl by the river had injected into Caipora's skin a potent venom which rapidly spread through her anaconda-crushed body and broken ribs. The Shaman's potion had neutralized the venom which would otherwise have slowly but surely brought an end to Caipora's life.

Some days after regaining consciousness Caipora asked for her belongings but her carer merely shook her head. Otherwise, she was treated with kindness and attention: served with fresh nourishing food and the Shaman's medicine administered as instructed. But despite this, Caipora's recovery was slow. Even after the venom had been neutralized, searing pain screamed through her rib cage with every breath. The Muiraquita Stone was no longer around her neck nor did the vials of potion hang from her belt.

Contrary to Caelia's warning, the Yonukari were surprisingly kind and friendly. When after two weeks she was at last free to move about the village, Caipora watched the women weave baskets from palm fibres and string, made of bark and roots - just as the women in her tribe had done, although the Yonukari shaped and decorated them differently: having dipped the baskets into a pot of red dye brewed from berries, the women chewed charcoal, spat it into bowls and, dipping sticks into it, decorated the red baskets with black circles, lines, dots and waves. At other times Caipora watched them weaving the cotton they had grown into string, cords, hammocks, loin cloths and slings in which to carry their babies. But she was an outsider, an observer, and for the first time in her life, although surrounded by people, she was lonely. She was apart from them, without purpose or meaning, without identity. She was no one in this tribe.

As Caipora grew stronger she began to accompany the women - babies in slings hanging from their shoulders - and older girls into the forest to harvest wild honey and collect nuts, freshwater mussels, land crabs, insect larvae, fruits, medicinal plants, fish, small animals and insects. The young children searched enthusiastically for termite nests and other grubs, laughing gleefully with every discovery of the crawly things and carefully putting them into baskets to be roasted over the family hearth that evening.

Weeks later and much improved, Caipora joined the women on fishing expeditions. They first made a powder from leaves dried for the purpose and threw it into the water. Harmless to people, the powder stunned the fish which floated to the surface of the shallow river where young children splashed about laughing and picking them up, loading baskets with fish for everyone.

One morning Caipora noticed a group of men sharpening darts for blowguns for their hunting expedition. On the ground beside them, in a basket covered with a grass net, squatted a blue poison dart frog. When their darts were sharp, the men pricked the frog's back with them. Immediately, a powerful toxin oozed from the punctured skin of the frog and the men covered the tips of their darts with it. In Caipora's tribe the men used to stroke the sides of the frog, which also caused it to excrete the poison which they then boiled down to concentrate its potency and stored it in a safe place. It remained toxic for a year. Unlike other poison dart frogs, the blue wasn't dangerous to humans.

Life with the Yonukari was very similar to how it had been in Caipora's tribe: the men made daily expeditions to hunt for peccary, tapir, deer and jaguars as well as armadillos, snakes, fowl and monkeys. The meat they returned with was highly valued by everyone - but no hunter ate what he himself had killed. Instead, he shared it among friends and family and in return was given meat caught by another hunter.

When at last she was able, Caipora worked with the women and girls to carry firewood and water for the village as well as tending to gardens of bananas, sugarcane, mangoes, sweet potatoes, papaya, manioc and many other crops. Every day she helped prepare the evening meal for the family she lived with and each night after dusk, when the fire had been stoked, they retired to their hammocks made from banana leaves to swing gently by the warm flames. All night the shabono glowed with a fire in each nano, murmuring voices filtering through the dancing shadows of the fluttering light.

As Caipora's participation in village life increased, a new-found happiness and contentment filled her heart. Carrying out her responsibilities brought meaning and purpose to her days, together with a sense of fulfillment and security as her work was rewarded with appreciation and acceptance as a worthwhile member of the tribe. She recalled how she had yearned for freedom from her responsibilities in her own tribe, longed to be unencumbered, to follow her heart - especially after Sema had been forced to marry some one else: it had simply been too painful to see him every day with another girl, even though she knew he loved her and not his new wife. But now she wondered, who would have appreciated her on her own? What would she have contributed and to whom? She realised now that she would have been solitary and lonely, belonging nowhere and to no one. She had been somebody in her tribe and through the contribution of her work she was now somebody again, here with the Yonukari people. The peaceful co-existence she enjoyed with them, the routine of her days, was a soothing respite from the stress and strain of the past months. The Toad had become almost a memory and she shied away from the thought of fighting through the jungle again, of facing further unimaginable evil. A certain complacency had set upon her. It was as if all those horrors had occurred in a different life and were now irrelevant to her.

One morning, the Shaman summoned her to his nano. "A moon and a half has passed since you were brought to us Caipora and I can see that you are now strong and well and no longer require the medicine you have been taking every day. It will be reserved for someone else who might need it," he informed her.

Three days later - three days without the medicine - it was as though a fresh breeze had blown a heavy fog from Caipora's mind and she saw with crystal clarity the reality and urgency of her true situation. She hurried to the headman who was most surprised to hear that she wanted to leave. "You cannot leave the village," he calmly informed her. "You must stay and marry one of our men. We need more women and more children so that we may grow stronger and more powerful."

Aghast and alarmed at his words, Caipora shouted, "I can't stay here and marry anyone! I have to get on with my mission! I have to find the Toad and save....."

"Silence! You will not speak or act against my wishes!" the headman commanded, instantly irate at her protest.

"You don't understand! I have to go and......" Caipora persisted but, with a signal from the headman, two men instantly grabbed her and hauled her into the nano where the Shaman did his healing. There, both her ankles were tied to ropes attached to a pole. She could move about but not go far. The headman immediately called the tribe together. Caipora, he informed everyone, was now well and wanted to leave them. As every member of a Yonukari tribe had an equal say in such matters, a vote was taken - the unanimous decision being that she should stay and marry one of their men.

So Caelia had been right to warn her about the Yonukari: Caipora had been saved only to produce children for them and the Toad would now have free reign to destroy the forest and its inhabitants. Devising plans of escape was pointless: not only was she tethered by thick ropes but two men guarded her day and night. When she needed the toilet they took her there, turned their backs, but did not leave her side. How suddenly her life had changed again: one moment, a useful member of the tribe, part of a family and the next - far worse than the outsider she had once been: a prisoner! Stripped of every freedom! No meaning or purpose in her life other than to produce children!

One morning, she finally she understood why she had wanted freedom from her tribe: a happy fulfilling life was not a life free of responsibilities, as she had misguidedly imagined, but a life with the freedom to choose those responsibilities which would allow the seed within you to grow and through its growth, allow you to become what you were meant to be.

She had taken on the herculean responsibility of saving the forest and its inhabitants. Yes, she had owed it to the

Nevae, but it had still been her choice. Here and now she was merely a prisoner, but beyond the Yonukari tribe the vast forest community was depending on her, supporting her, helping her in every way possible. She knew now who she was: not a member of her own tribe; not a member of the Yonukari tribe, but a vital member of the greater forest community - and their only hope! Her elders had often said: "We know ourselves through our relationships with others. We are defined through our relationships with others."

It was the forest community that defined Caipora. Defending it and saving it was her life's purpose.

It wasn't simply that Fate had chosen her for this mission. This is was what she was meant to be - this was her seed which needed to grow: the purpose of her existence was to care for the forest community. That was her family now. Alone in the dark, rubbing her chafed ankles, this realization brought her great solace. It also brought her strength. No! She would not stay a prisoner. Nor would she marry anyone. She *would* be free! She lifted her face to the universe, drew its power into her mind and saw herself free; *believed* she would be free; *visualised* herself capturing the Toad, freeing Verita and Fyglia. Believed it! Every day for two weeks, as she watched the sun rise and set from the end of the rope holding her captive, Caipora focused all her energy on this belief: on visualizing herself free and accomplishing her mission.

One day a woman, face contorted with heartbreak, entered the Shaman's nano, a little girl no more than three years old lying limply in her arms. Firelight danced on the child's pale face - the only movement on her small inert body. Mother and child were soon followed by the Shaman and a group of Indians. For three whole days the Shaman chanted, roared and danced frantically around the child, shaking his rattle and pouring drops of potion between her lips, but the child remained unresponsive on the grass mat. At dusk on the third day he spoke briefly to one of the men who then left the nano, returning minutes later with the whole tribe who gathered around the sick child and, to the slow beating of drums, began a mournful lamentation, heavy with heartbreak and woe.

The Shaman gently picked up the inert body of the child and carried her to her mother's arms. Nothing more could be done. The women began to wail. The mother pressed the child to her breast and let forth a heart-wrenching scream. It was clear they were now beginning a ritual for the dead.

"I can help!" Caipora called sharply above the wailing. Every voice hung throttled in the air and all eyes fell on her.

"I can help! I can heal the sick child."

Silence thudded though the nano.

"If you untie me, I promise I will heal the child. Please let me help her!" Caipora begged. In all the time Caipora had spent with the Yonukari, not once had she mentioned any special healing powers she might have. They had been kind and welcoming but since her refusal to marry one of their men, they had turned against her. Now they stared in amazement, disbelief, condescension twisting their mouths into sneers. Did she believe herself to be more powerful than the Shaman? She was just a girl - a girl who couldn't even save herself from an anaconda! They pointed, laughed and ridiculed her.

But Caipora continued pleading, promising again and again that she would heal the child - she just needed her possessions! Still they refused to believe her. Finally the mother begged the Shaman to let her try. Mumbling something incoherently at the ground, he reluctantly agreed. One man untied Caipora's ankles, another brought her belongings - but held onto the machete, the knife, the bow and the quiver. Caipora quickly pulled the healing vial of potion from her sack - and the Muiraquita Stone, which she tied at once around her neck and then hurried to the little girl in her mother's arms.

"Open her mouth," Caipora instructed. The mother, her face a torrent of tears, gently held open her child's mouth. Caipora let three drops fall onto the girl's tongue. Gasps flew from wide-open mouths, then silence as all eyes held fast to the sick child. Within moments her eyelids opened. She smiled at her mother and "Mamma", like the soft whisper of butterfly wings, fluttered from her lips.

An uproar exploded through the nano! The Indians leapt about shouting, dancing, rejoicing, incredulous at the miracle! The mother, sobbing, smiling, rivulets of joy streaming down her face, rocked the child in her arms, holding her close, stroking her hair.

That night a feast was held in celebration of Caipora's powers. The Indians pierced their bottom lips and cheeks with thin sticks and drove another stick horizontally through the septum of their noses; they painted their faces and bodies red, then decorated them with black paint. Headdresses thick with brightly coloured toucan and parrot feathers adorned their black hair and earrings fashioned from tufts of dried grasses, feathers, flowers and leaves swung around their cheeks like colourful birds' nests.

The forest throbbed to the beat of many drums, bulged with the sounds of singing and rejoicing while the village glittered with clouds of red sparks billowing from an enormous fire around which countless red loin cloths flapped like flocks of alarmed macaws. Caipora sat in the place of honour, face painted, head adorned with a headdress of brilliant feathers as the Indians danced around her, worshiping her. Only shortly before dawn, after copious quantities of food and exotic liquids had been consumed, when exhaustion won out over exuberance, did the festivities begin to fade.

Caipora was free again - more than free: elevated to a place of honour in the tribe. She thanked the universe for empowering her mind to believe in herself.

***

The following morning she again asked the headman for her equipment and expressed her need to be on her way. "We cannot let you leave!" he cried out in wide-eyed alarm and astonishment.

"What? I must go! I have to go!"

"We cannot allow someone with your great powers to leave! You are far too valuable! You must stay and marry one of our men so that your powers are passed on to your children!"

"No! No! You don't understand! The power is not in me! It's in the magic potion and when that's used up there will be no more power. I don't know how to make the potion. It was given to me by the wood elves - the Nevae. They are the ones who made it, not me."

The headman stared blankly at Caipora. He knew nothing of wood elves nor where he might find them and he had never heard of the Nevae. "Then you must take us to these wood elves. They must live with us so that we may always have this powerful medicine!" The morning was over before Caipora could bring the headman to understand just how far away the Nevae lived and why they could not possibly live with the Yonukari.

She explained to him her mission: the Toad and his evil spirits; the threat to the rain forest and all its inhabitants.

"He lives in a place called Stinky Lake, on top of a mountain somewhere nearby. I'll know when I'm getting close because the smell is so bad it can kill you!" When the headman and those around him heard these words their faces twisted in agitation. They knew the forest was being cut down in areas near their sacred Pico da Neblina, but they were helpless to stop it. They began to talk among themselves in great alarm. Finally the headman spoke.

"We never hunt near that mountain there," he pointed to the east, "The stench is so foul that it makes us sick for days." Having heard Caipora's story, the Yonukari believed the two-summit mountain to the east to be the one where the Toad lived and promised not only to release her but also to guide her to its base. They would not take her all the way however, certain the stench would kill them if they came too close.

"How do you plan to cross Stinky Lake to get to the Toad? How will you get him out of there and how will you put an end to him?" the Shaman asked.

"I need to give that some thought," Caipora replied, nodding to herself.

"At the very least, you will need a canoe," the headman advised. "We will build you a canoe and help you get it most of the way there." Work began immediately. The Yonukari carved their own canoes from tree trunks - a time consuming activity producing excellent but heavy canoes. Caipora's would be different. A day and a half later she was presented with a waterproof canoe made from bamboo, palm fronds and layers of liquid latex, light and small enough for her to carry on her own. A sturdy bamboo pole with blades carved from lightweight balsa wood served as a paddle.

The following morning the entire Yonukari tribe gathered in the centre of the village. Many heartfelt thanks were exchanged as they bid farewell to the young warrior escorted by two guides who carried her canoe and would take her as close as they dared to Stinky Lake Mountain.

PART FIVE

Capturing The Toad

CHAPTER 19
Towards Stinky Lake Mountain

No sooner were Caipora and her Yonukari guides on their way than thunder boomed through the blackened lightning-slashed sky. By dusk the deluge had emptied itself onto the land leaving the forest sagging under its weight; a chorus of heavy drips tinkling through the night. Moonlight gleamed in silver puddles on the forest floor, dappled the travelers' glistening skins, glittered on mossy rocks and danced on the scales of the snakes the Yonukari had caught during the day and now prepared for cooking.

The following morning the twin peaks of Stinky Lake Mountain, crisp and clear, reached up through the distant canopy, piercing the azure blue of the sky. About a day's walk, they guessed. The Yonukari would stay with her until midday, then turn back. When the sun was high, Caipora bid her friends goodbye. They'd strapped the canoe and paddle to her back, leaving both her hands free. While it weighed little it was cumbersome and slowed her down considerably. Tied to her back at an angle - one end above her left shoulder, the other protruding from behind her right leg - it often caught in the undergrowth and knocked sharply against tree trunks. No sooner were the Yonukari out of sight than the capuchins jumped down from the trees in front of her. Caipora stared at them wide-eyed. "Yes! I'm sure you must be surprised!" said the eldest indignantly. "You'd forgotten all about us, hadn't you?"

"Not a thought for us after you were captured!" reaffirmed an affronted second voice.

"You didn't even look in the direction of the forest when you were able to walk again! It was as if we'd never existed - no concern for us at all! And all the time we were so worried about you!" another voice accused.

"Look at all the weight I've lost just through worrying about you!" said the littlest one, clearly worried and sorry for himself.

"We were too frightened to go into the shabono to get your magic potions even though we knew where they were hidden. There was always someone about, even at night, and if we were to have been caught we would certainly have been cooked and eaten," the eldest explained, as though feeling guilty of inaction.

"They might even have served us to you and you would've eaten us without knowing!" the littlest one cried on the verge of tears.

"Can you stop jabbering at me for one moment so that I might say something too?" Caipora interjected. "I'm very happy to see you of course, and I'm glad you're all well, but yes, it's true, I wasn't worried about you because I knew you could take care of yourselves."

"Well, at least she's honest about it," they muttered disgruntedly among themselves.

"And while I appreciate your company, despite all your whinging, I have to tell you that you can't come with me all the way. The stench will kill you. You can come only as far as the base of the mountain - and even that could be dangerous for you."

Darkness found them around a blazing fire at the bottom of Stinky Lake Mountain. The smell was horrendous but not yet bad enough to make them ill. Caipora retired early to her hammock, exhausted from fighting through the jungle with the canoe on her back. If all went according to plan, tomorrow she would face the Toad. It was unimaginable to her that she had come this far. How had she survived the terrifying hurdles and the evils that had tried to stop her? And what horrors would confront her tomorrow? Her imagination ran wild and fear began to creep in. She unconsciously caressed the Muiraquita Stone and the words of her elders again spoke in her mind: we are all part of the universe and its power is within us. The words were comforting, filled her with a sense of security. Caipora turned her eyes to the stars and drew their white light down to her, absorbed it; visualised herself succeeding and believed she would. Falling into sleep, she remembered the words Sema had whispered to her after he had been married, as they passed one another in the village: "In my heart, I will always be with you." He would be with her tomorrow as would the power of the universe. She would be alright.

At first light, Caipora bid her troop goodbye. "It's time for us to part. You need to go far away from here. Don't wait for me. If the wind changes and the stink moves in, you could all die. You've been an enormous help and saved my life more than once. I want you to know that I deeply appreciate all you've done but now there's nothing more you can do to help me. I must go on alone." The monkeys didn't argue. They parted from their leader a second time, not knowing when or where they would meet again - if at all.

CHAPTER 20
The Evil Spirits on Holiday

Confident that Caipora was either dead from Boiuna's venom or would be forever held captive by the Yonukari, the evil spirits, believing their job was done, decided a well deserved holiday was in order and took themselves off to the Bahamas to play around in the Bermuda Triangle.

Corpo remained in Brazil, in need of some peace and quiet and a rest from Jurupari's caustic comments. Besides, unlike the others, he didn't have the power to fly and would have had to be transported there by his colleagues - a highly uncomfortable experience for all concerned. Furthermore, sitting in the hot sun in the Bahamas would only burn his delicate flesh making the crispy bits more likely to break off, and the coconut milk and pineapple juice would just run straight through him, bringing him no pleasure at all.

He decided instead to visit the Toad to discuss with him the things he'd need and would like when he moved into his majestic castle: the private swimming pool, the nurse, the pillows and of course, the new body parts. Jurupari and Boiuna, on the other hand, were enjoying themselves immensely. Having already sunk two ships, they were lying on Pink Sand Beach thinking about bringing down a plane when a black hawk alighted on the sand next to them.

"I have a piece of news for you," it squawked. More than surprised, the evil spirits instantly sat to attention and heard from the hawk that Caipora had not only been set free by the Yonukari but had actually been helped by them in her mission - and was about to climb Stinky Lake Mountain. This was alarming and frightening news! If she were to succeed in freeing Verita, they would find themselves under another five hundred year spell! With great alacrity, Jurupari launched himself into the air and flew off at great speed towards Stinky Lake Mountain.

"No need for you to come. I'll wipe her off the face of that mountain in an instant," he shouted to Boiuna as he disappeared over the palm trees. "I'll be back soon!"

The Toad had no idea Caipora was climbing his mountain. He continued to calmly wallow in his stinking hollow and swim in Stinky Lake now and then, confident that the evil spirits had everything under control. In his mind he was drawing up plans for his castle. Men were working for him near the base of Pico da Neblina, cutting down the rainforest, and lots of money was coming in from the timber sold. He also had men panning for gold in the foothills of Pico, the sacred territory of the Yonukari. One head man, a corrupt individual whom Boiuna had bought with the promise of great wealth, was taking care of all the business. Things were going very well indeed for the Toad. Soon, he thought, work would start on building his castle.

Oh! What a life he was going to lead!

CHAPTER 21
The Ascent to Stinky Lake

Caipora began her ascent up the mountain under clear skies. She fought and hacked her way through twisted, tangled undergrowth, but greatly impeded by the canoe on her back. The higher she climbed the steeper and more rocky the ascent grew and the more cluttered with fallen deadwood and spiky branches. The trees thinned and occasionally clusters of large boulders blocked her way, forcing her to go around them while the nauseating stench caused her bouts of retching. The sky was rapidly growing heavy and dark and just as Caipora was negotiating an almost vertical rocky section, the heavens disgorged their contents with explosions of thunder that brought rocks clattering down, narrowly missing her. Spears of lightning threatened to impale her; rain slashed at her face and body as terrific gusts of wind threatened to rip her off the face of the mountain. Teeth gritted, she screwed up her face and eyes against the battering needles of rain and clung to the rock face with fingers white from the strain.

A bloodcurdling scream pierced the air and the horrific Jurupari burst through the black clouds, red scaly wings flapping ferociously as he charged at Caipora through walls of rain, face snarling, claws outstretched, fiery flames spurting from his mouth, nose and ears. Terrified, Caipora clung to the mountain side: "This is the end! There's nothing I can do!" Jurupari was almost upon her when the black shape of an enormous bird fifteen times his size shot across the sky, head on at him. So shocked was Jurupari that for a moment he halted in mid air. Hung there upright and still. Then, as the bird was about to grab him with its gigantic claws, the devil ducked sideways and down. The bird swooped after him, was almost upon him when Jurupari lunged sideways and shot straight up. Fast as lightning the bird was behind him, grabbed him and wrapping the entire devil in his claws, soared up and out of sight.

Shocked and shaken to the core, Caipora clung to the rock face. With the storm raging around her she hadn't noticed the heat of the Muiraquita Stone - but even if she had, she would not have been able save herself. How was it possible that such an enormous bird could exist? Where had it come from? Had it known she was about to die? Trembling and exhausted, Caipora sheltered from the storm under a rock ledge. The canoe on her back, she lay on her side and, weak and ill from the stench, took a few drops of the potion and a good deal of the pudding. The universe had saved her. No greater power existed. She closed her eyes, secure in the belief that it would save her again.

When she woke, the storm had abated but the rain still fell in sheets. Conscious of time lost, she was quickly on her feet, picking handholds and footholds across the now slippery and treacherous rocky terrain. As she wrapped her hands around a large rock to pull herself up, it gave way and she fell backwards down the mountain side, the rock falling after her, striking her on the head.

CHAPTER 22
Argentavis

Caipora woke into a soft, warm, heavy darkness, aware of only two things: a bed of grasses beneath her and a blanket of blackness covering her. She sank her fingers into the softness of it and the blanket began to move and lift itself off her - and hovering above her was an enormous mass of feathers supported by two scaly yellow legs the size of tree trunks, gigantic feet and claws on either side of her. A huge curved and sharp beak lowered itself towards her until she was face to face with the pink and grey head attached to it. A crop of upright black feathers curved over a pair of fiercely gleaming black eyes and descended between them to almost meet the top of the beak. From there they crept under eyes and down the sides of the head. Terrified, Caipora stared mutely at the creature, expecting the flesh-eating beak to shred her to pieces.

"It's good to see you're still alive!" the bird's words rolled out deep and gravelly, touched with a hint of surprise.

Caipora's heart pounded in her head while her eyes remained fixed on those of the bird. "Who are you?" she finally squeezed out the thin strained words.

"I'm Argentavis, the biggest bird in the world and I'm here to help you."

"So you're not going to eat me?" Shock, surprise and relief flooded Caipora's senses.

Argentavis let out what must have been an Argentavian chuckle. "Haw, haw, haw, haw! No! I'm certainly not going to eat you. I promise!"

"What a relief.....what a relief...." Caipora breathed out the words, barely audible, as her eyes fell shut.

When she woke again, she lifted her head to look around but it instantly fell back onto the grass. "Where am I? And why does my head hurt so much?" she asked as her fingers ran over the lump on her skull. "Ouch!"

"You were hit by a falling rock on the mountain."

"I do remember a sudden terrible pain, but nothing after that. How do you know a rock hit me?"

"I saw it happen. I saw you fall."

"You caught me and saved my life?"

Argentavis nodded, his beak alarmingly close to Caipora's face.

"It was you who saved me from Jurupari too, wasn't it? He was swooping down on me and you snatched him up and flew away."

"Yes, that was me. I got rid of him and came back to see how you were doing."

"But you're a bird! How can a bird be so big and strong?"

"I've already told you: I'm the biggest bird in the world."

"Yes, I certainly believe that! I've never seen a bird as big as you before!"

"No, not many people have. Everyone thinks I'm extinct, but that's because I live a very secluded life. I don't go out much, you see. There used to be lots of us six million years ago......but, nothing ever stays the same," he added a little sadly. "Now I'm the only one left."

"Oh, I'm so sorry to hear that all your relatives and family have gone," Caipora said, wondering if he felt lonely.

"Thank you. I do get a bit lonely sometimes," he continued, as if reading her mind, "but I have a friend now, in my nest on top of my mountain!"

"Well that's wonderful! Is it another bird? Where is your nest?"

"You're lying in it!" Argentavis chuckled a gravelly chuckle.

"What?" Caipora looked around. It was true. Argentavis had removed the canoe from her back, untying the ropes with his beak, and laid her down in his comfortable nest. She sat up, groaning, to get a better look. It was enormous! It had to be to hold the gigantic bird: from head to tail Argentavis was about the length of four tall grown men lying head to foot! Looking around, Caipora saw that they were in a huge cave in a mountain side where a ledge above the entrance held out the rain.

"Oh! So I'm the friend in your nest! Well I'm very glad indeed to be your friend - in your nest on top of *your* mountain!" she laughed, walking around on the grassy bed which could hold at least a dozen Caipora's.

"Good. Glad to hear it," said Argentavis pleased that the girl was happy with her situation. "Now my friend, I've heard about you and your mission: the young warrior out to capture the Toad and save the rainforest. I hope I'll be able to help somehow."

"You've already saved my life. I can't see how you can help any more than that. Thank you. Thank you very, very much. I'm certainly glad to have you on our side," she said. "But how is it that you know so much about the Toad?"

"Information travels quickly through the forest. I've heard a lot about what you've been through and what you've survived. There's not one forest creature, big or small, who doesn't know who you are. Not one who wouldn't give their life if it meant saving yours. They call you their Amazonian Warrior. Their saviour - no, I should say *our* saviour, *our* Amazonian Warrior. We are all one family."

"Really?" Caipora's astonishment left her open-mouthed.

"Yes, really. We're all with you, every step of the way. And you're almost there now. Not much further to go - but this will be the hardest part."

"Yes it will be the hardest part. I haven't yet had time to think about it, you know - how I'm actually going to capture him. And I really don't know what to do with him after I get the keys."

"I could do with him what I did with Jurupari," chuckled Argentavis, wishing he could smile - but his beak wouldn't let him.

"Oh yes! What *did* you do with him? You just disappeared into the clouds......."

"Haw, haw, haw!" the bird chuckled again and the feathers on his head stood up as though the thought of what he'd done startled him. "First I dug a big hole at the base of a rubber tree, then I scratched a V-shape into the bark until the latex drained out and into the hole. Then.....haw, haw, haw.....then I dropped him into the hole....haw, haw... and rolled him around with a stick in my beak until he was well and truly covered and his wings firmly glued to his back. Then....haw,

haw... I stuck branches into the latex all over him to hold him together more firmly and then...haw, haw, haw......then I picked him up, flew west and dropped him into the crater of a volcano! It hasn't erupted in a long time. Must be due soon! Haw, haw, haw!"

"Did you really?" Caipora asked, incredulous at the bird's words. "The Mother of the Muiraquita Stone said the stone would protect me as long as I didn't harm anyone."

"Unfortunately, being the evil devil that he is, it won't hurt him much. He probably bounced when he hit the bottom with all that latex around him! Haw, haw, haw! He'll be uncomfortable for a while but he'll eventually get out somehow. I just like to revel in the possibility of the volcano erupting before he's able to escape and I do like to think of him crisping up nicely in all that hot larva! Haw, haw, haw! Anyway you didn't do it. I did. The only regrettable thing is that I still have some latex stuck between my claws!"

"It's not for me to punish the Toad. Maybe after I capture him you could put him somewhere until I free Verita and she can decide his fate?" Caipora asked.

"Sure, I can do that. I know lots of good hidey-holes in the surrounding mountains into which I could stuff him."

"That sounds perfect!" Thrilled and relieved, Caipora could barely believe that this enormous problem had been solved.

"Good," said Argentavis. "I have a plan. It's too late in the day now, but in the morning I'll fly you back to Stinky Lake Mountain and put you right on the top. You get the Toad and signal me when you have the keys. I'll fly by, pick him up and stuff him into one of my crannies where I sometimes hide my food. Just make sure you stand well back from him so that I can swoop down and grab him without stopping. Then I'll come back for you and we'll fly to Pico - if you're happy with that, of course. I don't want to impose myself on you."

Caipora couldn't believe what she was hearing! Argentavis knew Verita was on Pico da Neblina - and even knew where it was! It was as though all her troubles had simply melted away - well, almost. She still had to actually *capture* the Toad and get the keys, but her long trek to Pico and all the dangers that could entail, not to mention climbing it - all that hardship was suddenly gone!

"I don't know what to say," she replied, stunned by his offer. "That would be fantastic! Simply fantastic! I can't thank you enough!"

"No need for thanks. You rest here and we'll fly out first thing in the morning."

"That's an excellent idea. I need a good rest. It wasn't easy carrying that canoe up the mountain."

"Good. Right now, I'm going to get some food. Is there anything you'd like?" the bird asked. Taken aback by his offer, Caipora could do no more than smile and shake her head. Never before had a bird offered to bring her food!

Argentavis launched himself from the mouth of his cave into the serenity of the evening and glided soundlessly through the silence until he was no more than a speck which the purpley distance swallowed. Caipora looked down from the cave. Far below, the ripe sun threw its orange-pink gossamer rays across a lush verdant valley and all around majestic green mountains reached for the azure sky while gleaming yellow rivers flowed like molten gold around their feet. On the horizon, its summit engulfed by cloud, one mountain towered above the rest: Pico da Neblina. She could almost hear it calling her.

That night Caipora slept soundly under the feathers of the enormous black bird. He settled down in his nest on top of her just like a bird sits on its babies to keep them warm: not at all suffocating - just soft; very soft and warm.

***

"I'll carry your canoe in my claws while you sit on my neck" Argentavis said as they roused themselves from his nest. "You'll be more comfortable and the aerodynamics will be more efficient."

"An excellent suggestion!" said Caipora as Argentavis' huge beak gently closed around her and lifted her onto his shoulder where she grabbed hold of his feathers and climbed onto the back of his neck.

"Hold on tight!" the giant called and launched himself from his cave. Gliding through the golden rays of morning light, in and out of white vaporous clouds, over mountain tops and deep green valleys, Caipora's hair streamed in the breeze like a tasseled black flag against the blue sky, as if heralding doom and gloom for the Toad.

"There it is," said Argentavis, breaking through a thick cloud. "The mountain with two summits covered in green vapour. The Toad lives on the flat one. I'll set you down in a clearing by the lake. Signal me when you want me to pick him up. Any questions?"

"No. No questions. Just wish me luck," said Caipora.

CHAPTER 23
The Capture of the Toad

Traveling with the wind in their approach to Stinky Lake, Caipora and Argentavis were spared its stench, but on descending, Caipora began to gag and once on the ground, instantly took a few drops of the potion. It stopped the symptoms but didn't stop her smelling the stench!

Finally, after months of diabolical challenges and fighting evil, Caipora stood on the shore of Stinky Lake - the Toad not more than one hundred metres away! It was surreal. Soon she'd have the keys to the lanterns holding Verita and Fyglia! Soon they would be free and the Amazonian rain forest with all its inhabitants would be saved! It had seemed impossible. Unimaginable. Yet here she was, by the sludgy waters of Stinky Lake, heavy green vapour biting and putrid in her nostrils.

A thick wall of reeds blocked her access to the water and as she thrashed through them with her machete, they seemed to come to life, rustling and jerking about, bending this way and that. Small creatures scurried across her feet, bumped into her legs and leapt out of the reeds, running across the top in an effort to escape the thrashing machete: thousands of mice surrounded her! She stopped thrashing and stood still, whereupon a squeaky little voice by her feet spoke out defiantly. "Stop it! Stop it! Why do you want to chop our heads off?"

"Oh! I'm so sorry!" Caipora apologised to the white footed climbing mouse next to her leg - as big as her foot. "I didn't know you were in the reeds. Don't you normally live up in the trees?"

"Yes, we do. But on sunny days we often come here to entertain ourselves. We're normally safe on the ground as there are no other creatures on this stinky mountain to harm us - but now you've turned up - and with a machete, no less!"

"I'm not going to hurt you, I promise. But how can you bear to live in this stench? Doesn't it make you sick?"

"Well you see, our ancestors inhabited this mountain before that wretched Toad arrived. The stench wasn't so bad at first and and, through the generations, we just became immune to it. We don't really notice it any more," the mouse explained.

By now all the mice had gathered around Caipora, excitedly squeaking: "Who are you? Why are you here? How did you get here? That's a very frightening knife you've got there!"

Then one much older mouse emerged from the shadows and plopped down on her soft white haunches in front of Caipora. "We don't get much news here," she said. "It's the smell. No one wants to come here. Certainly, you're the first human who's ever set foot here. And as for that enormous bird, well, we nearly died of fright believing he was going to peck us all off our mountain top! So, why are you here?" Her tone demanded an explanation.

Caipora told them her story.

"So you alone have taken on the mammoth task of saving our world! That is truly heroic! Of course, we will help you in every way possible. Do you have a plan to get the Toad out of his rotting mound?" the mice asked.

"I'm going to throw my spider silk hammock over him, tie it to my canoe and tow him back to the shore. When I've got the keys for the lanterns from the pouch under his mouth I'll signal Argentavis to pick him up. He's going to stuff him into a cranny in a mountain while we free Verita and Fyglia."

"It won't work, with your hammock, I mean," the oldest mouse shook her head and long thin whiskers from side to side. "He'll thrash about so much in the water that if he doesn't escape he'll certainly capsize your canoe. And if by some miracle you do get him to the shore he'll simply hop out of the hammock, croak on you in the hope of killing you with his breath and hop back across the lake to his stinking mound! Besides, do you really want all that foul slime on your hammock? You'll never be able to sleep in it again! You're going to need some help here."

"I didn't think of the stinking slime sticking to my hammock," Caipora grimaced. "You're right - it would be impossible to get off. Help would be great, of course," said Caipora, "But how can anyone your size help me?"

"We're actually very large for mice you know!" a good number of indignant voices protested at being made to feel inadequate. "And we're a lot stronger than we look! Besides, we have connections!"

"What do you mean, connections?" Caipora inquired, puzzled.

All the mice turned their heads towards an enormous tarantula approaching them. Then another and another, until eight stood around them. Caipora had never seen tarantulas with a leg span as wide as her arm was long! She'd always quite liked the huge arachnids, and not just because they tasted nice. Now, surrounded by them, she felt no fear - only a slight discomfort, guilt perhaps, wondering if they might somehow sense that she'd eaten their kind in the past.

"We heard you talking about capturing the Toad and we believe we can help," the nearest tarantula addressed Caipora in a thin spiky voice.

Surprised that he was offering help and vaguely wondering if all tarantulas had spiky voices, Caipora thanked him. "That would be great. What did you have in mind?"

"You need something strong - and disposable - with which to tie him up. We can spin silk thread from our spinnerets. It's so strong that almost nothing can break it, just like your hammock," said the tarantula. "And we can make it as long as you like. It wouldn't take much time with all of us spinning."

"That's an excellent idea!" Caipora enthused.

"Yes, but there's more," the tarantula continued. "You can't get out of the canoe and onto the reed mound to tie up the Toad - you'll sink. You're far too big. Furthermore, you'd probably die from the putrid slime all over you."

"Yes, yes that's true," the mice nodded, murmuring together. "Smaller is sometimes better."

"Indeed it is," the spiky voices concurred.

"We can easily get onto the mound," squeaked an enthusiastic mouse, "and tie him up with the silk thread and then tie him to the canoe. We're very fast and nimble and we're immune to the slime!"

All the mice excitedly agreed. "It would be fantastic to be rid of him and have the mountain clean and fresh again! We'll get into your canoe with the silk thread," they continued planning the details, "and jump onto the reed mound, dig out the Toad and wrap him up so tightly he'll barely be able to breathe!"

"I'll all be done before he can even croak!" laughed one little mouse gleefully. "What fun it will be!"

"There's just one thing," one of the tarantulas advised the mice. "Our silk thread is sticky and will stick to your paws. You'll need to cover them with a gel from a special plant. We'll show you which one to use."

And so it was agreed. The tarantulas spun silk thread and wound it into balls while the mice covered their paws with the recommended gel. Meanwhile, Caipora continued slashing a path to the edge of the lake. Surprisingly, the water was clear for about six metres in from the shore, after which it turned sludgy and putrid, emitting green vapours which cut out the sunlight, thickened the air. The stench was horrendous. Caipora's head throbbed with pain and she struggled to keep herself from vomiting. With trembling fingers she pulled the stopper from the vial and swallowed more potion.

Caipora pushed the canoe half way into the water and held it while the mice hopped in, forming a soft layer of white fur across the bottom of the boat. Then she gave the canoe another push and jumped in as it moved off. The mice sat on their haunches, every pair of paws clutching a ball of silk thread. Paddling was easy until they came to the sludge, putrid and thick as porridge. Caipora grunted and strained, struggling to move the canoe through the moldy rotting reeds. The green vapour ate into her eyes, making them water so copiously that she could barely see.

At last the faint shape of the Toad's mound oozed through the blurry distance. Caipora's fingers gripped the paddle more tightly and her stinging eyes focused on the shape emerging eerily through the vapour. Clearer and clearer it grew, closer and closer they drew until the rumblings of heavy snoring engorged the foul-smelling air around them. The mound itself visibly shook from the vibrations.

And then they were upon it! Caipora rammed the canoe into the reeds so that it stuck and held fast. Soundlessly, and fast as quicksilver, the mice hopped out, balls of silk gripped in their sharp little teeth, dozens of tiny white feet scurrying over the mound so that it looked like a gigantic pile of mice before they disappeared over the top and into a hollow. Moments of silence - then a frenzied thrashing as clumps of reeds flew into the air! Deep guttural roars reverberated across the lake and the sludgy water trembled. Throughout the pandemonium, the high-pitched squealing of the mice and the fearsome screaming of the toad cut through the thick green fog to the shore where hundreds of mice and tarantulas waited in tremulous tension for the outcome of this daring exercise. The scuttling, grunting, groaning and shrieking raged on and on while clumps of rotting reeds sprayed every which way until the mound disintegrated and the Toad was at last revealed: completely wrapped in silk just as a spider wraps its prey!

Finally the mice rolled the howling Toad to the edge of what was left of his reed island, deftly twisted together lengths of silk thread into a long rope, tied one end around his neck and the other to the boat, leaving a good distance between the two. The Toad was huge - at least up to her waist in height, Caipora guessed.

With the mice on board, Caipora pushed the canoe off the mound with her paddle. Towing the Toad was far more difficult than she'd expected. Breathing heavily from the effort, she took in more and more of the toxic green vapour until, unable to hold back any longer, she leant over the side of the canoe and vomited. Progress was slow as she dragged the shrieking amphibian behind her and she began to doubt she'd have the stamina to reach the shore when the sludge around the boat began to ripple and bubble and within moments, exploded into a frenzy of small toads hopping, burping, croaking, jumping into the air and flopping back into the lake. Many landed in the boat while those in the water began to pull the Toad and the canoe backwards!

The toads in the boat threw themselves at Caipora, smacking into her chest, climbing up her legs and plopping onto her head. One especially revolting one sitting on the stern of the canoe took aim at her face and with one giant leap and a loud smack landed right on her nose and mouth, covering them with its disgusting slimy belly, planting its front feet over her scrunched-up eyes. She smacked it so hard that it flew off into the murky water but still its fetid stench clung to her nostrils.

By now the boat was covered in toads. With the onset of the attack the mice had curled up into tiny balls and buried their heads in their paws - but seeing Caipora almost covered with the disgusting creatures, they plucked up their courage and joined the fight. Far more agile and speedy than the fat toads, they hopped and leapt and scurried about the boat nipping at them with their razor-sharp teeth, clinging to their backs, sharp claws in their necks as they gnawed at their heads. Screaming hideously, the toads leapt back into the sludgy water, leaving the canoe empty of the foul creatures - but now they were all in the water pulling the boat and the Toad back to his mound! There was nothing Caipora could do. The poisonous fumes were taking their toll: nauseous, head throbbing, she could not move the boat forward through the sludge.

All at once a terrific splashing exploded around the canoe. Toads flew into the air left, right and centre, emitting frightful screams as they fell back with a heavy splat and floated lifelessly on the sludge - a thin silvery shaft sticking out of their fat stomachs. And while the sludge grew thick with floating toads, the air above swarmed with Warrior Forest Fairies, the green vapour iridescent with their lights. Armed with bows and silver arrows they darted this way and that, zipping here and zipping there with buzzing green wings. They whooshed up high and plunged down low with lightning speed, rolled into tiny balls and turned somersaults to avoid collisions. Their silver shafts whistled through the air with a "Whit! Whit! Whit!" before plunging with a "thunk" into the slimy creatures. The battle raged until all the small toads had either swum away to save themselves or floated lifeless on the sludge. Their job done, the Warrior Forest Fairies disappeared as suddenly as they had arrived.

Caipora swallowed more potion and paddled hard again towards the shore where she dragged the Toad back and forth through the clear water to wash off some of the slime and sludge. Then, pointing the canoe at the path she'd cut through the reeds, she rammed it onto the shore where mice squealed, leapt and scrambled in an effort to get out of the way while those in the boat jumped out and ran about excitedly recounting their adventure. The tarantulas listened with great interest.

Caipora cut the Toad free, dragged him into the clearing and faced the task she'd been dreading most: slitting open the pouch hanging under his mouth. His legs were strapped to his body with the silk thread but his head remained free. Huge yellow red-rimmed eyes bulged from it and his lip-less mouth stretched half way around his head. The body, partly visible through the silk thread, was a mottled grey-green, splattered with pink and purple patches. The entire creature was covered in ugly lumps and although much of the slime had been washed off, the sight and smell remained horrendous.

Knife in hand, Caipora stood over the evil creature, ready to cut open the pouch - yet hesitated. Would she really have to put her hand into it and feel around for the keys? Even though she was immune to the poison on his skin, the thought of touching him made her stomach heave. One of the mice came up to her. "The expression on your face tells me you're not looking forward to this," she said.

"No, I'm not. No one could possibly look forward to this but there's no other way. I have to get the keys." With those words Caipora stepped forward and bent down towards the Toad. As the tip of her blade touched his skin he began to scream hysterically, bulging eyes almost exploding from his head.

"Don't cut me! Don't cut me! I'll spit the keys out for you! Just please don't cut me!" he whimpered and begged in a high voice, thin as a thread.

Caipora couldn't believe the turn of events! What a relief! At the same time she thought, what a wimpy Toad! For all the torment and unimaginable suffering he had brought upon countless lives, he himself was incapable of enduring the minor pain of a small slit in his skin! Instead of stoically facing the situation he grovelled for mercy, bereft of all dignity, willingly surrendering the precious keys that would open the door to his own downfall!

Caipora welcomed his offer without hesitation. "All right, but be quick about it. I don't have time to waste. If you're going to take all day, I'll have to use my knife!" she ordered authoritatively. Strange gurgling and grunting burbled from the Toad's throat as he tried to get the keys from the pouch into his mouth. Finally he seemed to both burp and spit simultaneously as one key flew out, landing near Caipora's feet.

No one moved. Everyone - except the Toad - stared at it: it was difficult to grasp that one of the priceless keys was suddenly within arms' reach. Although thrilled to see it, Caipora hesitated in picking it up, dripping as it was with putrid slime and saliva. The stench of the Toad's burp alone was making her ill again.

"I'll get it!" An energetic mouse leapt forward, picked up the slimy object and ran to the water's edge where she washed it and rubbed it thoroughly with sand to get all the foul stuff off. Meanwhile, all eyes were on the odious creature as he worked hard to get the second key up into his mouth. Finally, with another violent burp and sickening splatter of slime, it flew out and bounced onto the ground whereupon another diligent mouse hopped forward, picked it up and ran to the water's edge to wash it.

Caipora tucked the clean keys into the bottom of her sack. High above, a black silhouette against clear blue, Argentavis circled the mountain. She lifted her arm and waved. The bird instantly swooped down and within moments, even before the mice had time to run and hide, was high in the sky again, toad in his claws. Caipora watched Argentavis dwindle to a small black spot and disappear, taking the Toad's frantic screams with him, and, surrounded by mice and tarantulas, sat down and swallowed more potion. Reluctant as she was to use it so frequently, she knew that if she allowed herself to fall gravely ill and die, even though she now had the keys, Verita and Fyglia would remain locked in their cages and die before anyone else could free them. She had to take care of herself to complete the final task of her mission.

"Are you all right?" asked a caring mouse, noticing Caipora's pale, grey face.

Caipora sighed heavily. "I have to admit that towing the Toad through that thick sludge took a lot out of me and I still feel sick from the stench - but the drops will soon fix me." She closed her eyes and let her head fall back to the tree trunk against which she rested.

"You did an amazing job!" a squeaky little voice piped up.

"Yes! You were incredible!" another concurred and the rest joined in, squeaking and squealing their admiration of Caipora's courage and strength in the face of the swarming attack by the repugnant toads.

"No," said Caipora. "It was you who were amazing. There's no way I could have done this without your help: you and the tarantulas deserve all the credit. It was your idea and your help that got this job done and I thank you from the bottom of my heart."

"You're very welcome! I don't think we've ever had such fun, have we?" a little mouse enthused, beaming at her friends.

"No we haven't! It was terrifically exciting!" they all agreed, delightedly re-living their unexpected adventure.

"Can we have your canoe?" one eager young mouse asked.

"Of course you can. I won't be needing it any more."

What joy! The canoe was instantly overrun with frolicking hopping mice devising endless games to play in their new toy.

***

Revived by the potion, Caipora stood knee deep in the clear water by the shore, scrubbing herself hard with sand to get the slime off her skin. When Argentavis returned, he too walked back and forth in the water, scratching one foot with the claws of the other over and over again to scrape off the muck. The mice were nowhere to be seen.

Capturing the Toad had taken longer than expected and it was now too late in the day to set out for Pico da Neblina. They'd fly there in the morning. Again the enormous bird picked Caipora up in his beak and she was quickly snuggled into his soft warm neck feathers. "Hold on tight!" he instructed, launching himself into the air from the edge of the summit. Far below, silvery rivers twisted through green forests and filmy veils of clouds meandered across their path in the sky. Soon Caipora was ensconced in the great bird's nest.

Despite many draughts of the potion, the young warrior's condition deteriorated rapidly. Burning pangs cut like knives through her body and excruciating pain pounded in her head. Unable to feed herself, Argentavis pecked out small pieces of pudding with his beak and dropped them into her mouth, but she vomited up every one. Seeing that she would soon be dehydrated, he flew back and forth to the river carrying water in his beak. Wrapped in her hammock, Caipora lay in his nest opening her mouth like a baby bird as he let droplets of water fall into it.

For three days Caipora drifted in and out of consciousness, her mind a frenzy of nightmares, hallucinations, evil spirits, the massacre of her tribe. She screamed in terror, burned with fever, vomited and gasped for air. In her delirium, Sema wiped her feverish brow, gave her water to drink, just as he'd done when she'd been seriously ill from snake bite. In her more lucid moments, the conflict between Fate and the power of her mind raged inside her. Why did Fate try to sabotage her efforts to achieve the very goal she had set for her? "Fate tests the strength of your mind," the voices of her elders finally answered. "You have an obligation to use the strength the universe has given you, to develop it - to strive for perfection."

She had tried to be strong and through all that she had overcome, had learnt that the power of her mind was great and her memory leapt back to her wishing for freedom from the laws of her tribe and she felt the tremendous power of her mind in that wish. It jolted her from the delirium, sobbing and screaming "I'm sorry! I'm sorry! Please forgive me! I'm so deeply sorry!"

Alarmed by her agonized cries, Argentavis, who had not left Caipora's side for three days other than to bring her water and find food for himself, lovingly stroked her with his enormous beak. "Hush, hush," he whispered."Everything's all right. Everything is fine."

When at last she was fully conscious and opened her eyes, "I don't deserve to live," were the only words to float on her feeble breath. Little by little Argentavis coaxed Caipora's story from her lips.

"No," his great beak slowly moved from left to right, his gravelly voice deep and serious. "You are not responsible. The elders of your tribe should have been prepared for the attack. It was the responsibility of your warriors to defend you. You are not responsible for their negligence. As for Fate, some allow themselves to be governed by Fate, like a leaf at the mercy of the whim of the wind. Others carve their own path, make their own decisions, determine their own future. It is your choice whether you take charge of your life or let Fate run it. And as for freedom, other than freedom of choice - what does it really mean? Even I am chained to the sky!"

His wise words made sense and soothed Caipora who, finally recovered from the deadly poison of Stinky Lake, ate her pudding, slept peacefully at last, and rested another day.

CHAPTER 24
Flying to Pico da Neblina

Once again Caipora firmly gripped the silky feathers of the great bird as they flew off to Pico da Neblina. "Landing might be problematic," he observed as the perpetually cloud covered summit drew near. "That cloud can be so dense that it's impossible to see the mountain-side until it's too late. I don't want to fly into a rock wall!"

At 2,994 metres, the peak was well above the tree line and its uppermost, almost vertical sides were bereft of trees and foliage. The rocky summit, sparsely covered with low-growing vegetation, was so small that landing was both difficult and dangerous for a bird the size of Argentavis. He circled the peak several times but unable to even glimpse the rock face, flew around and around the cloud, flapping his enormous wings to disperse it. Eventually it thinned and on his third attempt he finally landed.

Standing on the summit of Pico, the enormity of her

achievement did not enter Caipora's mind.

Her eyes immediately scanned the summit, urgently searching for any sign of where Verita and Fyglia might be hidden. She moved whatever rocks she could - nothing. Argentavis dislodged others with his beak and shifted larger ones with his claws - nothing.

Only one possibility remained: an enormous boulder - impossible to shift. Verita and Fyglia had to be under that monolith, but there was no way of getting to them! Despair got the better of Caipora: she sat on a rock and buried her face in her hands. After everything she'd overcome to get here, was she really to be defeated by one boulder? To make matters worse, black storm clouds surging over the horizon would soon bombard the summit with thunder, lightning and fierce winds. The summit of the highest peak in the land was not a good place to be in a storm! The situation looked hopeless and just as Caipora felt the Muiraquita Stone burn her chest a violent orange light exploded around the mountain and a gargantuan fiery dragon with monstrous scaly wings charged screeching at them both. Caipora threw herself to the ground but Argentavis, unable to duck, was knocked off the summit. Instantly regaining control, he turned to confront his fearsome opponent.

The huge dragon, despite its size, was faster and more agile than Argentavis. It circled him, looped over and under him, spewing scorching flames at his feathers. Caipora watched terrified, shouting 'duck' time and again as the dragon swooped down from above and behind the bird where he couldn't be seen. The battle raged on and on and Argentavis was beginning to tire. Caipora felt helpless, useless - and desperate! But there was no giving up. Not at this point - not ever! There had to be a way! There had to be something she could do! Casting emotions aside, rationality flooded her mind. "Verita! I have to free Verita!" she shouted. "She's the only one who can help now! I *have* to move this boulder!"

"Use the potion for power," spoke a voice in her head. "The potion for power!" Frantically Caipora rummaged through her sack and snatched up the silver vial. Her memory voiced Ravan's words: "You can do whatever you want with this as long as you believe you can."

Caipora swallowed a few drops and, standing in front of the boulder, saw herself lifting it. Was she just imagining it? Did she really feel stronger? Were her muscles bigger? She didn't have time to check. Knees bent, she pushed her fingers into tiny gaps under the monolith, sucked in a deep breath and heaved. Nothing happened. Another deep breath and heaved again.

"I *will* lift this!" The words surged defiantly through gritted teeth. Knees shaking, her legs began to straighten as the boulder moved upward! Grunting, groaning, she pulled harder until her legs were straight. Then flooded with the strength of her belief, she pushed the bolder away from her until it fell back with its own weight and rumbled down the face of Pico da Neblina!

The sight beneath it snatched her breath away: side by side in a hollow lay two glass cages. Verita lay against the glass in one. Pale. Inert. Fyglia looked in better condition, having been locked up for a shorter time. For just an instant, the Goddess glanced at Caipora, then her eyelids fell shut again. "Hold on! Hold on for just another moment! I'm getting you out right now!" Grabbing the key from her sack, Caipora's only thought was "It can't be too late! It can't be too late!" Amid the snarling, roaring and thrashing in the sky, Caipora unlocked the cage holding Verita. The moment she lifted the lid the Goddess gasped a breath of fresh air. In a flash her wand uncurled itself from the base of the cage and sprang into her hand. Verita's fingers grasped it, but otherwise she still did not move. Caipora lifted the limp white body into her lap. The long dark hair falling across it and the thin dress covering the slight frame did nothing to provide much needed warmth. "You'll be all right. You'll be all right!" Caipora pulled the stopper from the gold vial, parted Verita's blue lips and carefully let several drops of potion fall into her mouth.

"Who are you?" the goddess whispered feebly.

"I'm Caipora. Caelia sent me to free you."

"You're so young - a child. How did you manage such an impossible task?" Weak and drowsy, she continued without waiting for a reply. "I don't know how long I've been here.... but thank you...." again her eyes shut for a moment. "What's that terrible noise? What's happening?" She turned her head to the sky.

"I'm certain that dragon is Boiuna. She and Jurupari and Corpo Seco have been trying to stop me from reaching you. They're working for the Toad. You have to save the big bird! Without him I wouldn't be here! Without him I fear all will still be lost!" Caipora pleaded urgently.

"Give me another drop of two of the potion and I should be able to do it." This time Verita opened her mouth herself and Caipora let at least three drops fall into it. "That's better," said the Goddess, sitting up in Caipora's lap, but just as she got to her feet, the dragon swooped down and snapped her up in its claws, knocking Caipora to the ground!

"No! No! No!" Caipora screamed. Gleaming on the ground lay Verita's wand: she was in the grip of the demon dragon without it! Almost powerless! They were all doomed!

Seeing the dragon snatch Verita, Argentavis charged at

it with almighty force. Hurtling down on it from above and behind, he dug his claws into its scaly back and violently shook it back and forth. The dragon turned its head and shot hot flames at the bird, scorching his burnt feathers even further. The bird lunged at the dragon's neck, digging into its scaly skin and shredding its flesh with his knife-sharp beak. The dragon screamed while Argentavis held his grip and grabbed onto its neck even harder, preventing it from turning its flaming jaws back at him.

Caipora watched in horror - then remembered Fyglia! Within moments the second cage was open and Fyglia was swallowing the resuscitating drops. "You have to help! You have to help somehow! Verita's in the dragon's claws without her wand!"

Half the size of Verita and sitting on Caipora's knee, Fyglia rubbed her eyes, shook herself, took the vial from Caipora's hand and throwing back her head, gulped down a good swig of the potent potion. "OK! I'm ready!" she announced with some ferocity and grabbing Verita's wand, took off faster than Caipora's eyes could follow.

Seconds later there appeared in the sky an horrendous two-headed winged serpent, three gleaming black horns protruding from each head. Flames shot from both mouths and vents in the sides of the luminous green monstrosity. It charged head on at the dragon, snarling and thrusting its metre-long razor sharp tongues at it, all the while whipping its great tail left and right - a tail flicking a sharp arrowhead at its end. Incredibly, the instant the two collided, the flaming green serpent disappeared, leaving the dragon searching the sky in confusion for its new opponent. While it was thus distracted, Fyglia, who had changed from the green serpent into a small bird, zipped down to the dragon's claw which held

Verita and thrust her wand into her hand. Armed with her magic weapon, the Goddess instantly waved it at her captor, causing it to vanish into thin air.

No sooner had the two monsters disappeared from the sky, than Verita and Fyglia appeared in front of Caipora, leaving a baffled Argentavis still circling above them, scanning the sky for his two fiery opponents. Finally he landed, somewhat unsteadily, on the summit. Disheveled, scorched feathers sticking out in all directions, he looked down at the three figures at his feet.

CHAPTER 25
The Spells

Caipora proudly stroked a thick scaly yellow leg. "This is my friend Argentavis. I wouldn't be here without him. He saved my life." Verita and Fyglia craned their necks to look up at the gigantic bedraggled bird.

"It looks like you could use some help yourself now," said Verita and with one wave of her wand Argentavis was smooth and sleek again, shiny black feathers gleaming all over him.

"Wow! Thanks! That feels much better - even better than before!" he enthused.

"I'm Verita. I believe you played a big part in saving my life too," she said.

"And I'm Fyglia. Thank you for your help."

"Any time," replied Argentavis. "But what happened to those flaming monsters?"

"One of them was me!" laughed Fyglia. "I was the two-headed one! I flew up to distract the dragon and give Verita her wand."

"And then I changed the dragon, who was really Boiuna, into a worm," explained Verita. "She fell from the sky and for the next five hundred years will be living in the ground eating rotting plants and producing manure to improve the growth of the forest!"

"Oh! Well done Verita! What a fantastic spell!" exclaimed Caipora.

"Now I just have to sort out the Toad, Jurupari and Corpo Seco," the goddess continued.

"Argentavis dealt with the Toad after I captured him," said Caipora.

"Did you? And how did you do that?" a surprised Verita asked the bird as she stood on a rock, again craning her neck upwards to meet his gaze.

"Well, I would have disposed of him for good, but Caipora thought you should decide his fate, so I stuffed him into a cranny in the side of a cliff not far from here. He's all tied up and can't get out."

"Yes, and Argentavis dealt with Jurupari too!" Caipora proudly boasted.

"And what did you do with *him*?" Verita enquired, even more surprised at the big bird's impressive efficiency.

"I dropped him into a volcano, but only after I'd glued him up with latex and wrapped him in lots of branches. Unfortunately, the volcano wasn't erupting at the time! Haw, haw, haw!"

"I see," said Verita, eyebrows raised. "That certainly was imaginative of you, although I don't expect that if it did erupt it would do him any harm. He is a devil after all you know, and quite used to fire. Hopefully he'll still be there so I can put him out of action for a really long time without wasting days looking for him."

"He's not hard to find. Just fly west to Columbia. There are six volcanoes there all in a row along the Andean Mountain range. He's in the northernmost one, just west of Bogota. But I wouldn't go there now if I were you," Argentavis advised, glancing at the thunderous clouds almost overhead. "That storm is about to break right over us!"

"Yes! We have to get off this mountain now!" Caipora exclaimed.

"Wait! I just felt something!" and Verita flew off without another word. They waited nervously under the blackening sky as the impending storm rapidly rumbled towards them, lightning flashing and cracking nearby, gusts of howling wind whipping their faces. Verita returned moments before the storm broke "I sensed Corpo Seco nearby," she said. "And I was right. He was making his way up the mountain. We had a little chat and I told him I'd organised a place for him to stay for the next five hundred years: a cave high in the side of a sheer cliff. I've covered the entire place with mirrors - even the floor - and blocked the entrance with a boulder so that he doesn't have a view. But I did leave a small opening at the top to let in just enough light so that every time he opens his eyes he'll be confronted with his ghastly reflection wherever he looks. He's there now, getting to know himself a little better I think. Now I just have to deal with the Toad and Jurupari."

Black clouds gulped up the light. Their thunderous claps and rumblings shook the mountain as water fell in solid sheets and jagged lightning bolts cracked around the summit. There was nowhere to hide.

"Everyone on my back!" Argentavis shouted above the thunder. "Caipora stand here so I can lift you up - you know what to do. Get the others under my feathers!" And the bird threw himself off the summit and swept down the mountain side to the river where, flying just above the water's surface and well below the treetops, they were safe from jabbing bolts of lightning. He followed the watery path as it wound its way through the valleys and when it reached the foot of his mountain he soared up to his spacious cave where they sheltered comfortably from the storm, the bird in his nest and Caipora, Verita and Fyglia snuggled into the soft warm feathers of his neck.

The following morning they flew through a fresh clear sky to the mountain where the Toad was stuffed into a cranny. "You, Toad, have learned nothing from the previous spell I cast on you," Verita pronounced. "You sat in that stinking mound for five hundred years and learned nothing! Since you've been free you've followed only your greed, willfully wreaking horrific damage upon the forest and causing shocking pain, trauma and death to its animals. As punishment, for the next five hundred years you will feel excruciating and incapacitating pain every time you think an evil or selfish thought!" Verita waved her wand and it was done.

Instantly the Toad groaned in agony from his immediate evil thought: "I'm going to lock you up again as soon as this spell is over!" Again and again he groaned and moaned as the evil thought flew violently around in his mind.

Having dealt with the Toad, Verita and Fyglia flew to Nevado del Ruiz in west Columbia, the volcano into which Argentavis had thrown Jurupari. They found the devil lying on a ledge of hardened larva half way down the crater - a bundle of broken branches, leaves and twigs, glued together with latex. It was difficult not to laugh at the sight of him: slanting red eyes glowered behind the leaves and a sharp hooked nose, nostrils bulging with dirt, poked out between them. A sneering mouth oozed blobs of white latex.

"It's time to pay for your evil ways Jurupari," Verita informed him. "When this volcano erupts and you are blown out of it and released from your latex binding, you will be free to resume your vile deeds again. But that won't bring you any joy because for the next five hundred years, every evil thing you do will turn to good. The more evil you try to do, the more good there will be!"

Groans bubbled through the latex of Jurupari's glued-up mouth and his glowering eyes almost exploded from their sockets as Verita waved her wand at him and flew off with Fyglia by her side. Her job was done.

***

Argentavis' feathers bristled with excitement as his claws dragged the screaming Toad from the cranny. Verita had granted his wish to fly the creature to the driest place on Earth and leave him there and so with Caipora on his neck, they headed south west, across Amazonia and their own country of Brazil, across Bolivia and the Salar de Uyuni - the biggest salt lake in the world - to the Atacama Desert in northern Chile. High-flowing air currents propelled Argentavis silently and effortlessly over mountains and valleys, through forests of billowing clouds, their serenity disturbed only by the frequent groaning of the Toad as evil thoughts crammed his head.

When at last the vastitude of orange sand that was the Atacama Desert stretched across the breadth of the horizon where only occasional rocky outcrops and volcanoes disturbed the flat expanse, Argentavis zoomed down onto a volcano from the top of which he would be able to take off again. His enormous wingspan of seven to eight metres would not allow him to take off from flat ground: his wings would hit the dirt as he tried to flap them.

The moment he landed, the big bird broke a thread of the silk binding the Toad with the tip of his beak and holding the end, released the blotchy creature to roll down the side of the volcano as the thread unraveled. Eventually the Toad came to a stop at the bottom - on the burning desert sand.

"I'd start digging if I were you. There's water under the ground - a long way under," Argentavis advised as he flew down and hovered over the creature who was now hopping about like an energetic flea in a hot frying pan. And so the Toad began to frantically dig, hoping to find some relief in a little cooling water. Surrounded by one hundred and five thousand square kilometres of desert, he was doomed to stay underground forever because if he were to come to the surface, the burning sun would fry his skin and the scorching sand turn his feet to crisps. He was now in a very different environment from the succulent rain forest which he needed to live comfortably. Here in the winter, the temperature at night often fell below zero and not one patch of shade offered shelter from the piercing sun during the day. Forced to stay underground to survive, it would make no difference how hard the Toad might scream for help: the evil spirits in Amazonia would not hear him - and had their own problems to deal with.

CHAPTER 26 Returning Home

"What do you think? Are you ready to go home?" Argentavis asked Caipora.

Home. Was it really all over? Had the unimaginable horror of the Toad and his evil spirits finally come to an end? Could it truly be that Amazonia and its inhabitants were safe? It was difficult to comprehend that life would once again be normal.

"Home....yes....home would be nice," Caipora spoke more to herself than in answer to the question, the image of the hut where she'd spent only one night instantly in her mind. The thought of being there again, of making it her own, filled her both with excitement and with solace.

"And where is home?"

"It's a hut in a clearing by a river, not far south of the Amazon. I'll show you on my map."

A brief glance was all Argentavis needed. "OK. Looks like all I have to do is fly directly north. It's quite a way, but I think we'll just make it before dark."

The sun was a flaming ball low in the West, the Amazon a vibrant glittering pink on the horizon when Argentavis announced "We're almost there." Silence. "Hello! Are you there?" He turned his head and gently nudged Caipora with his beak.

"Mmm.....yes.....I'm here....was just sleeping," yawned Caipora, stretching herself out of the bird's warm, cosy feathers. "You do make the most comfortable bed I've ever slept in."

"Sorry to wake you, but I need you to look out for your hut, if you think you can recognise it from the air."

"I should be able to - I've never seen a hut like that before. I believe it was built by a white man a long time ago."

"I'll fly lower so you can get a closer look." Argentavis descended so they could clearly see the small rivers but still get a broad view of the surrounding area.

"That's it! That's it over there to the right! I'm sure of it!" Caipora shouted, her voice shrill with excitement. Argentavis veered right and flew lower still. "Yes! Yes! I'm home! I'm home!"

Argentavis landed on the roof. "I can't believe it's all over," Caipora said, looking up into the large dark eyes of the extraordinary bird.

"Believe it. It *is* all over and *you* did it!"

"I did, but not without vital help from you and many others. There's no way I could have done it on my own."

"And there's no way it could have been done without you."

"Will we ever meet again?" she asked.

"We *will* meet again, and not infrequently. I'll come by every so often and we'll take a trip somewhere, if you'd like."

"Oh, I *would* like that! I'd like that very much indeed."

"Then we won't say goodbye. We'll say 'until we meet again'." Argentavis lowered his head and very gently brushed Caipora's cheek with the tip of his beak.

"Yes. Until we meet again," she lovingly stroked his gleaming feathers.

No sooner had the enormous bird dissolved into the dusky sky than a loudly chattering troop of monkeys bounded towards her, gleefully turning somersaults on the way. "It's you! How did you get here so quickly?" Caipora exclaimed, stunned to see her troop so far from the bottom of Stinky Lake Mountain where she'd left them not more than a week ago.

"It seems Verita's powers have no limits!" they laughed and recounted their adventures since their parting, talking and shouting over one another, as always. Finally the eldest got a word in edge ways. "We've been sent by Caelia to take you to the Underworld. She wants to see you right away."

"I'll be ready in a moment. I just want to have a look inside my hut."

"No, no! No time for that. The hut will still be here when you get back. You must come at once! They've already been waiting a long time for your return." Caipora breathed a sigh of resignation and followed the capuchins. What was the urgency? Not another mission, surely? When was she to rest? She would help, of course - she just needed to rest and recover!

At the entrance to the Underworld Ravan greeted her with his wide beaming smile. "Congratulations a thousand times over! You have achieved a feat far beyond the normal capacity of humans, let alone of someone so young!"

"Not without your invaluable help," she replied.

No cheers, no jubilation greeted Caipora as she entered the cave. The Nevae, heads bowed, knelt on one knee, hands over their hearts. All the animals, no longer mutated, stood quietly, heads bowed. Only the Queen walked towards her through the silence, arms extended. Taking Caipora's hands into hers, she spoke. "Words cannot express our joy at your safe return Caipora, nor how enormously grateful we will forever be to you. We, Amazonia and all its inhabitants are indebted to you for our existence. Your courage and determination have been awe inspiring, but we expected no less. Not for one moment did our faith in you falter. We ask that you accept this crown as a token of our eternal gratitude and a symbol of your place of honour in our family," and Caelia's eyes filled and glistened as she crowned Caipora with a garland of precious flowers. Then she turned and addressed the crowd. "Let us show Caipora our appreciation."

The entire cave reverberated with cheers and exultation while Verita and Fyglia flitted about beaming at the unrestrained jubilation. Again they sat at tables laden with an opulent feast. Speeches praised Caipora's intrepid courage and unrelenting resolve to achieve her goal. The capuchins too, were applauded for their bravery, for saving Caipora's life and for their commitment to stand by her and the cause at all costs. Laughter and merriment fused with music, dancing and singing. Even the fireflies seemed to bounce about with unfettered glee.

How young she had been when she first sat at this table. And how frightened. Yet they had all believed in her, although she had not then believed in herself. Only six months had passed but she was now a different person: she knew what commitment meant and understood the meaning of freedom and responsibility. As she watched those around her, she heard the words of her elders again:

"We know ourselves through our relationships with others. We are defined through our relationships with others." It was the forest community that defined Caipora; defined her life's purpose. She was part of it now. It was her community.

When at last the energy of the revelers began to ebb, Caipora bade her farewells. The capuchins escorted her to the verge of the forest, to her hut, promising to visit often. Darkness had long since chased dusk beyond the horizon and drawn its blanket embroidered with moon and stars across the sky. The water level had receded to the riverbank and the inviting wooden structure stood in the grassy clearing on its tall stilts, weathered boards silver in the moonlight.

That she would make this her home, build a new life - that she would be sheltered and safe in this place - brought joy and serenity to Caipora's heart. And to be so close to her new family filled her with a deep sense of belonging, security and comfort. She stepped lightly through the darkness towards the hut.

A light burst through the window! Fell at her feet and stopped her in her tracks. It pulled the ground from under her and flung her into a dizzying black abyss where nothing existed but the light shattering her hopes, her dreams!

Aghast, horrified, she stood staring, but couldn't, *wouldn't,* simply surrender her treasure and walk away. She had to discover who had stolen her home. Confront them. Heart pounding, she crept up to the hut and climbed the ladder. A creak squealed into the night. She froze. Waited. Silence. She climbed further; stepped onto the landing. Another creak. Stopped. Waited, frightened; held her breath and crawled to the window. Slowly, tremulously, she drew her eyes up to the ledge.

A gasp escaped her mouth! In the flickering golden light of the candle stood Sema.

A note from the Author

If you enjoyed this book, I would be very grateful if you could write a review and publish it at your point of purchase. Your review, even a brief one, will help other readers to decide whether they'll enjoy my work.

Acknowledgements

I would like to express my heartfelt thanks to my brilliant and dear daughter, Kate Burbeck, for her honest and insightful critique of my work. Without her candid appraisal, this book would have been lacking in so many ways.

My deepest gratitude also to Andrew Burbeck, Vivien Atkins and Vizma Bell for their uplifting support, exacting proof reading and valuable suggestions.

About the Author

Liene Burbeck is a graduate of the South Australian School of Art. After moving to Melbourne, she gained a B.A. in Politics and Sociology from Monash University. Liene raised two children while establishing her own small advertising/illustration business. Years later she qualified as a teacher of English as a Second Language and taught in Prague, Latvia and Australia. After painting for some years in water colour, oil and pastel, as well as producing pen and ink drawings and being awarded prizes in exhibitions, Liene finally turned to writing, which had been her passion since her early teen years. While she has had poems published, "The Power Within Her" is Liene's first novel. Liene has travelled extensively and spent almost a year in South America. "The Power Within Her" is born of Liene's love of the jungle, of wild things and of the challenges of surviving in the wild.

www.ingramcontent.com/pod-product-compliance
Lightning Source LLC
Chambersburg PA
CBHW030614170726
48283CB00002B/600